A Flickering Flame

REVA SPIRO LUXENBERG

authorHOUSE®

AuthorHouse™ LLC
1663 Liberty Drive
Bloomington, IN 47403
www.authorhouse.com
Phone: 1-800-839-8640

Published by AuthorHouse   03/06/2014

ISBN: 978-1-4918-7116-4 (sc)
ISBN: 978-1-4918-7115-7 (e)

Library of Congress Control Number: 2014904385

Dedicated to

FATHERS RIGHTS FOUNDATION

Acknowledgment

With gratitude to my editor, Jill Herring

Chapter 1

MOST BABIES ARE BORN nine months from conception, but Jeffrey's soul sensed the world wouldn't be a happy place when he made his appearance in the tenth month on a scorching day in July in Nassau Hospital in Mineola, Long Island.

*　　*　　*

Ricky watched her husband gobble down the cheese omelet holding the fork in his left hand. How quaint it is that Europeans always use their left hands while we use our right hand, she thought. After eleven months of marriage, she learned more and more about him, that he wasn't four years older than he had told her before their marriage—twelve years was more accurate, that every night he woke from nightmares sweating heavily—that the three-bedroom, split-level ranch house he alleged he owned, really belonged to the Conservative congregation.

"The lawn needs mowing and you need to do it," Simon ordered with the authority of Napoleon.

A momentary flash of anger showed in Ricky's hazel eyes. "I'm so huge, my back hurts, and the baby is kicking. I think I'll lie down."

"What? You'll mow the front and back lawns and be quick about it." Simon rose to his feet and glared at his wife. He raised and lowered the yarmulke on his head, a nervous habit he had. "I have to practice the new song for next Friday night's service. The Rabbi asked for a different tune for Adon Olam."

Ricky put her hands on the table and raised her unwieldy body, left the house, and waddled to the back lawn where the shed was located. She opened the door, yanked hard at the hand mower, and pulled it out aware that a pregnant woman who was ready to give birth shouldn't be doing this. Her heartless, sadistic husband wouldn't take no for an answer and so she knew not to object.

With a strong sense of unfairness, she began the tedious job of rolling the mower back and forth over the tall grass. *Just because Simon's a Cantor, doesn't excuse him from doing a man's work.* The used red maternity top, that her cousin Lillian had given her, was soon soaked with sweat. The sun beat relentlessly on her brown straight hair that Simon insisted she not wash or cut.

"Brush it for ten minutes," he used to say, "and then the curl will come out." He hated her naturally curly hair. She wondered if he liked anything about her.

Pushing the mower around one of the seven stately oak trees, Ricky, her mouth dry, stopped for a minute to rest in the shade. But afraid Simon would pop out and find fault, she continued watching the clippings grow into piles that would have to be raked. The dark green grass, mixed together with lime-colored blades and dotted with dandelions, bravely endured the lack of watering. If the spring hadn't brought showers, there would be no grass at all since Simon practiced his singing and did

2

nothing else with the exception of bossing his wife. With a sigh of disgust, Ricky resumed propelling the mower thinking about Simon's protestations of love during the four months he courted her. His so-called love had proved as ephemeral as a puff of smoke.

Her reverie was interrupted by the startling moo of the cow in the field next to her home. Her neighbor's house was old and so was its only occupant, a grumpy man who kept to himself, raised corn, and kept a cow as old as himself. Ricky glanced up at the soft blue of the sky and the slow passing clouds, as she shaded her eyes from the blazing sun, and wiped her wet brow. Short hair would have cooled her, but Simon forbade it. She was supremely vexed with herself for not realizing that a man who had been in six concentration camps during the war must be scarred for life and would make a miserable husband. But he had kept this from her until after the wedding when they went home.

His sister stayed with them the first night of their marriage as Simon said she was flying back to Denver the next day and he didn't want to ask her to stay in a hotel. Ricky thought it was inappropriate as a newly married couple should have privacy, but she kept silent. That night he told her about how he had suffered in concentration camps during the war. Truly she felt sorry for him, but it didn't take long before he turned into a harsh man and she cringed at the thought of divorce as she kept the mower revolving over the overgrown lawn. She couldn't work with the responsibility of a baby or move back with her aging parents in a small, three-room apartment, and was convinced she had to make this marriage work.

* * *

With extreme clarity, Ricky recalled the night a week after they were married when Simon woke up screaming.

"What's wrong?" she whispered.

"Another nightmare."

"Tell me about it."

"I'd rather not."

Ricky put her hand on Simon's shoulder. "Maybe if you talk about it, it'll go away."

"It'll never disappear. It's based on the reality of when I was in Dachau. There was a chubby Nazi officer who used to like to talk to me since I spoke German. He liked to discuss World War I and how it led to the economic decline of Germany and the rise of Hitler. I agreed with him."

"So how does that lead to your nightmares?"

"One day he approached me and asked if I would like more privileges including more food. Of course I said yes as I was starving. He told me if I learned how to use a rifle, I could guard the other prisoners in my bunk. I told him I knew nothing about shooting because I had been a Yeshiva student and was used to studying religious texts."

Ricky had turned on the bedside lamp and looked at her husband who was as white as the sheet that covered him. "Go on."

"To make a long story short, I learned to use a rifle and one day, when I was a good shot, I was told to display my talent in front of a group of Nazis. An officer led me outside and said I was to shoot at the bull's-eye in a flag they had draped about thirty yards from me. I aimed, pulled the trigger, and hit the bull's-eye exactly in the center. They applauded and, when they took down the flag, I saw a dead woman on the ground. When I looked closer, it was my younger sister. I murdered my own sister.

I'll never forgive myself and I'll carry the guilt to my dying day. So you see the nightmares will never go away."

Ricky's face flushed as red as the fiery sun. She had known that the Nazis were barbarians but never suspected such cruelty. *Is it a wonder that Simon needs therapy? How could anyone have walked away from such torture without a scar in his heart? No wonder he screams at night, waking up covered with perspiration from a black nightmare.*

How awful. His mother and younger brother murdered in a concentration camp and his sister dead from his own hand.

She was so affected she couldn't utter a sound, but put her hands on his shoulders and rested her head against his in a futile effort to console him. Much of the humanity he possessed as a youth, Hitler had erased. She could do nothing to bring back the humanity.

After that night she tried to forgive all the heartless things Simon did to her because of his traumatic past.

* * *

Ricky kept mowing the lawn but stopped for a moment to gaze across the street at the ramshackle house that stood like a reminder of the day that it was picked up and relocated to that plot of land. How disappointed she had felt when a copse of beech trees had been downed and the house, which was tilted like an old bent woman, replaced it. She had watched with astonishment as the frame house moved down the street propelled by a trailer, and she still missed the woods and yearned for the past. But supposedly felling trees and relocating houses was progress as more and more people moved to the small town in Long Island.

She let the mower fall to the ground as she grabbed her huge stomach when the first contraction hit like a locking vise. *Why did Eve listen to the snake? Why did she tempt Adam with the apple? Giving birth with excruciating pain was her fault.* I hate Eve, Ricky thought as the contraction stopped and she hurried into the house and upstairs to the bed. She waited breathlessly for the next contraction and it didn't come for fifteen minutes. Simon came up to complain that she hadn't finished mowing, and, when Ricky told him that the labor pains had started, he shrugged, left the bedroom, went downstairs and continued practicing his singing.

The contractions were coming regularly every ten minutes when Ricky decided that she could take a chance to run downstairs between contractions. She had embroidered a baby quilt but still hadn't made the aprons she wanted to wear after the baby came. When she didn't know the baby's sex, she had bought pink and blue towels and intended to make them into aprons to protect her dresses.

After running up and down the stairs for hours, Ricky completed five aprons.

"Fix my supper," Simon ordered in a harsh voice.

"Fix your own," Ricky said weakly. "I'm not supposed to eat or drink and I'm in too much pain to make food for you." His cold black eyes were as hard and unmoved as a predator as he stared at her, turned on his heel, and stalked down the stairs to the kitchen.

At night, when the pains moved quickly from five minutes apart to three minutes and her breath came in panting gasps, Simon drove Ricky to the hospital. Without warning, the contractions came fast and furious at one minute apart. Ricky moaned, "It hurts so much."

Simon looked dark and irate as his eyes bored into her. "You don't know what pain is. Pain is when you march for hours in the snow, without food, without warm clothes, when men are dropping like flies all around you, but you want to live so you put one bloody foot in front of the other, dragging yourself to the next concentration camp. That's real pain."

Biting down on her quivering lower lip, Ricky kept silent.

At the hospital Simon checked her in, then turned and left without a goodbye. His acrimonious departure left Ricky feeling abandoned, frantic, and wretched at his unmitigated arrogance. A nurse gave her a shot and disappeared. Ricky became nauseous and began to be afraid she would vomit on her hospital gown, disgusted with herself and the fact that she was there with no one to help her through this trying time, horribly miserable after being in labor for twelve hours. Unable to control the nausea, she opened her mouth and the contents of her stomach spurted out.

She waited for what seemed like an eternity until the nurse returned with a disgusted look at the smelly hospital gown. As the nurse changed the gown, Ricky fell into a deep, dreamless sleep that lasted for three hours, and at 6:15 a.m. without regaining consciousness, she gave birth to a 7 lb. 6 oz. boy.

Chapter 2

Ricky inspected her baby for the first time through the nursery window and frowned. His head was covered with a mop of brown hair, a wide face, and a nose as large as a lemon. It's all right, Ricky thought, a boy can be ugly; it's a girl who needs to be pretty. Time was frozen in a moment so sharp that she felt she'd always remember that having a baby would ensure she'd never be alone again.

Later that morning Simon came to the hospital, pleased with his newborn son, but brought no offerings like flowers or candy, no words of praise, no tenderness. He stood at Ricky's bedside and announced in a harsh voice, "I've been fired from my job."

A shiver of dread flowed down Ricky's spine. Overwhelmed with the prospect of having a newborn with an unemployed husband, she moaned. "Why?"

"I was teaching my Hebrew class when one of the younger boys was disobedient," he grumbled. "He was the son of the President of the Congregation. I warned him to behave himself and he didn't, so I sent him home in a taxi. You'll be in the hospital for a week. I'm going to Florida for an interview as a Cantor. Pray that I get the job. Pray hard."

"Pray hard," she echoed as she thought about the

iciness of this man who came to the hospital without words of gratitude or even a solitary rose.

She looked at the woman next to her with eight people gathered around her bed. A dozen vases with colorful flowers filled the room with a heavenly odor. The woman's husband's eyes were brimming with tears of love and concern as he patted her shoulder.

With a cold wave of his hand, Simon left Ricky alone. The episiotomy hurt, the hemorrhoids as a result of childbirth hurt, the suckling baby hurt, but the pain from her husband's lack of affection hurt her even more. She remembered the time before she met Simon how she had pictured a future with a loving husband, two perfectly behaved children, and a home with modern furniture, manicured green lawns, and tall trees. By the time she was in her late twenties, none of the girls she knew from college weren't married with at least one child. She, as an American woman, had rushed into a marriage to a foreigner without examining Simon's background. She bitterly regretted her mistake. Now she had the home without knowing for how long, but not the loving husband; on top of that, a baby to care for made it impossible for her to work. Life seemed unbearable, the future terrifying.

And then, as if nothing could get worse, it did. The poor mother in the bed adjacent to Ricky's had given birth to a Down's Syndrome baby. Day and night she sobbed, and was on the telephone constantly. For four nights Ricky got no sleep and gradually her memory ebbed like a stream that turns into a trickle. Simon had promised he would bring her kosher food, a false promise now that he was gone, and she made due by not eating the meat or the shellfish. Her body was weakening from the constant pain and poor nutrition.

Four days later her father came with a box of Barton's candies, saying that her mother had a cold and couldn't come. He recognized something was wrong when his daughter didn't remember where the bathroom was. When he accompanied her down the hall to the bathroom, Ricky told him about her husband losing his job but she was sure he would get another in Florida where he was now. She wasn't a person to complain to her parents and preferred to keep her problems to herself.

"I don't want to leave you and mother, but a wife has to go where her husband is and I may have to move to Florida."

Her father left with a bellyful of rage, saying nothing, thinking a person doesn't have the right to interfere in a marriage.

Three days after, Ricky was discharged from the hospital and Simon brought home his wife and baby. On the ride home, with a crying infant in her lap, Ricky asked, "Did you get the job in Florida?"

Simon's face lit with bitter triumph. "No. They were a Sephardic congregation, a group of Spanish Jews, and I am Ashkenazi, and I don't want to sing their songs."

"You could have changed your accent, just a couple of sounds to change. I can speak Sephardic or Ashkenazi. It's not so hard."

"I despise Spanish Jews, their customs, their foods, their arrogance. Maybe you could do it, but I don't want to," he declared fiercely. "I made the trip for nothing and had to sell your engagement and wedding rings that you left at home."

Her silence lasted a dozen heartbeats. With a shocked gasp of outrage she said, "How could you sell the rings you gave me? You didn't even ask me?"

"I needed the money for the flight and the hotel."

Her heart thudded wildly. "You could have borrowed the money from my father. He would've been glad to give you a loan until you got another job."

With a sputter of indignation, Simon answered, "Your Hungarian father? I hate Hungarian peasants. I wouldn't ask him for a pencil."

"My father was born in Manhattan. He's as American as they come. He served in the Army in World War I. His mother came here from Hungary, his father came from Poland."

"It makes no difference to me. I'm a decent Jew from Poland, but your father has Hungarian blood and they are lower than cattle."

A blazing tension escalated in the car as they continued driving home. *I can't stand the outrageous things he does. Now I have a baby, but not a wedding ring. How much longer can I endure this crazy behavior? He hates my parents. He hates me. He hates the whole wide world.*

The next day the members of the conservative congregation gathered in the living room of the house for the circumcision of the eight-day-old infant. Ricky remained in bed agonizing over the pain she imagined the baby felt. Simon had named the baby Jeffrey after his father who had escaped to the United States before the war and died in New York prior to his family's immigration. After the ceremony, a lavish spread with bagels, lox, and salads, platters of fruits, whiskey, wine, soda, and cakes were served. Weary from her lack of sleep, Ricky was bleary-eyed and starved from the lack of food and love.

That evening, eight days after giving birth, Ricky's mind played tricks with reality. "I see people who are huge, blown up like balloons," she confided to Simon in their bedroom.

"I'm calling my psychiatrist," Simon said as he turned, left the bedroom, and went downstairs to telephone.

A warning voice clamored in Ricky's tortured mind, a threat that she was helpless to heed.

His jaw set in grim, tight anger Simon returned and ordered his wife to put on her bathrobe. "Where are we going?" Ricky asked.

"I'm taking you to see Dr. Chase. It's a forty-mile drive. Go to the bathroom first."

Ricky winced at his sharp tone as she donned her bathrobe. "Let's take the baby."

"He's sleeping. He'll be all right without us," Simon said heartlessly.

Simon dragged her down the staircase as she tried desperately to pull back. He pushed her into the car and drove silently on the Long Island Expressway. By the time they reached the psychiatrist's office, Ricky kept thinking about her wretched marriage and her week of despondency in the hospital. Though she wasn't one to shed tears, her body and mind gave way. She wanted to pour out her sorrow to the doctor, but couldn't when her eyes overflowed with tears and hysteria took over.

At 3 a.m. she was admitted to a local hospital in Long Island, left alone in a ground floor room for three days that crept by with surprising slowness. By the third day, after eating and sleeping normally, she peered out the window with a mind that had cleared, although she suffered a nervous flutter in her stomach, and yearned for her motherless baby who was now without breast milk. She was in a perilous situation, married to a dangerous man who would do or say anything to hurt her. He was in charge of her life and she couldn't help herself. She held herself rigid, feeling dread, wondering why she married this man. At twenty-eight years of age, she should have known better.

She began to remember how she had met Simon. The April before last when she and her parents spent the Passover holiday in a hotel in the Catskills, a young man approached her with an engaging smile. When she returned to Brooklyn he began dating her. He wasn't exactly what she had in mind for a husband: short, just her height of 5'7", not bad looking with prominent check bones, intelligent dark piercing eyes, an upward tilted nose, a head of chestnut hair, a high forehead, a wide mouth with full lips, but not an American.

What Simon had going for him was his brilliance and his dedication to a traditional Jewish life. He was pleasant and polite and spoke seven languages, English without a foreign accent. When he emigrated to the United States, he attended Harvard taking various courses and perfecting his English. He was looking to marry a religious woman who wanted children the way he did, and he could provide nicely for a family as he had a home already in Long Island. He held a position as a Cantor in a Conservative Temple, and additionally had the job of teaching children Hebrew and preparing boys for their bar-mitzvah. He asked her for advice on how to decorate the new home he had just moved into as she had told him she had taken courses in interior decorating in college. She was flattered by his attention, his seriousness, his maturity, and was duly impressed by a man who already had a home, a real home, a home that she had yearned for her whole life.

Ricky put aside these memories and sat down on her bed wondering what the future with this heartless man could be. During the time she spent in the hospital where his psychiatrist had put her, he hadn't even come to see her. And then to her surprise, on the fourth day, Simon opened the door of her room and stood there with his arms folded over his chest.

"You're discharged. I brought you underwear and a dress for you to put on. Get dressed quickly," he urged. "I'm taking you to Queens to see our new apartment."

"Queens? I've never been to Queens. New apartment? Why there? What's been happening?" Her insides clenched as a cold chill came over her.

"I got a job teaching in a Hebrew school and moved the furniture from the house to the apartment."

Oh, I can't take these changes, so many, all at once. Help me, Lord. I need your help.

Ricky breathed deeply and asked aloud the gnawing question that was screaming in her mind, "Where is my baby?"

"Jeffrey is being cared for by my sister in Brooklyn. He's gained weight. But before we go to the apartment we're going to a shelter for babies. My sister works in her grocery store and can't devote enough time to a baby, so I want you to see where I'm placing Jeffrey."

"I'm better and I'll take care of our baby. He needs his mother."

"You're not ready. You have to get completely well, and, after you see the apartment, I'm taking you to a private mental hospital in Manhattan that has a fine reputation."

She stared at him, open-mouthed, heat flooding her senses. "But I am better. My mind is clear and I want my baby. I don't want to go to a mental hospital."

Simon gave a malicious smile. "It's already arranged."

Ricky fought for breath as a strange panic startled her.

She couldn't speak. Nothing that she would say would make any difference to this man.

As Simon drove the car along the parkway, Ricky looked through the passenger door window at the private homes, many with plastic children's pools in the backyards and couples who lived there in a carefree existence, people who didn't have to move because the husband had lost his job due to poor judgment, wives who didn't suffer mental anguish and were threatened with hospitalization in a mental jail, babies safe in the arms of their mothers.

Simon came to an abrupt stop in front of a rundown building. "Get out. This is the orphanage. We're going in."

Ricky bit down hard on her chapped lips. He hadn't brought her lipstick and her lips were dry without it. She closed her eyes tightly after she looked at cribs with babies in diapers, all alone, deserted, and orphaned, no one to sing to them, caress them. "I won't agree. You can't put Jeffrey here," she said with her last weak breath. "Not here. Not in this terrible place."

"I'll think it over," Simon said.

A strange panic left Ricky fighting for breath. After they left the orphanage, Simon drove along the parkway, finally parking in a space facing a line of compact two-story houses, each containing an apartment that looked like they were designed by a man without any imagination. When they emerged from the car, a pregnant woman approached them.

"Is this your wife?" she asked as she turned to Simon with a puzzled look.

"Yes," he answered.

"But you told me she was dead."

"No, I didn't. I said she was sick."

The woman waddled away shaking her head.

Ricky knew the pregnant woman heard correctly. *He wishes I was dead. He only wants the baby, not me.*

Ricky groaned after they entered the small four-room apartment with the furniture spread around haphazardly, boxes scattered on top of the sofa and the mattress, the box spring against the wall, everything helter-skelter on scratched wooden floors. "We can't stay here," she said as her eyes swept across the mess.

"I'm taking you to stay with your friend overnight," he said as they re-entered the car.

Simon drove to Brooklyn and parked the car in the street next to a twelve-story apartment building where Paula lived with her husband. Ricky remembered her friend, Paula, from the time they lived in the N.Y.U. college dormitory. He rang the bell of an apartment on the sixth floor and, when Paula answered, he asked if he could leave Ricky overnight.

"Of course," she said. "I have a guest room and Ricky is welcome to stay as long as she needs."

"Thank you," Simon said. "May I speak to you in private?"

Paula and Simon stepped into the kitchen while Ricky examined the living room furnished in American colonial style. She sank down carefully on a Windsor chair groaning as her hemorrhoids burned like a bonfire. Her eyes moved to the carved wood writing desk topped with a cobalt blue ginger jar stoneware lamp that matched the drapes on the window. In the corner of the room a seven-foot grandfather clock clicked away each minute. *Oh God, the time is flying minute by minute. Where will he put me tomorrow? Maybe Paula can save me.*

After Simon left, Paula sat down on a ladder-backed chair next to Ricky.

"What did my husband have to say?" Ricky fisted her hands.

Paula, a blonde with shiny blue eyes, clamped her lips together and rubbed her diamond clad hand on her navy slacks. "He said you tried to kill your baby."

Ricky moaned. "What else?"

"He said that I should keep knives away from you as you already attempted suicide."

"Lies, all lies. I fear Simon greatly. He said he's putting me in another hospital tomorrow. He probably told them the same story about my being suicidal and that I made an attempt to kill my baby. Believe me, he hates me the way he hates the whole world."

Paula stood up and put her hand on Ricky's shoulder. "I see your mind is clear. I believe you. Frankly I never thought you should have married him. When I first met him, I had a bad feeling about the man."

"Please, Paula, don't let him put me in the next hospital."

"Don't worry. I won't let him take you."

Chapter 3

THE NEXT DAY PAULA was in the shower when the bell rang. Ricky froze and didn't open up until Simon's fists beat at the door. As soon as she let him in, Simon pulled her out without a word to Paula. Her insides clenched as a chill spread in the pit of her stomach.

In the hospital the nurses assigned her to a private room that was clean and bright and looked like a room in a five-star hotel, not like the jail she imagined she would be in. But it was a jail, with nurses quietly efficient with icy eyes and cold ways. Ricky trembled with a gnawing anxiety and prayed she were any place but there.

An hour later, Dr. McLeish, a man in his forties with a broad brow and a full head of blond hair, interviewed her in an office with files piled high on a mahogany desk. He picked up a pen and held it over a lined pad.

"How do you feel?" he asked kindly.

Ricky bit down on her dry lips as her bloodshot hazel eyes filled with tears. *He asks how I feel. I'm an unwilling patient in a mental hospital. I have no cosmetics, no brush or comb for my thick tangled hair. I feel embarrassed just looking at the dirt on my white print dress. I lost so much weight the dress hangs on me.*

Trying to protect herself, Ricky crossed her arms over her chest.

How does he expect me to feel after giving birth less than two weeks ago, losing my memory in the hospital, losing my baby, and then my home; and married to a psychologically damaged man in charge of my life, a man I never should have married? I feel lousy.

"I'm a little depressed," Ricky said in a low voice.

"We have something to make you feel better," the psychiatrist said with a slight smile.

The following morning Ricky was placed in a queue in a corridor with ten patients. The hospital was air-conditioned and the corridor chilly. Ricky pulled her black sweater close to her trembling body.

Without warning, one of the white-haired patients, fourth in line, screamed with tortured breath, "Let me out of here. I don't want to go. No! No! No!" Two hospital guards seized her as she broke away and started running. "Let me go," she yelled, but the guards held her firmly as they dragged her to the front of the line.

Ricky's knees felt rubbery as she entered the room that had a large machine next to a table where she was placed and strapped down. *I feel like I'm a victim in a concentration camp.*

She was then quickly injected with a needle. *It's the bite of a poisonous cobra. I'm in Hell.*

She became unconscious after being hooked up to the psychotron apparatus.

Electricity ransacked her weak body with convulsions, and, when she was held up by two nurses and led back to her room, she was completely disoriented. Nothing on this earth could be worse than this experience. The room with the machine was her torture chamber, her snake pit. Brain damage was the result, even though some psychiatrists believed otherwise. Years later, she was sure she had lost her 140 I.Q. and many of her stored memories.

After nine shock treatments, Ricky couldn't remember if she used a fork in her left or right hand. Europeans use a fork in their left hand, but she didn't know who she was. The nurse said, "Your husband is coming to see you."

"I have a husband?" She didn't remember being married.

A man entered the day room and stopped at the table where Ricky sat alone, her hands crossed over her chest as if protecting herself from further abuse. She studied him through cool, narrowed eyes, not recognizing him. He took a seat next to her, gave her a wry look, and laconically announced, "The baby is doing well."

Somehow Ricky remembered she gave birth to a baby. She couldn't be married to such a short man, but she supposed she was. She sent him a reproachful glance, straining her eyes, as she couldn't see well and didn't know where her glasses were.

If he were my real husband, he would have brought me cosmetics, clean clothes, and glasses. What proof do I have that he's telling the truth?

"You're being discharged," the man said impatiently.

"Where will I go? Will I have my baby?" Ricky was wildly excited, breathless with anticipation.

"You are not well. You don't remember me, do you?"

Ricky hesitated. Wretchedly, she said, "No, I don't know who you are."

"That's why you have to go to a voluntary hospital so you can remember and recuperate. You're lucky that this hospital has room for you. I'll take you there and I'll visit you. The baby is being cared for. Just concentrate on getting well."

Flustered, Ricky said, "I don't want to go to another hospital. I'll get well at home. Where is home?"

"We have an apartment in Queens and the hospital isn't far from there."

"Will you bring me clean clothes, a comb and brush, cosmetics, my glasses?"

"Yes, tomorrow I'll come with all those things, and I'll bring you a picture of the baby and your prayer book. Today you're going to the hospital."

"Do I have to go to another hospital? Will they put me on the machine?" With a pleading look, Ricky looked at the man who claimed to be her husband.

"Yes, you must go in order to recover. The doctor told me there will be no more shock treatments. I'm driving you there as soon as you're discharged from here," Simon said in an icy tone.

Chapter 4

SIMON'S STRONG FINGERS CLENCHED the upper part of Ricky's arm, as he dragged her along a path that led into a hospital behind high brick walls. Ricky struggled uselessly to free herself from Simon's tight grasp. Inside an aide took her arm and led her away. Without a word, Simon strode away leaving her alone and dejected, feeling weak in every muscle and bone in her body.

Her room was unadorned, twin beds, a dresser, no pictures, no window. She was shut away in a tomb. A slightly overweight young woman with dirty blond hair and a bad permanent sat on one bed reading a book. She looked up.

"Welcome. I'm Sharon, your roommate.

"I'm Ricky."

Sharon opened the closet. "There are hangers in here for your clothes and the bottom two drawers in the dresser are yours."

"I have no stuff yet. My husband says he'll bring my things tomorrow."

Ricky looked at the mirror over the dresser and almost failed to recognize the pale woman with the long dark tangled hair and frightened eyes who stared back at her. She was behind bars, a prisoner with no way to escape.

She sat down on the edge of the bed, her arms crossed, hugging her shoulders.

"Why are you here?" Sharon asked with a warm smile.

"The doctor told me I have post-partum depression. I gave birth to a boy in July and now it's September." Ricky reached into the pocket of her sweater and drew out a picture of a newborn with dark hair and thick lips. She handed it to Sharon who studied it and said, "He sure looks like a healthy boy."

"I had nine shock treatments that made me lose my memory. Why are you here?"

"I turned on the gas and put my head in the oven. There are times I try to commit suicide. My two kids are home and my husband is taking care of them. It isn't so bad here. The doctors are nice and the food is passable."

The next day to Ricky's surprise Simon did bring everything that Ricky wanted, and he rushed away without asking how she was, just saying he had to go to work. Ricky sat down in the day room with *The New York Times* and read the news, hoping her memory would come back soon so she could go home. She turned to the obituary page and gasped as she read that her Aunt Sari had died, an aunt who was like the grandmothers she never had. Aunt Sari was twenty years older than her mother, an angel on this earth who never raised her voice, a kind, considerate person, a softer individual than her own mother. Ricky sat in a fog of discomfort and depression.

The next Sunday Ricky's parents visited and found her sitting like an island in a corner of the day room. Comprehension crashed through her when she remembered them as her mother and father. Her spirits lifted a little. Her father was frowning as he carried a shopping bag that seemed to weigh him down. When he took off his hat, the large bald spot on the top of his head was dotted with freckles. Her mother, a short stout woman looked sad.

"It's a long trip for you to take," Ricky said as she gave them a wan smile.

"You're our only child and we'd go to the ends of the earth for you," her father said. "It only took a little over an hour, not bad for an old Chevy."

"Can you get me out of here?" Ricky asked wretchedly.

"We spoke to the doctor and he told us you're still depressed and not ready to be released," her mother said as she looked at Ricky with sympathy.

"What about my baby? Have you seen him?" Ricky glanced from her father to her mother and back again.

"Simon refused to let us near him." Her father's jaw tightened. "He claims your mother and I are responsible for your breakdown."

"How ridiculous; I don't understand that cruel man," Ricky said as she felt both anger and sadness. I won't be able to be a teacher when I leave here. I have to make a living since I can't rely on a man who calls himself my husband. Please bring me my typewriter and I'll practice typing so I can get a job as a secretary."

"All right, I'll bring it next Sunday," her father said as he nodded his bald head now glistening with perspiration. "I can't come sooner as I'm working every day." He reached into the shopping bag and drew out a box of chocolates and fruit. "We brought some Barton's candy, bananas, apples, and chocolate chip cookies. You're so thin and drawn that you have to make sure you eat well so you'll get home faster."

Ricky opened the chocolates and popped one into her mouth, rolling it around her tongue, trying to remember how she used to enjoy the sweetness. She embraced her mother and father who hugged her back. "Thank you for being you. I love you both."

Ricky kissed her parents goodbye and sat alone with tears welling in her eyes. She put the chocolates, fruit, and cookies in her bureau drawer.

The next day it was gone.

"My food has disappeared," Ricky told Sharon disgustedly.

Sharon looked sympathetic. "It's Elsie. She steals everything she can get her hands on. She's a nasty kleptomaniac. The guard always goes into her room and finds what she's stolen and he gives it back to the patients. And then she goes and steals some more. I never got back my favorite bra."

The next day as Ricky was sitting alone at a table in the day room while two aides talked in the corner, an unshaven man who looked like he was in his early twenties approached hesitantly. He took a seat next to her and Ricky, propping her chin on the heel of her hand, studied his brooding eyes.

She felt his eyes scourge her face. Then his mouth curved in a shaky smile. "Hi. I'm Bill. What's your name?"

I don't need to complicate my life with another man so I'll tell it like it is. "I'm Ricky. I don't have a wedding ring, but I'm married."

He laughed, making a kind of eerie sound. "That's okay. I wasn't coming on to you. I just needed to talk and you look like you might be a good listener."

"Talk away, Bill. I have nothing to do so I can listen all you want."

"I'm a statistician, good at my job. Then something strange happened one day. My mind opened up and I kept doing more and more complex math problems until my folks got frightened and the doctor said I needed hospitalization. Now they put me on a drug and I can't even add two plus two. I hate it here. What's your story?"

"I hate it, too. I gave birth and then I saw people blown up like Humpty Dumpty and my husband had me put in two hospitals and this is the third. I had shock treatments and when I see some people I can't remember who they are. The doctor told me to play the piano." Ricky turned her head and pointed to the piano in the corner. "I can't remember how to play the piano. I can't even remember my marriage. My husband is a stranger to me although I remember my parents."

Bill nodded. "That's normal for shock treatment. Maybe it's good you can't remember your husband. Was he a good husband?"

"I don't know. When he comes here he smiles and tells me about my baby. He writes me letters and each letter lists the time of day and what he does during that time, as if I'm interested in his schedule. All I know is that I'm miserable."

After that time, Ricky and Bill met often in the day room and shared their wretchedness.

One morning after another sleepless night, Ricky heard a commotion in the corridor. She sat up in bed wondering what was happening. The noise increased so she quickly put on her flannel robe, stepped out, and moved next to Sharon who was looking through the open corridor door at the men's side.

"What's going on?" Ricky asked. "Who's the man in the strait jacket with his back to me?"

"That's Bill," Sharon said. "He became manic and managed to cut his wrists during the night. They put him in restraints and will keep him in a locked padded room until the doctor medicates him."

"That poor young man," Ricky said in a whisper. "He's so nice. I feel sorry for him. Wish I could do something to help him."

"Well, you can't," Sharon said as she stepped back into their room with Ricky following, her head hanging down.

*   *   *

Every week a group of doctors and nurses like a flock of ducks walked around and spoke to each patient. The chief in charge of medication approached Ricky. She didn't like his grim mouth and the hard expression in his cold eyes.

"How are you today?" he asked her as his eyes scanned each inch of her body.

"I still can't remember and I'm not happy about that," Ricky answered, her eyes cast downward.

"We'll try a medication for you." The doctor wrote the prescription on a pad on a clipboard he carried.

"I don't want any medication. I just want to leave here."

"Not right now, young woman. You're not ready to be discharged."

The next afternoon when the nurse came around the corridor with the medication trolley and the patients lined up, Ricky stayed in her room. The nurse, thin as an electric wire, stepped in with a pill in a paper cup. "You have to swallow this, doctor's orders."

"I don't want it," Ricky cried. "You can't force me to take it."

The nurse's face turned cherry red in sharp contrast to her stark white uniform. "I can force you and I will."

She called in a male aide whose muscles bulged from his short-sleeved white jacket. "Hold her down," she ordered.

The aide pushed her down on her bed while the nurse took a needle and stabbed her. Shaking and furious with the abuse, Ricky vowed to accept the pill without objecting. The following week Ricky's vision clouded until she was almost completely blind. She begged her psychiatrist to stop the pills, but he said he wasn't in charge of medication.

One day, as the women lined up to go to the dining room Ricky, who now was completely blind, felt her knees go rubbery and she collapsed in the corridor. A short young woman helped her to her feet. *I'll never forget the kindness of this woman.*

Ricky sat on her bed that night and tried to figure out a way for the horrible Thorazine pills to be stopped. Three weeks the pills were forced on her. She felt more despondent than ever. Every night when she couldn't sleep, she tried to come up with the solution to the horror of the effect of the pills. She kept mulling over in her head what Dr. Zeki, her Turkish psychiatrist, had said. "Why are you depressed?"

This meant that he felt she shouldn't be depressed. She was young and had the future ahead of her. Her health was good. Her parents were supportive. Ricky decided not to be depressed. If she told her psychiatrist, Dr. Zeki, she was feeling better, it might make a difference.

It did make a world of difference. The pills were stopped. Her vision returned. *Thank God. But how long will I have to remain in this unendurable mental hospital?*

Chapter 5

Ricky dwelled on Dr. Zeki's question, "Why are you depressed?" Gradually her attitude changed and she realized that one day she'd be out of the hospital and have her baby back, and it isn't a big deal if she couldn't remember certain things which weren't important anyway.

The next month, Dr. Zeki gave his permission for Ricky to visit her baby and she was elated, but as she sat in the passenger seat of Simon's car and looked up at the dark sky with raindrops loud like pellets, a shiver of dread flowed down her spine. She didn't trust this man. Who knew what he was up to?

Simon parked in front of a six-story apartment house whose bricks were dark with grime. They took the dirty elevator to the third floor and entered a gloomy apartment with shabby furniture and the smell of urine. The heavy rain spattered against the living room window and a forty watt bulb illuminated the white crib with nursery rhyme figures on it. Ricky remembered how she had taken pains in selecting the most attractive crib in the store, and now it was in her sister-in-law's apartment.

Her baby lay in the crib clutching the quilt she had embroidered for a month. He was a good-looking infant, not the homely baby she first remembered when he was born, but he didn't seem like the baby that was snatched away from her. This baby was a stranger to her.

"May I hold him?" Ricky asked Simon.

"No. You'll frighten him. He doesn't know you."

Ricky's heart throbbed with desperation.

A three-year-old boy approached the crib, put his small hands through the bars, and with the force of an older child began to punch Jeffrey. Her infant started to bawl in pain. Her stomach twisted in knots.

"That's Jeffrey's first cousin," Simon said. "He's jealous of the baby. Stop it, Moshe. Don't hit the baby."

Moshe's reaction was to pinch the baby and stalk away from the crib with his thumb in his mouth.

Simon's stout sister, Leah, opened the front door and entered the living room. She had been working in her grocery around the corner. Leah wore a dirt-spattered apron over a housedress the size of a pickle barrel. Ignoring Ricky, she took a jar of baby food and with a spoon stuffed it hurriedly into Jeffrey's mouth. The blood rushed to Ricky's face as she observed how her son was mistreated by her nephew and sister-in-law. Simon seemed to take it all in stride while Ricky's heart pounded.

Her brother-in-law walked in from the bathroom dressed only in boxer shorts. Shocked, Ricky noticed that he had pieces of toilet paper hanging down from his shorts.

Ricky looked with surprise at Simon who offered an explanation. "He has dysentery from the concentration camp. My sister's baby was thrown to the ground by the Nazis and killed, and that's why she wants to take care of my baby even though she has to rush from their grocery. She's doing a good job and you should be grateful."

Grateful, he says. I should be grateful for the

mistreatment of a poor innocent infant? I'll do anything I can to get out of the hospital and get my baby back.

When Ricky returned to the hospital, she pleaded with Dr. Zeki. "My baby is being abused. I must be discharged."

"Tomorrow there's going to be a conference of doctors, a nurse, and a social worker to determine if you're ready for discharge. You may be present if you wish." Dr. Zeki placed his elbows on his desk and steepled his hairy fingers.

"I want to be there." Ricky had a determined expression. "I've been here seven months, that's long enough. I've been separated from my baby for nine months. I can't take it any longer."

At 10 a.m. the next morning Ricky sat in the middle of a long oak table in the conference room. She offered a weak smile to Dr. Zeki who returned an encouraging smile. Seated at the head of the table was the medication doctor, Dr. Richardson, the chief nurse, and a social worker fidgeting with her fingers looking like she wanted to be somewhere else.

"How are you feeling today?" Dr. Zeki asked.

"I'm okay. I'd like to be discharged." Rivulets of sweat ran down from Ricky's armpits but she wouldn't reveal how nervous she felt.

Dr. Richardson shook his head. "I don't think you're ready to go just yet."

"Why not?" Ricky asked in a thin voice as she picked at a loose thread on her sweater.

"Your husband told us before you were admitted that not only did you try to commit suicide, you also attempted to murder your baby. We can't take a chance that you would do this again."

"Those are out-and-out lies," Ricky raised her voice to

almost a cry. His gullibility had engendered a feeling of anger. She rose to her feet.

"Take your seat," Dr. Richardson said.

Ricky sat back down as adrenaline rushed through her. She looked at him as if he were an open wound draining pus.

"Why would your husband lie about something so serious?" Dr. Richardson asked as he opened his dark eyes wide.

"I don't know." Ricky's jaw tightened. "I think he hates me. He wants his sister to keep my baby."

"I doubt that very much, but I thank you for your input. We'll let you know our decision tomorrow. You may go now." Dr. Richardson pointed to the door where a male aide stood waiting to accompany her.

As usual, Ricky couldn't sleep that night. She tossed in her bed like a schooner in a storm.

The next day at her session with Dr. Zeki, he said, "The committee reached the decision that you are not to be discharged, but that every weekend you may stay with your parents. Perhaps you'll be able to sleep when you're away from the hospital."

"At least that's some concession," Ricky reflected with chagrin.

The wind howled like a wailing wolf, but the March sun shone brightly when Simon visited Ricky.

"I have good news," Simon said as he gazed at Ricky with an evil eye. "It's a beautiful day and I have permission to take you for a walk outside. It's windy, so put on your coat."

Ricky could feel the tension in him. She didn't want to walk with him but didn't know how to refuse, so she walked alongside of him shivering from the wind and the bad emanations from her husband. He was like a live wire sputtering with dangerous electricity.

"How do you feel walking around the hospital?" Simon asked.

"It feels a little strange. I haven't been outside except for the time we went to see the baby."

Simon pointed to an immense building many blocks from the hospital. "Take a good look at that place. It's Creedmoor, a mental hospital for the severely disturbed. I'm going to put you there for the rest of your life."

Ricky cowered with fright as panic seized her. At that moment she realized she could never live with this evil man.

* * *

On Friday afternoon Ricky waited in the day room, her coat on, her hands in her lap.

"It's warm in here," Sharon said. "There's time enough for you to put on your coat when your father comes."

"The minute he comes, I'm leaving." Ricky made a concession by opening the top button of her coat.

"Here he is," Sharon said as a medium-sized man holding a felt hat walked in. She noticed he wore a winter coat with shredded button holes. The dark hair around the sides and back of his bald head was sprinkled with gray. Ricky's hospitalization had aged him.

His face lit up when he spied his daughter. "Have a good visit," Sharon called out as she walked to the other side of the room.

Ricky felt comfortable sitting in the passenger seat while her father drove his old Chevy from Queens to the Midwood section of Brooklyn. It was like an escape from Alcatraz, and she heaved a sigh of relief.

The four-story apartment house looked just like it did when she had lived there in the small three-room apartment on the second floor in the rear. There was a little flower garden on either side of the entranceway where Rose of Sharon bushes were planted. Gone was the foliage, but the blooms would return in late spring.

She held onto the bannister as she climbed the narrow marble staircase remembering how many times she had done this while going to junior high school, high school, and college. When her father took out his door key, her mother pulled the door open and planted a kiss on Ricky's cheek. Her mother, a head shorter than her daughter, had added twenty pounds to her stature from the fattening Jewish diet. She wore a flowered polyester dress and her silky black hair was peppered with white. Her features were well-proportioned and, even in her sixties, one could see where she might have been an attractive younger woman. Her husband had wedded her thirty-one years ago although she was eight years older than he, but he never mentioned the difference in age and never minded it.

"I prepared candles for you to light. Shabbos is almost here," her mother said as they entered the small kitchen. The kitchen table was covered with a white tablecloth and two polished sets of candlesticks, one brass and the other silver. The table was propped against the wall with three chairs around it.

Before lighting the candles her mother had something to do. Ricky smiled knowingly as she noticed the laundry hanging from the unique retractable clothesline on the ceiling. Quickly her mother untied the rope, lowered the ceiling-mounted clothesline, opened the clothes pins, and gathered the dry clothes in a plastic basket. Then she tugged at the rope and it rose to the ceiling. *My poor mother still does the wash by hand.*

Her mother lit the candles first, then said the prayer, as her eyes brimmed over with tears that slid down her rosy cheeks. Ricky recalled that her mother always cried every Friday night as she remembered the loss of her parents, her grandmother, four brothers and one sister. Ricky had seldom shed tears since the time when she was five-years-old and her mother had told her not to cry when they saw a sad scene in a movie with Shirley Temple.

The meal was the same one as every Shabbos, first chopped liver followed by gefilte fish which was not a fish but a ball of chopped white fish and pike mixed with egg, sugar, salt, and matzo meal and dropped into boiling water. Cold gefilte fish was always partnered with red horseradish. Ricky took a nickel full of the sharp stuff and poured on a teaspoon of sugar as she didn't like the sting of the horseradish. Then her mother served the chicken soup with kneidlach, another ball of matzo meal and eggs.

The main dish, that her father served, was a chicken breast with string beans, a sweet potato, and a side of cranberry jelly. Dessert was tea and sponge cake. The cutlery and the dishes never matched, but everyone took this for granted. *How wonderful to be eating at my parent's home. Every dish is kosher and in the hospital I have to eat only fruits, vegetables, bread, and dairy. I haven't had chicken for seven months. If only I could stay here with my baby, I'd be so relieved.*

After the meal Ricky's father opened the prayer book and recited 'Grace After Meals' in Hebrew as Ricky and her mother said it in low tones. The lengthy prayer took ten minutes to complete and, when it was finished, it was her father's job to put away the leftovers in the old refrigerator. He had to employ ingenuity to find places in the tiny refrigerator for the leftovers they would eat for lunch tomorrow on the Sabbath after they went to the synagogue. The leftovers would be heated on the asbestos pad that covered one lit gas burner, as it was forbidden by strict Jewish law on the Sabbath to open gas or electricity.

Ricky slept on the red couch in the living room. On the Sabbath, a lit floor lamp offered the light they needed to read. After Ricky said her nightly prayers, she closed her eyes, feeling loved and secure, and in fifteen minutes she was asleep.

On Sunday, Ricky approached her father after he had finished his daily morning prayers and put away his tephillin and tallis in a blue velvet pouch.

"Daddy, I slept last night."

"That's great."

"I never could fall asleep in the hospital." Ricky looked straight at her father's pale amber eyes. "I don't want to go back to the hospital. I want to stay here with you and Mama. I can never live again with Simon as he said he will put me in Creedmoor for the rest of my life."

"You're not discharged, but I'll call the psychiatrist and see if you can stay."

Ricky's father went into the kitchen, and picked up the phone on the little table next to the window. He returned to the living room where Ricky was folding the bed linens. "The doctor says if you're comfortable here, he sees no reason for you to go back to the hospital. It's a voluntary hospital and you don't have to be discharged. He recommended that you continue to see a psychiatrist."

As Ricky kissed her father on his unshaved cheek, the bristles rubbed against her lips but she didn't mind. Her eyes lit up like Sabbath candles. She didn't have to return to the mental hospital. Then she closed her eyes and felt the beauty of freedom. *How wonderful!*

Chapter 6

FOR THREE LONG DAYS after Ricky came to live with her parents, she spent all her time reading in the apartment. Her father had retired as a clerk in the main post office in Manhattan, but he still kept his job as a messenger on Wall Street. When he came home on a sunny day, he hung up his overcoat, took off his hat, and put on a yarmulke. He sat down on the sofa next to her and she closed the book she was reading.

"What are you reading?" he asked.

"Just a mystery by Agatha Christie. I don't know what else to do. Mama doesn't let me cook or clean and I feel useless."

"You'll get depressed doing nothing but reading."

"What do you suggest?"

"First of all I want to tell you about the inscription on the general post office building where I worked. It says, 'Neither snow nor rain nor heat nor gloom of night stay these couriers from the swift completion of their appointed rounds.' This means nothing should keep you from getting better and leading a normal life. You have to leave behind the sadness and keep going on your appointed rounds."

"I'm mystified. What appointed rounds do you mean?"

"How about going to school? I'll pay the tuition. There's a business school a few blocks away."

Ricky put her hand on his arm. "That's so generous of you. But my mind couldn't absorb anything right now. I had nine shock treatments. I don't think I'm up to it."

"But you were typing in the hospital. Couldn't you at least try?"

"I don't think so, Daddy."

Her father cleared his throat. "I'm offering you this opportunity. Don't turn it down."

"All right, I'll try. Maybe I could learn to type faster, but I'm not so sure how I'd do in stenography."

"Wouldn't you like to go to school?"

"Yes, I would."

The next day, when Ricky walked the few blocks to the school, she had diminished expectations of herself. Unsure of her ability to concentrate, her breath came in spurts. The wind whistling through the trees seemed to say, "Watch out. Watch out." She didn't want to disappoint her father but her mind wasn't as clear as before the shock treatments.

The school occupied the top floor of a two-story building. Ricky, her heart racing, held heavily onto the banister as she climbed the dark staircase.

Can I do this? Is my mind working right?

Suddenly a young woman bounced down the stairs almost knocking her over. *Should I turn around and go home? I don't know what to do.*

The young student turned to her. "Sorry, I didn't expect to see anyone. If you're looking for the office, it's the door on the right at the top of the stairs."

It didn't take long for Ricky to be admitted, given text books, and told to come back tomorrow at 9 a.m.

It poured the next day as Ricky's fingers tightened around her umbrella, and her heart beat as fast as the cold rain that splashed and plunged all around her. She couldn't bear the possibility of failure and that's what she was faced with. Ricky remembered the rage and bitterness in Simon's voice when he threatened her with a mental hospital for the rest of her life. She wouldn't give in to negativity. No. She would go on and do the best she could in the business school.

Her Gregg stenography teacher, Miss Blare, a middle-aged woman whose hair was a mess and who swallowed half her words, asked her to read back her notes.

"I can't. You're dictating too fast for me."

Miss Blare grunted. "I'm dictating only 100 words a minute. Keep trying. You'll catch on."

In three days Ricky could read back her notes. Also, her typing improved rapidly. Ricky's self-confidence rose like an air balloon and she was delighted that her father sent her to the business school that was only a ten-minute walk door-to-door.

A woman in her forties, Diane Davis, befriended Ricky. She encouraged her, and one day, while waiting for the typing teacher, Diane praised her progress. Diane had a soft, comforting voice and wore her hair short with long bangs over her forehead.

"How come you're going to business school?" Diane asked.

"I was in a hospital for many months and I need to prepare myself to make a living."

Diane put her lips to the soda can and took a hefty drink. "I was also hospitalized. How are you paying the school?"

"My father is paying my tuition."

"If you apply to New York State Vocational Services, they'll pay the bill and give you money for lunch and transportation."

To Ricky's amazement, the government gave her the grant.

One evening Ricky and her parents were watching 'The Danny Thomas Show' on TV. When the commercial came on, Ricky said, "I want to get my baby, but I have to prove that I'm a fit mother as Simon will try to prove I'm mentally sick."

"You need to see a psychiatrist on a regular basis," her father said. "My sister told me she would be happy to help you out. She'll pay for each visit."

There was a beat of silence in the small room as Ricky absorbed this fantastic gift. "Oh, I'm so glad. She's a wonderful aunt."

"You bet," her father agreed. "Carrie has money put aside to help you, and her husband need never know as he wouldn't approve."

After Ricky graduated from business school, she began to have regular sessions with a psychiatrist in Manhattan. Dr. Berger was a pleasant man with a short trimmed beard and mustache who encouraged her to return to college and take more education courses.

Ricky enrolled in Brooklyn College and her mind absorbed learning like a clean sponge. Meanwhile Simon refused to let her see the baby. There was no money for a lawyer, so Ricky applied to Legal Aid and got a lawyer *pro bono.*

Many months had passed, and the baby was now thirteen months old. One hot day in August, Ricky and her father walked to the grocery on Kings Highway near Ocean Avenue.

"I'm going to go to court to get custody of Jeffrey," Ricky said.

"Perhaps you should leave him where he is," her father said. "It would be easier for you than to raise a child as a single mother."

Ricky's stomach clenched tight at the thought that her father didn't understand the pull a mother has to care for her baby. "It will be hard, but it's what I want to do."

Legal Aid assigned a lawyer to represent Ricky. He was a sloppy dresser, but he was on her side and they went to Family Court where the judge ordered a psychological examination for Ricky once Simon reiterated his false claim about her attempt to kill the baby.

"What was your diagnosis from the hospital?" the psychologist asked in a kindly way. She was a woman in her thirties, svelte and attractive with blond hair in a French knot.

"They told me I had post-partum depression. I had nine shock treatments and couldn't remember many things, but I know I never tried to kill my baby even though my husband said I had."

"I doubt you had post-partum depression eight days after giving birth. What you told me about not sleeping or eating well in the hospital for the first week you were there could've brought on the symptoms you describe. It didn't help that your husband was absent the entire time. I believe you're able to care for your baby, and you should pursue this course."

Ricky returned to Family Court and still the judge wasn't convinced that she should be awarded the infant. He looked down at her with pale blue eyes from his perch on the bench. "I order that your husband pay for a psychiatric examination for you."

Ricky stared at him with a grim look. *If Simon pays for the psychiatrist, he'll find that I'm not well enough to get custody of my baby, but I have no choice and I'll go to his psychiatrist.*

As Ricky sat next to the window in the subway car, with a tight jaw and a quivering stomach, her eyes were on the passing scenery but her mind was on the coming interview by the psychiatrist Simon selected. *How can the doctor be impartial? It's impossible. If only the Lord will help me, I'll be a good mother. I promise.*

Ricky sat like a rock in the leather armchair in front of the psychiatrist. His expression was grim as he asked her what she had been doing since she left the hospital.

"I'm living with my parents. I graduated from business school and I've been taking education courses in college. I eat well and I sleep well and I don't take medication."

"Sounds fine," the psychiatrist said. "But your husband has made the assertion that you tried to kill your baby. What do you say to that?"

"It's not true, but I have no way to prove it. It puts you in a tough position, doctor. If you say that I'm able to care for my baby, and then I go and kill him, you'll be responsible. What are you going to do?"

"You're a bright lady. I will send you to a psychologist who will administer tests and she will have the final say."

Once again, Ricky had to be subjected to testing, but the psychologist was kind and understanding and his report said that Ricky was well enough to get custody of her infant.

Chapter 7

IN COURT SIMON DID everything in his power to stop Ricky from obtaining custody. And then the fateful day arrived, when Jeffrey was walking and talking at the age of fourteen months, when the judge ordered that Ricky could take him to her parent's apartment. Her emotions went from a high of ecstasy to a low of doubt that she could be a good mother. *I have no experience. I won't know what to do.*

Climbing onto the front seat of her father's old car, Ricky was perturbed, not knowing if Simon would release Jeffrey. Her father accelerated onto Bedford Avenue. They passed Brooklyn College and, with warmth, she remembered the day she graduated with a Bachelor's Degree in Science. Never in her wildest imagination would she ever think that she'd be married to a damaged husband who tried with lies to keep her baby from her. Now her baby was with his emotionally impaired aunt in a dark, smelly apartment, but soon he might be in her loving arms.

When they became enmeshed in traffic near Flatbush Avenue, her father slowed down, cleared his throat, and attempted to calm Ricky's electrically charged nerves.

"Don't worry, everything will be all right. Your mother and I will be there to help you."

Ricky fisted her hands. "I can't help worrying. I don't know anything about caring for a fourteen-month old baby who's been abused."

"You're a mother. It'll come naturally to you."

They stopped at another traffic light that changed and her father pulled across the intersection. After traveling another few blocks, he parked in front of the apartment house.

Simon's sister stood outside clutching Jeffrey to her enormous chest while Simon stood guard over the crib, carriage, high chair, playpen, and boxes filled with baby things. Ricky's father opened the trunk and without Simon's help loaded the lot into the trunk and the back of the car. When everything was tightly packed, Ricky held out her hands to the baby who remained in Simon's sister's arms.

"You lazy bitch! I've taken care of the baby for fourteen months. You have no right to him. This is my baby," Simon's sister screeched as she spit on the sidewalk.

Ricky, breathing hard, tried to ignore this outpouring of rage. She snatched the baby from her, and patted him on his back. Suddenly, Jeffrey clung to her and called out in a clear voice, "Daddy."

Ricky turned to Simon. "Why doesn't he call me, Mama?"

Simon with an evil grin said, "We never taught him that word."

"I'll teach it to him," Ricky said as she entered the car and sat on the passenger side holding Jeffrey on her lap. They drove away as Jeffrey looked at her with interest and seemed happy to be leaving. Again he called out, "Daddy."

"Mama," Ricky said. "I'm Mama."

"Daddy," the baby said. "Daddy."

Chapter 8

WITH THE BABY IN her arms, Ricky entered the three-room apartment on the second floor. This was her dream come true and she felt a surge of strength. Her mother, in the same polyester dress she wore almost every day, held out her arms for the baby to come to her. He pulled back and began to cry.

"It will take time for him to be comfortable with you," Ricky said holding the baby on her lap trying to comfort him as she sat down on the daybed in the living room.

"Where do you want the crib?" her father asked as he brought in the crib in sections.

"Perpendicular to the daybed but not blocking the doorway to the foyer," Ricky said as she kept patting her baby on his back.

After the crib was assembled, Ricky attempted to change the baby's diaper. She struggled with the diaper pin since she had never held one before, but the baby lay quietly looking with interest at her, and she was proud that she had mastered the skill of diaper-changing.

The crib was next to a large mirror with a ribbon shaped gilt frame. Jeffrey peered at himself in the mirror and, holding on to the sides of the crib, he bounced up and down.

When Ricky's father held out his hands to the baby, Jeffrey looked alarmed, pulled back, whimpered and called, "Daddy."

Ricky picked him up and put him in his high chair that had a design of a clown on the top. "Don't worry, he'll get used to you. I'm going to feed him banana and cereal now. He must be hungry."

Jeffrey clamped his lips shut when Ricky put the spoon with the food next to his mouth. "It's all right, Jeffrey, I know how she hurt you with the spoon. I'm putting the spoon down now." Ricky picked up the food in her hand and placed her fingers near the baby's mouth. He opened his mouth and let her feed him.

"Poor baby," Ricky whispered. "A spoon is now your enemy. I'll feed you from my fingers as long as it takes for your fear to disappear."

Ricky noticed that Jeffrey wouldn't drink his bottle unless it was held for him. One day when Jeffrey asked for his bottle when Ricky was pushing his carriage on Kings Highway, she handed him the bottle.

"From now on if you want to drink from your bottle you have to hold it yourself," Ricky said firmly.

Jeffrey gave her a sharp look, took the bottle in his hands and began to suck. I'm learning fast to be a good mother, Ricky thought with pride.

One rainy day when the baby was stuck in the apartment, Ricky called Sharon's home. Her husband barked, "My wife will be discharged next week."

Two weeks later Sharon called Ricky and invited her and the baby to her home.

"We're going visiting," Ricky told Jeffrey as she dressed him in a three-piece outfit. He looked cute in shorts, a shirt, a vest, and a bow tie. Underneath he still wore his diaper and plastic pants. She put him in his carriage and walked ten blocks to a private home where Sharon, her husband, and her two school-aged children lived.

When Ricky rang the doorbell, Sharon opened the door, and with a hug she greeted her. Jeffrey looked at the stranger and cried until his cheeks were covered with tears. "I feel so bad," Ricky said, "that my baby was so mistreated that he fears people, can't eat with a spoon, and calls me 'Daddy'."

"I'm so sorry," Sharon said as she stood in the doorway. "Give it time and he'll come around. He calls you 'Daddy' and clings to you because he knows you're his mother. How did you feel when you saw him after so many months?"

"Truthfully, I felt like I lost my baby and this was a baby I was adopting, but nevertheless I looked forward to loving him."

"It's only natural to feel that way. You both need time to bond," Sharon said as she stepped back. "Come again next week and see if he still will be frightened of me."

When Ricky returned to her parent's apartment, her mother was making a lemon meringue pie in the kitchen. She beat the egg whites, and turned the bowl over to test if they were stiff.

"Jeffrey was afraid of Sharon," Ricky said in her normal voice.

"What did you say?" Her mother had a wry smile.

Ricky remembered that her mother was deaf in one ear ever since she had diphtheria as a child. She raised her voice, "I said that Jeffrey cried when he saw Sharon. He's afraid of strangers."

"That's too bad." Ricky's mother kept beating the

egg whites. "I think you have to teach him to call you 'Mommy', and he should call me 'Mama'."

Ricky winced, left the kitchen, took Jeffrey to the living room and set him down in the playpen with blocks for him to play. She returned to the kitchen, and flopped down into a chair. "I'm his mother; he should call me 'Mama', and you 'Grandma'."

"That's too formal. No!" Ricky's mother said with her authoritative air. "I want him to call me 'Mama'. It's easier to say. You'll be 'Mommy'."

I can't argue with my mother, a woman who demands respect. I never could argue with her or contradict her. She always gets her way, but as soon as I can go to work, I'll move out, and Jeffrey will call me 'Mama'.

By the time Jeffrey was eighteen months, he called his grandma 'Mama' and his mother 'Mommy'. Ricky took a notebook and jotted down his extensive vocabulary for three days. It amounted to eighty words and sentences. It was obvious he was a bright toddler. He also began to accept food from a spoon and was comfortable when they visited Sharon.

Ricky enrolled in another education course in Brooklyn College. When Mr. Morgan, the thin male teacher, spoke about how pigeons were trained to play a tune on a toy piano, she absorbed every word. When Jeffrey was two-and-a-half, it was time to toilet train him. She used what she had learned in the education course and thought about how she could reward Jeffrey for the behavior she wanted.

Band-Aids would do it. She bought the kind that had pictures on them. She also bought a child's toilet that was close to the ground. And she spoke to her intelligent child.

"Jeffrey, it's time you learned to be toilet trained. These

are pretty Band-Aids and, when you urinate in this plastic pot, I'll give you one. Every time you sit on the small toilet and have a bowel movement, I'll give you two Band-Aids. Do you understand?"

Jeffrey nodded. "Yes."

"Okay, now we won't go outside until you learn to tell me when you have to go to the bathroom. I'm removing your diaper. You're a big boy now and you'll learn fast."

In a week Jeffrey was completely toilet trained.

By court order, Simon was awarded visitation every Sunday between noon and 5 p.m. Ricky, upset as a loser in a prize fight, dressed the baby in his clean clothes and waited for Simon to show up. When he rang the bell, Ricky held Jeffrey in her arms and opened the door.

"Come to Daddy," Simon said as he grabbed Jeffrey and walked down the stairs carrying him awkwardly.

Ricky called after him. "Jeffrey takes a nap at 2 p.m."

Simon ignored her. He brought the baby back a half-hour after the appointed time. Jeffrey's face and clothes were dirty and he looked exhausted.

"He had a good time," Simon said, as he handed Jeffrey over to Ricky whose eyes blazed with anger. "Now that you're functioning, I was wondering if you want to move back with the baby and me."

"You must be kidding," Ricky laughed like the sound of the musical scale. "You wanted to put me in a mental hospital for the rest of my life. I'd never go back to you. You will soon hear from my lawyer about an annulment."

The court procedure passed quickly and the annulment was granted to Ricky on the grounds that Simon had lied about his income. The baby was declared legitimate, and Simon was ordered to pay $40 a week.

Ricky got a part-time job teaching typing in a private

school. Her father gave her the use of his car, and parked it for her when she went to her job and when she drove it home. Since she wanted to be independent, she took one successful lesson in parking and no longer needed his help.

It was a comfortable day in summer when Ricky pushed Jeffrey in his carriage on Ocean Avenue in front of the library. He was twenty months old and his vocabulary was increasing by leaps and bounds. Jeffrey had his eyes on the moving traffic and noticed a black convertible pass with the top down. He had never seen a convertible.

"Car broke?" Jeffrey asked. Ricky laughed and that evening bragged to her parents how clever her son was.

One afternoon when Ricky came home from work from her job teaching typing in a Yeshiva, her mother handed her an official looking letter.

"I hope you're not in trouble with the government," her mother said waiting for Ricky to tear open the envelope and read the letter.

"I'll read it after I kiss Jeffrey and take off my coat."

"Read it first," her mother said as she wiped her hands on her apron.

Ricky stepped into the living room, bent down to Jeffrey's playpen and picked him up, planted a kiss on his soft cheek, put him back down, and removed her coat. She read the letter silently and frowned.

"What does it say?" Her mother asked.

"It says that I'm to report to the Internal Revenue office in two weeks."

"Did you lie on your income tax?"

"No! Why would I lie?"

"Well, aren't you worried?" Her mother lifted her brow where deep creases had already formed.

"I'm not worried. I didn't do anything wrong. I don't want to discuss this anymore. Now I'm taking Jeffrey out for a walk."

"Make sure you dress him with a sweater under his jacket. It's chilly outside."

"I'll dress him appropriately," Ricky said as she opened a drawer and took out Jeffrey's lighter jacket, no sweater.

On the appointed day, at the appointed hour, Ricky showed up at the downtown branch office of the Department of Internal Revenue. She stated her name and a man who looked like a walking skeleton approached her.

"Please follow me and take a seat at my desk," he said.

Ricky sat down on a government-issued metal chair while the skeleton sat at his government-issued metal desk. He said in a thin voice, "Your husband declared on his income tax that he is paying you alimony, and since we consider alimony as income and since you haven't reported it, this is the reason why you were asked to come here."

Furious at Simon for trying to get her into trouble, Ricky's eyes blazed as her voice rose dramatically. "That man is not my husband since I have an annulment and that means that the marriage never took place. Furthermore, the annulment states that he is to pay $40 a week. It doesn't stipulate that the money is for me. I use it for child support and that doesn't have to be declared."

The agent looked puzzled. "Do you have the annulment papers with you?"

"I do," Ricky said as she opened her purse and drew out the papers. "Here they are."

"I haven't come across any situation like this. I have to consult with my supervisor."

Ricky sat in the office fiddling with her curly hair for

an hour before the agent returned. "It was decided that the money is for child support and you're excused."

I wish Simon would just disappear from the face of the earth.

Ricky's wish came true. Simon disappeared and so did the $40 a week.

Because of the financial burden, Ricky went to work full time, but after three weeks she had to resign. Jeffrey cried like a lost lamb when she disappeared for hours and she didn't have the heart to abandon him for eight hours. She was still Mommy, but she desperately wanted to be Mama and knew she had to wait until Jeffrey was old enough to be left alone and then she would be able to move into her own apartment and her mother would have to accept being called 'Grandma'.

There were times that Ricky was amazed by Jeffrey's astute comments. Once, when he was two, she took him with her to the bank. It hadn't snowed yet in December but it was chilly and Jeffrey was bundled up in his carriage with a blanket around his legs. There was a cardboard figure of Santa Claus in the bank. Jeffrey studied it. "That's Rabbi Claus," he remarked.

Another time, Jeffrey noticed a nun in full habit strolling on Kings Highway. He had never seen a sister before. He wrinkled his forehead. "Man? Woman?"

Ricky chuckled. "That's a woman."

By the time Jeffrey was three, Ricky felt it was time for her to move out.

"Mama, we're very crowded. Three adults and a baby in a tiny three-room apartment is uncomfortable for all of us. I'm thinking of getting my own place."

Her mother's jaw dropped. "I don't want you to go. Please don't move."

"But we're jammed together like sardines in a can."

"Let's look for a larger apartment," her mother said in an effort to ward off the split.

They searched the paper and looked at some four-room apartments that weren't feasible. Finally there was a ground floor apartment available in Flatbush opposite a ball park in a nice neighborhood. The rent was higher but Ricky felt she could teach and contribute money for the rent. She liked the apartment in a modern apartment house that wasn't far from shopping. Her mother agreed and they gave a deposit, only to have her mother change her mind the next day.

Now Ricky had no choice but to look for her own apartment. First she was appointed as a teacher in a junior high school not too far away. Then she found a ground floor four-room apartment on Ocean Avenue six blocks from her parents.

The day she moved out, her mother stood with her arms folded and a sour expression on her face. Her father had retired as a messenger on Wall Street and offered to take care of Jeffrey for forty dollars a week. Ricky took him up on it. She knew that he was devoted to Jeffrey and would take good care of him.

It seemed that the toddler adjusted to her absence as long as he had his grandfather around. When the house across the street caught fire and the fire engines responded, Jeffrey looked at the spectacle from the living room window and excitedly jumped up and down.

One day when Ricky came home from work, she sat engaged in making a dress at the Singer sewing machine. She listened with one ear to the TV and suddenly bounded up, gave her whole attention to the broadcaster, and slumped while her eyes filled with tears.

"What is it, Mama?"

"President Kennedy has been shot. He just died. Why is there evil in the world?" Ricky bit down hard on her lips.

"I don't know why, Mama? Why?"

"Because God gave us free will and some people are bad. We can all be bad but we have a choice, and that's why there are good people in this world."

Chapter 9

SIX MONTHS PASSED AND one blustery day in March Ricky came home from teaching, tired and hungry. She kissed Jeffrey, fixed a snack, and turned to her father who had a worried look.

"What's the matter?" Ricky asked him as she bit into a Delicious apple.

"I'm sorry but I can't take care of Jeffrey any more. I'm returning to my job as a messenger on Wall Street. I like delivering stocks and bonds and I know the financial district like the back of my hand."

"You have a life of your own," Ricky said drumming her fingers on the kitchen table. "I'll just have to hire help." *I'm disappointed but I have to make the best of the situation. Like my father's favorite saying, 'It can always be worse.'*

Mark, a good looking young fellow of eighteen, seemed like a sensible choice as a sitter for Jeffrey. He was enrolled in college at night and his days were free. Furthermore, he didn't object to the low wages that Ricky could afford to pay. She thought he would be a good role model for Jeffrey who liked the idea of a young man taking care of him.

Three days later, when she stepped into the apartment, Ricky was astonished to find pizza boxes scattered on the floor, bottles of soda and booze on the table, and her living room in complete disarray.

She screwed up her face. "What went on here?"

Jeffrey laughed loudly. "Mama, we had a great party with girls and boys and food and drinks."

Mark attempted to explain that it had been his birthday and it was a surprise party his friends threw for him.

Ricky nodded before she said, "Here's another surprise. You're fired."

The second person she hired was a black, middle-aged woman. She lasted three months. "Do you like Hedy?" Ricky asked Jeffrey.

"Yes. She took me on the subway and we went to Manhattan. I like to go on a train."

Ricky sat down at the kitchen table opposite Hedy who cast her eyes on the linoleum of the floor. "Why did you take Jeffrey to Manhattan?"

Hedy averted her eyes.

"I asked you why you took my son on a train. You were hired to watch him in this apartment, or take him to the park. What's going on?"

"I'mmm sorry," Hedy stammered. "I'm getting divorced and I had to go to my lawyer."

"I'm sorry, too, but I have to let you go."

The next woman, Janice, had white hair, and no obligations. She lived alone, had experience taking care of children, and was happy to get the job. She worked a couple of months and it appeared that life was getting easier for both Ricky and Jeffrey. Ricky cooked nutritious meals and liked raisin bread so she kept buying it.

One afternoon when she came home from work, she was tired, from having to stand on her feet lecturing to

A Flickering Flame

sewing classes about how to lay out a pattern, and helping the girls one after another. The principal had visited one class while she was fixing a sewing machine, and he always made her nervous. She ate a cream cheese on raisin bread sandwich for supper and went to sleep early.

The next rainy morning she rushed around getting herself and Jeffrey washed and dressed, but the small rug in the bedroom wasn't anchored and she slipped. She tried to hang on to a chair but couldn't reach it, and like a slow-moving snowflake, she fell on her back and wrenched it so much that the pain was like a hammer hitting her and she couldn't get up.

"Mama, why are you on the floor?" Jeffrey cried as he stood next to her motionless body.

"I fell and it hurts, but, when Janice comes in, she'll help me stand."

Ricky gritted her teeth and waited fifteen minutes until Janice arrived. When she heard her turn the key in the lock of the door, relief flooded her.

Her white hair perfectly groomed, Janice stood at the bedroom door. With hardness in her eyes, she gazed down at Ricky on the floor and stood with her hands on her hips.

"All you have for my lunch is raisin bread, not rye bread, or white bread, just raisin bread. I quit right now. You can send me my check."

Janice stalked out. Ricky's eyes filled with tears. After ten minutes Ricky crawled over to the phone and called in sick.

The next day she sat at the kitchen table and wrote a check for Janice Cohen. She called her mother who came over to take care of Jeffrey. There was only less than a month until the end of the school year. And for a short time her mother agreed to watch Jeffrey while Ricky went to work.

"How do you feel?" her mother asked right before Ricky went out the door.

"Lousy."

"Will you hire another baby sitter?"

"No. I've had it with sitters."

"Will you move back with us? I don't mind being cramped."

"No, thank you anyway." Ricky looked forlorn.

"How can you go to work if you don't have a sitter?"

"I won't work." Ricky pressed her hand to the small of her back where the pain was.

"Then how can you live?" Her mother wrinkled her brow even more than before.

"There are many single mothers who go on relief. I'll apply for public assistance."

"You'll starve."

"I'll make do."

*   *   *

It didn't take long before Ricky received a subpoena from Small Claims Court stating that she hadn't paid Janice her salary.

"I paid you," Ricky said on the phone. "Why didn't you call me if you never got my check?"

"My son is a lawyer and he told me to sue you. I'll see you in court."

Ricky investigated and found that the check had been cashed by a Joseph Cohen who lived in the same apartment house as Janice Cohen. It was a real mix-up and

Ricky was disgusted with the whole procedure, especially that she had to go to court for nothing.

*   *   *

Once Ricky made up her mind to get relief, she followed through and applied.

The investigator in the Public Assistance office was a stout man with a Charlie Chaplin mustache. Ricky noticed he sat a foot from his desk to make room for his bulging stomach.

"You're eligible for Aid to Dependent Children, but the $138 a month you pay for rent is excessive, and you'll have to move to a cheaper apartment."

"Oh, my," Ricky said.

"We don't pay for a phone, just the electricity and gas, and we provide for medical care."

"All right, I understand."

Ricky moved to a two-room apartment in a dilapidated building as she saw no way around the regulation. *It's just for a year. Then I'll put Jeffrey in kindergarten and I can go to work.*

Public assistance wasn't a pleasure. Ricky had to do without a phone and her first cousins who were supervisors in the department were embarrassed when she told them she was a recipient. The government paid the $85 a month for the three-room apartment from hell. The amount for food was $1 a day and her parents didn't help except for taking care of Jeffrey once in a while.

When the police came to an adjacent apartment and arrested a neighbor, Ricky shivered. When the downstairs neighbor, a bachelor with a leering look, kept ringing her doorbell, she decided to move.

Jeffrey was staying with his grandparents one winter day, when it started to snow. Ricky put on her winter coat and immediately went downstairs to shop for groceries. As she stepped down from the street into the gutter and walked to the middle of the road, she slipped on the wet pavement, fell on her back, and couldn't get up. She saw a car coming her way, and since it was backing up a one-way street, the driver didn't see her on the ground. She believed that her good angel came in the form of a man who put his hand up and stopped the car. *I could have died but it's not my time.*

The man helped her up and she determined to find an apartment in a decent neighborhood. She was fortunate to locate an apartment with the same rent of $85, only this time it wasn't three rooms but a living room and a kitchen. She moved. One of her cousins gave her a gift of $5 and she never forgot her generosity. Another friend helped her by bringing a load of groceries once a week.

She remained on relief for a year.

Chapter 10

ONE DAY JEFFREY CAME home with a present that he gave his mother for Mother's Day.

Ricky sat at the kitchen table admiring a hand-painted porcelain box.

"Thank you, Jeffrey. It's a lovely gift. Where did you get it?"

Jeffrey looked sheepish. "There's a store in the basement of a private house down the block."

"How did you pay for it?"

"I took it when the lady wasn't looking."

Ricky's heart beat fast, but she kept her cool. "That's stealing and you should never take anything without paying. Show me where the store is and I'll pay for the box."

Jeffrey walked ahead of his mother and stopped at a brick home. Ricky rang the bell and a pleasant woman with a hooked nose came to the door. She escorted them to the side door and they went down to the store in the basement where she had a variety of pretty items.

"My son took a porcelain box to give to me as a gift and I came here to pay for it."

The woman laughed. "I wondered how the box had disappeared. It's ten dollars."

Ricky handed the woman a ten dollar bill and thought nothing more about the incident, but that was the first in a line of thefts that Jeffrey committed.

When Jeffrey turned four, Ricky enrolled him in a nursery in a local Yeshiva. Jeffrey was happy to be with other children except when the teacher asked them to call out their names in a loud voice. All the children gave their full names including their middle names. But Jeffrey wasn't given a middle name so he quickly he made one up. "My name is Jeffrey Jay Schulman."

For the rest of his life he kept the middle name he named himself, although he never changed it legally.

Jeffrey never listened to any directions Ricky gave him and she decided to have him tested. He was also obstreperous with his teacher and peers.

The psychologist had an office on Avenue U. The reception room was decorated with inexpensive green vinyl covered chairs, photographs of children on the light green wall, a table with various children's magazines, and a box of tissues if clients decided that life was rough. There was a box of toys with building blocks, crayons, and coloring books. Ricky had dressed Jeffrey in a matching suit, vest, and bow tie, so he looked spiffy and handsome.

After the psychologist ushered Jeffrey into his office, Ricky tried to read a woman's magazine in the outer office but she couldn't concentrate and read the same paragraph over six times. She wondered if Jeffrey was as emotionally disturbed as she surmised.

An hour later, Jeffrey emerged with a smile as big as the Holland Tunnel.

Dr. Gross said, "Jeffrey, I'd like to speak with your mother in my office. You can stay here and play with the toys or take some crayons and color the pictures in the coloring book."

Ricky took a chair in the psychologist's office. She leaned forward as Dr. Gross spoke to her about the outcome of the tests.

"As you probably surmised, your son is brilliant. His IQ is 160 which is in the superior range."

"Wow!" *He's much smarter than I. I was tested at 140. He can run circles around me.*

"Of course that means that he should have adequate mental stimulation so he doesn't get bored in school."

"What about his emotional status, doctor?"

"He's had a traumatic beginning and he shows many signs of insecurity. He could benefit from counseling. But he's a bright boy. I was impressed by his answer to my question, 'What do you want to be when you grow up?'"

Ricky gave a weak smile.

"The boy replied that he wanted to be an architect. Then I asked him what an architect does and he answered that he builds houses and bridges. An answer that clever I've never had from any other child I've tested. I recommend you set boundaries for him, and give him counseling and mental stimulation."

*   *   *

Ricky took her summer vacation in Miami Beach. She drove with Jeffrey in the new Dodge Dart she was paying for in installments. She stopped in Savannah, a city dotted with the splendor of picturesque wide trees with moss hanging down. They ate at the Pirates' Inn, and Jeffrey came away with a yellowed antique map of buried treasure that Ricky bought for a dollar.

She located a furnished apartment in Surfside and enrolled four-year old Jeffrey in day camp. He liked the camp and was thrilled with the baby elephant that lived across the street. Every day Jeffrey visited the elephant and spoke to him. "You're a pretty elephant," he would say.

He refused to change to shorts and Ricky gave up trying to convince him and let him wear his three-piece suit with a bow tie even though the weather was hot and humid.

When Jeffrey came home the last week of vacation, Ricky fed him, bathed him, and put him to sleep. At 3 a.m. Jeffrey began to whimper, then his cries became louder, and when Ricky looked at him it was evident that he was in excruciating pain. In a rush Ricky dressed and brought Jeffrey to the car. As she raced through the empty streets of Miami Beach, a police car pulled her over.

"What's the rush, madam?" the officer asked.

"I have to take my son to the hospital," Ricky gasped.

"Follow me." The officer hopped back into his car and in a few minutes Jeffrey was in the emergency room being examined by a stern Hispanic resident.

"What happened, boy?" the doctor asked.

Jeffrey wiped his nose with a tissue Ricky gave him. "I was playing Nok Hockey and I got the stick in my eye."

The resident spoke to Ricky in the corridor. "I can't treat your son as I'm not a specialist. In the morning the ophthalmologist will be in and he'll know what to do. Meanwhile, I'll sedate the boy. I think he'll lose that eye."

Ricky shivered. She held her breath. *Oh, no. Please, God, not his eye.*

Every minute until the doctor showed up Ricky spent praying. Finally the doctor examined Jeffrey's eye. "The cornea is cut. I'll put in drops. It'll take a while until it heals."

"Doctor, will he be blind?"

"Of course not. You have to put these drops in his eye and I'll put a bandage over it. Why did you think he'd be blind?"

Ricky wrung her hands. "I don't know." She kept the resident's prognosis to herself. She didn't like getting anyone in trouble.

* * *

Jeffrey was enrolled in the first grade in Yeshiva. One night at the parent-teacher conference, Mrs. Solomon, Jeffrey's teacher, leaned toward Ricky who was sitting at her desk, and quietly told her about Jeffrey's hitting children, and not following any rules.

"He's a smart child," she said, "but we can keep him only until the end of the academic year and then you'll have to enroll him in public school or another Yeshiva where they can handle him."

Ricky was disappointed. She had thought that a private school where Jeffrey could be given more attention, and at the same time learn about Judaism, would be good for her son. Counseling didn't seem to help him, and her lectures fell on ears that were stuffed with cotton.

Once when they were in the Prospect Park Zoo with her father and cousin Lucy, her cousin predicted that someday Jeffrey would get himself in deep water. Ricky prayed he'd straighten out. There was no one in her family who was a thief, a drunk, a jailbird, or on dope, but deep down she wondered if Jeffrey's life would soar or sink to the lowest level.

The next incident happened when Jeffrey was in public school. Ricky waited for him to be dismissed and he came out the school door accompanied by a boy in his class.

The boy smiled lazily at Ricky. "Jeffrey is a good friend of mine. He helps me with my homework."

"That's nice," Ricky said pleased that Jeffrey had made a friend and was assisting him. Then she heard something that chilled her.

"I think it's great that Jeffrey's grandpa was a General in the army."

First he steals and now he's lying. I have to sit him down and explain that it's wrong to tell a lie. But he always listens like he understands, and then does whatever he pleases.

As many times as Ricky spoke softly to Jeffrey and as many times as he listened with rapt attention, it did no good. There were days that she caught him in a lie. She brought him for the costly therapy, but that didn't help. Jeffrey was addicted to lying.

Ricky also spoke to her father about the gifts he was buying Jeffrey.

"I don't like that you keep buying my son guns."

"They're toy guns. He can't do any damage with them."

"But so many?" Ricky said exasperated.

"That's the only toy Jeffrey wants."

Ricky understood that there was no way to convince her father to stop giving Jeffrey toy guns. But they were only toys and she surmised that it would never amount to anything in his life, only she was wrong.

One spring Sunday when Ricky visited her parents, and her mother was out shopping at the grocery on Kings Highway, her father served her a cup of coffee and a piece of sponge cake at the table in the kitchen. Jeffrey was playing with his favorite gun in the living room.

"I want to tell you something interesting," her father said.

"What?"

"Young women were distributing samples of packages of cigarettes on Kings Highway. There were four cigarettes in every package. Grandma was in the bank while Jeffrey remained outside. He managed to take a few packages and he showed them to Grandma who said she would spank him if he dared to smoke them."

"Wow," Ricky said.

"She told me and I took Jeffrey to Kings Highway to a large tobacco shop. While Jeffrey listened, I said to the clerk, 'I want the very best cigar you have in the shop.' I bought it for $2.00 and then I took Jeffrey to the park."

"Really?" Ricky said wide-eyed.

"Yes. I said to Jeffrey, 'When you enter a board meeting on Wall Street, you find people of a higher class smoking cigars. You need to learn to smoke a cigar."

"You said that?"

"Yes. I removed the cellophane from the package and unscrewed the metal wrapper. Then I cut off the end, lit the cigar, and puffed away. I turned the cigar over to Jeffrey and told him to smoke it. He sucked heavily on the cigar and proceeded to cough for an hour. I knew that for the rest of his life he'd never smoke."

"I never would have thought of doing something like that," Ricky said as she went to the sink and washed the coffee cup.

*   *   *

When Jeffrey was eight-years old, Ricky took a walk with him to Ocean Parkway and they sat on a worn wooden bench on the wide thoroughfare that ran for miles from Coney Island to Prospect Park. Across the street were two parks with swings, seesaws, sliding ponds, and a roller skating rink. Jeffrey sat peacefully with his hands clasped together next to his mother.

"I have something important to tell you, Jeffrey."

Jeffrey's dark intelligent eyes widened.

"You know the man I've been dating?"

"I don't like him," Jeffrey said frowning.

"Nat asked me to marry him."

"Don't do it. He's not a nice man."

"I don't see anything wrong with Nat. He was married before, like me, but he doesn't have any children, and I think we could have a good life with him. We'll move into a larger apartment and you'll have your own room. I told him I'd marry him."

Jeffrey cried out, "Why didn't you ask me first?"

"I'm sorry you're hurt, but a grown woman doesn't need to ask her eight-year-old child for permission to marry."

"Will there be other children at the wedding?"

"Yes, Nat has many nephews and nieces and we have to invite them."

"Then I won't go. I want to be the only child there."

Ricky spoke to Nat and at first he objected to excluding his nephews and nieces from the ceremony in the synagogue, but he relented when Ricky said they could attend the luncheon afterwards in the vegetarian restaurant.

When they moved from the two-room apartment into the four-room apartment in the same apartment house, Ricky furnished the second bedroom with a new bedroom set for Jeffrey. Soon she learned that Nat ignored her son, never ridiculing him and never praising him. He was the type of man who was a loner, and the only praise she ever heard out of his mouth was that she parked the car well.

That summer Ricky enrolled in a school in Manhattan to learn upholstery. The living room set that Nat insisted on buying had a rough texture and she was determined to learn how to make her own slipcovers. The course was two years and the advancement was slow, so Ricky went around the school looking at projects that other pupils were making. In three weeks she taught herself all she had to know to make lovely printed blue and white slipcovers for the sofa and armchair. She spent the rest of the summer sewing. Jeffrey was in a day camp and seemed to be adjusting to his new environment, or so Ricky thought.

One August when Jeffrey was nine, the family spent a vacation in a hotel in the Catskills. There was an announcement in the dining room of an art auction to take place in the theater at 2 p.m. Jeffrey was excited and begged to go to his first art auction. It started off with the offering of a 3' x 5' oil painting of a sad clown with a green complexion.

The auctioneer called out in the same way auctioneers do, "Who will start the bidding for this unusual oil?"

No one answered. It was not a picture that evoked a positive response.

Again the auctioneer called for a bid. "Just look at the exquisite carving on the gold frame," he said, urging the crowd to bid on the painting of the sad clown.

Not one hand was raised. Many guests just frowned including Nat.

Jeffrey raised his hand. "I bid fifty cents."

"Sold to the young man in the three-piece suit. Enjoy your picture," he said as Jeffrey bounced along and climbed the steps of the stage to get his painting and bring it back to his seat.

Nat said, "That's an ugly picture."

Ricky nodded. "Yes, it is, but I'll repaint it and we can hang it in the foyer."

After Ricky turned the clown's lips up with a smile and repainted the face a shining pink color, Nat agreed that it was acceptable and it hung for years in the foyer.

Chapter 11

NAT AND JEFFREY NEVER warmed up to each other. Nat never offered any praise to the boy, and Jeffrey continued lying. He walked his own path, listening to his mother, but doing whatever struck his fancy. Ricky tried to make peace between them, but the cold war continued unabated.

Eventually, Nat became highly critical of his stepson who had been expelled from the Yeshiva and was now in public school. He had passing grades but his conduct was unsatisfactory. Authority was anathema to him.

Ricky was at her wit's end. She tried to encourage good behavior by rewarding Jeffrey with a toy car every month. He played for hours with the cars but, all in all, nothing she did worked.

One of Jeffrey's teachers recommended a neighborhood psychiatrist. Ricky paid for the doctor's time. She was still teaching and could afford the hefty fee.

Dr. Kantrowitz, a man with a pudgy face and a big smile, ushered Jeffrey into his office while Ricky sat with a magazine in the waiting room. When she tried to read a book she had brought along, she couldn't concentrate. A half-hour later the psychiatrist brought Jeffrey out.

"There are toys here for you to play with, Jeffrey," he said. "I want to speak privately to your mother."

Ricky sat in Dr. Kantrowitz's office looking at the diplomas on his wall. "Is it a hopeless situation, doctor?" she asked.

"Not at all. I think what would give Jeffrey the security he yearns for is if his stepfather adopted him. He would have your name and feel like he was part of the new family."

When Ricky spoke to Nat, at first he was vehemently against the adoption. "He and I don't get along. He never listens to me. Why would I want to adopt him?"

"His father is back in New York. He's married for the fourth time and will never support him and he doesn't want to see him. You don't have to support Jeffrey; just give him your name. The psychiatrist recommends this. It could make a big difference in his life. Please, Nat, let's try this."

"All right, but I don't think anything will change Jeffrey."

Ricky consulted a lawyer about the adoption. He told her that Jeffrey's biological father would have to be notified.

Although Simon didn't ask to see Jeffrey and didn't support him, he objected to an adoption and that was the end of that.

* * *

Jeffrey held the side of his mouth with his hand. Ricky was in the kitchen preparing chicken, carrots, and white potatoes for the next day's supper. She had discovered the usefulness of a crock pot. She put the pot in the refrigerator, and in the morning she would take it out, plug it in and set it on low. When she came home from teaching, they would have a ready-made meal.

Jeffrey groaned.

Ricky turned from the refrigerator and stared at her son. "Okay, what's wrong?"

"Nothing." Jeffrey took a step toward the kitchen door.

"I know you're in pain. Does your tooth hurt?"

"A little."

"I'm taking you to the dentist."

"I won't go," Jeffrey protested. "I won't open my mouth and let anyone look in."

Ricky knew the origin of Jeffrey's angst which stemmed from the time that his aunt had stuffed food down his throat when he was a baby. "The dentist will put you to sleep and then he'll fix your tooth."

Reluctantly Jeffrey went to the special dentist who had to administer gas to his fearful patient, and during Jeffrey's whole life he needed gas to have his teeth worked on.

*   *   *

When Jeffrey was ten, Ricky took him on an outing to see the Statue of Liberty. As the ferry sped through the murky water away from the tip of Manhattan toward the island, and as Ricky and Jeffrey stood at the railing, Ricky decided to open a risky subject starting with innocuous information.

"In the summer when I was your age, Grandma used to take me to Bedloe's Island to play on the grass in front of the Statute of Liberty. She said it was cooler than the heat in Brooklyn."

Jeffrey nodded. "The name was changed from Bedloe's Island to Liberty Island in 1956, but I bet you didn't know that. I read all about it in the encyclopedia Grandpa bought for me."

"No, I didn't know that piece of trivia."

"I like this ferry," Jeffrey said with yearning in his voice. "I wish we could have our own boat."

"We can't afford it."

"But you and your husband are working, so why can't you buy a boat?"

"I have news to tell you, and I hope you'll be happy when you hear it." Ricky took a deep breath. "You're going to have a sister or a brother in six months."

"Oh! If it's a sister, I'll throw it out the window. But if it's a brother, I'll keep it and teach him to box."

Ricky winced at Jeffrey's cruel words. She hoped that he would get used to the idea of a half-sibling regardless of gender. She would show Jeffrey love and give him as much attention as she was capable of and offer prayers that his attitude would change.

Her students teased her mercilessly with words and bags of pickles, and Ricky felt she could work only until she was seven months pregnant. The week after she resigned she spoke to Nat in the kitchen, saying that she wanted him to buy some pears. He did all the shopping now that she was popping like a jug of water.

"You're not bringing in any money since you're not working," Nat said belligerently. "We have to watch what we spend. Pears are too expensive. I'll buy apples instead."

"I'd be satisfied with just three pears, one for each of us," Ricky said as she stood up and faced him.

Suddenly Nat's face turned the color of a radish. He put his hand on her chest and pushed her violently. Ricky fell hard against the kitchen window but maintained her balance somehow. Her fear turned her hands to ice.

The next day after Nat went to work, Ricky consulted a psychologist. His opinion was that her husband had a low frustration tolerance and, at the time he assaulted her, he had been psychotic. If she decided to remain in this marriage, she should make her own life, pursue her own interests, and make her own friends.

It was a chilly day in April when they were sitting in the living room reading the newspaper. Ricky was blowing her nose as she had a cold. Before the baby's birth, they decided to have the apartment painted and the windows were open to help dry the paint. Jeffrey was in his room in bed, also with a cold. Suddenly the bell rang.

"Go answer it," Nat said. "But if it's your father tell him he's not welcome here. I don't like that he visits Jeffrey so often and he shouldn't be butting into our business and saying we shouldn't have painted and that it's cold in here and that's what gave Jeffrey his cold."

Ricky went to the front door. "It's my father," she called out.

Nat heaved himself off the couch and raced to the tiny foyer. "I don't want you in my house," he said.

Ricky's father frowned. "I won't bother you. I only want to see my grandson."

"Well, you can't."

"I have a right to see my grandson."

"Not in my house, you don't."

Jeffrey's grandfather took a step in. Nat put up his hands and pushed him out. The old man's face reddened. He pushed back. They started punching each other.

My God, my father never laid a finger on anyone. I'm pregnant. I can't stop this. I'm paralyzed. I can't even talk.

The old man stepped back and walked away, his chin on his chest.

He quickened his pace as he walked down Kings Highway on his way home. When his wife saw the sad look on his face, she cried out, "What happened? Is Jeffrey very sick?"

Grandpa sat down at the kitchen table. Grandma took off her apron and sat down facing him. "They didn't let me in."

"What? I can't believe that."

"It's true. Nat pushed me out and we got into a fist fight."

Grandma clenched her hands around her face. "Are you hurt?"

"Not really. I punched him back."

"Where was Ricky? What did she do?"

"She was there. She didn't say or do anything, just stood there. I left. I'm an old man but I never hit anybody before. He goaded me."

Grandma's face turned beet red. "This is awful. How could our daughter not stop him, not say a word? When the baby comes, we won't go to the hospital, we won't talk to her."

"That's going too far," Grandpa said in a low voice.

"I don't think so." Grandma put her apron back on and returned to the sink to wash the pots.

* * *

Ricky had been to her obstetrician a few days before the fighting incident. He had examined her and said the baby wasn't due for five weeks. The aggravation she suffered seeing her father hit was too much for her system. In the middle of the night she felt labor pains but decided to ignore them and went back to sleep. At 7:30 a.m. when she got up to go to the bathroom she discovered that her water had broken.

She told Nat and went into Jeffrey's room.

"Get up now, Jeffrey. The baby's coming and you need to get dressed. We'll be leaving soon."

She and Nat dressed, and Jeffrey kept lying in bed.

"I told you to get dressed," Ricky urged. "We have to leave for the hospital in Manhattan."

"I don't want a sister," Jeffrey said as he got out of bed and reluctantly put on his clothes.

"We don't have a choice," Ricky said, praying that the baby would be a boy.

Nat's father drove the Lincoln from Brooklyn, across the Brooklyn Bridge, and luckily, it was early morning so there was little traffic on the FDR drive. Ricky couldn't time the labor pains as they didn't exist, but the pain in her back grew more and more intense with every moment. She wanted to give Jeffrey something to remember, so when they passed a police car she told her father-in-law to hail them. He did and asked for a police escort to the hospital.

When the police accompanied them with the shrieking siren, Jeffrey smiled like the cat that caught a mouse.

At the hospital Nat and Ricky sat down on a bench near the reception desk while a young woman, who twirled her long hair around her finger, talked endlessly on the phone. Since Nat took no action, Ricky stumbled to the desk.

"I'm in labor," Ricky said.

"Sorry, I didn't know," the clerk said. "I'll get a wheelchair."

"See you later," Nat said. "Jeffrey and I are going out for breakfast."

Jeffrey never threw the baby out of the window since Ricky gave birth to a boy. Five days later when they brought Arthur home, Ricky presented Jeffrey with the gift of a red wooden garage and ten miniature cars. The circumcision was held in the apartment, and Ricky's friends thoughtfully brought Jeffrey a gift as well as presents for the baby.

Chapter 12

NAT SAID WITH DETERMINATION, "The baby is a year-old. It's time we moved the crib into Jeffrey's room."

"I don't know how Jeffrey will take to his having a crying baby in his room," Ricky said wondering if her difficult son would rebel.

"What do I care how he feels," Nat said, "or how he reacts? It's time he learned to behave himself."

Jeffrey complained bitterly about his lack of privacy and the result was that he was taken out of the small bedroom and placed in the living room on a chair that opened into a bed. He deeply resented this move, and his behavior deteriorated, but Ricky was at a loss and couldn't come up with another solution.

But there were times that Jeffrey treated Arthur with kindness and love. One time when Arthur was three-months-old, she put him on the sofa in a sitting up position. Jeffrey sat close to him looking at him with such love in his eyes that Ricky snapped a picture of them. This became her favorite photo.

Ricky's parents continued their silence once Arthur was born. It cut Ricky to the core that her parents had figuratively deserted her.

Arthur was six-months-old when Grandpa approached

his wife as they sat on the sofa watching the news on TV. Grandpa got up and turned off the TV.

"I think it's time we forgave Ricky for not interfering when Nat hit me."

"I don't think so," Grandma said. "It was a terrible thing to do, to stand by while your husband hits your father."

"But I miss Jeffrey and I miss Ricky. I could do without Nat but he is her husband. I'd also like to see our new grandchild."

"She should apologize to us," Grandma said with a shake of her head.

"I don't think she's going to. Why don't we consult the Rabbi?"

"Okay. You call and make an appointment."

Approaching the Rabbi with the problem of hurt feelings against their daughter and cutting off the relationship, the Rabbi listened attentively and advised them to pursue peace. They agreed, called Ricky, and saw their new grandson for the first time. No apology was made and they never discussed the situation but went on as nothing had happened.

* * *

When Arthur was almost three, Ricky decided to put him into a nursery school. At home, no matter how she scolded Jeffrey, he wouldn't stop boxing with the toddler.

"I'm not hurting him," he protested.

"I know you're not, but you're teaching him to box and as a result he's hitting the children in nursery school. You must stop that immediately."

Jeffrey continued to box with Arthur and Arthur continued to hit the other children.

That summer the family vacationed in a hotel in the Catskill Mountains. Ricky was at her wit's end, sleeping poorly, worried about the effect that Jeffrey was having on Arthur who was a happy baby and didn't understand that it was wrong to hit other children. She sat on a chair on the lawn without observing the beauty of the green, tree-covered mountains, but read a paper written for Jewish people when her eyes spied something of interest.

"Nat, it says here that there's a Jewish agency that has counseling for troubled youngsters."

"How much does it cost?"

"It says it's on a sliding scale," Ricky said as she passed the paper to her husband.

"Let's apply," Nat said. "Jeffrey is impossible. We just can't handle him."

The agency tested Jeffrey and interviewed Ricky and Nat.

The social worker, Mrs. Abrams, a sweet woman with a Jewish accent, sat at her desk and spoke to Ricky who sat in a chair opposite her. Ricky crossed and uncrossed her legs. She wiped the perspiration from her upper lip.

Mrs. Abrams said, "Our children's home was opened in 1969."

"That's the year my younger son was born."

"Yes, you told us his age. I understand there is a ten-year difference in age between your boys." The social worker continued to speak softly. "My agency sponsored the first orthodox group home on this continent. It's on a quiet, residential street and only twenty boys live there. Each floor is the home of ten youngsters who have houseparents. There is a homey dining room and the meals are nutritious. We have room for Jeffrey, and a staff of social workers, psychologists, and psychiatrists can begin to repair the damage of the painful past. We will also continue to see you for counseling. What do you think?"

"I don't know. Jeffrey will stop talking to me if I send him away."

"In time he'll adjust. He'll learn to get along with the other boys and feel comfortable in the home. We'll send him to a good Yeshiva and he'll continue with his studies."

"For how long will he live in the home?"

"He will stay there as long as he needs," Mrs. Abrams said.

Ricky went to the public school and spoke to Jeffrey about her heart-wrenching decision to send him to this group home. He listened, turned away from her, and didn't speak to her for four months.

It felt to Ricky like a dagger had pierced her. She missed him, but rationalized that Rebecca had turned Ishmael out to save her son, Isaac. It didn't take long before Arthur stopped hitting the children in his class, and she experienced relief but pined for Jeffrey to come home.

Arthur felt the loss of Jeffrey deeply. He kept asking, "When is Jeffrey coming home? Where is he? I want him?"

A few months later when Ricky visited Jeffrey in the home, he decided to speak with her and asked to come home.

"It's up to the doctors. When they feel you're ready, you'll come home."

The agency sponsored the bar-mitzvah for Jeffrey. It was held in the ballroom of a hotel and was a formal affair. Ricky made an evening gown of blue silk and dressed

Arthur in a suit and tie. Nat wore a blue polyester suit. Four boys from the home were being honored.

That evening Nat whined, "Let's go. We'll be late."

"I have to get the camera. I want photos of Jeffrey and all of us." Ricky felt jittery. In her wildest imagination she never pictured Jeffrey in a home that would sponsor his bar-mitzvah. She wiped the tears that were collecting in her eyes.

Jeffrey looked nice. He had grown a few inches and was as tall as she at the age of thirteen. His thick hair had been trimmed and he wore a dark blue suit, seemingly happy, and speaking nicely to all of them.

But Jeffrey never returned home. Ricky's heart bled for her first born.

There came a time when Jeffrey was fourteen the authorities decided to send Jeffrey home for a weekend. He behaved himself and he hugged and kissed Arthur who was ecstatic. On Saturday Jeffrey asked if he could visit his friends around the corner.

"Go ahead," Ricky said. "Enjoy yourself."

Jeffrey came home five hours later.

The next day after he left, Nat sat in the bedroom while Ricky changed her clothes. He said in a harsh tone. "I don't want Jeffrey to come here for any more weekends. He spent more time with his friends than he did with us."

Ricky was devastated.

Jeffrey never came home again.

* * *

Jeffrey, at seventeen, was reconciled to living in a group home in an upscale residential neighborhood in the neighborhood of Flatbush in Brooklyn. In the summer they sent the boys to an upstate camp and Jeffrey wrote often to his mother.

One letter read, *Dear Mom, Hi! How are you? Just got a letter from you. Does it really go faster for you if you type it? If I typed this, I would be here all day. Anyhow, I just finished breakfast which was a bowl of Rice Krispies and eight pancakes. Right now I'm resting from breakfast. We're listening to music. Later on this afternoon I'm going into town.*

There is a rifle range up here so all day yesterday I spent shooting targets which is lots of fun and I'm not bad. As far as hunting goes there are only two things around here- dear(Jeffrey was always a poor speller) and wild pig. Pigs are very dangerous and dear are too nice to shoot so I'll stick to targets. Got to go. Love, Jeffrey"

Ricky put down the letter. She was glad that Jeffrey was no longer angry with her but she wondered about his obsession with shooting. This could get him in hot water.

* * *

Since Jeffrey needed more excitement in his life, when he was twenty he enrolled in the Army Reserve. He looked forward to the rigorous training and especially becoming adept at various fire arms. He loved guns like a bear loves honey. Carrying himself like a General, he was proud of his muscular figure in khaki which harmonized with his dark brown eyes and hair.

Jeffrey met other trainees from all over the country. Most of them weren't Jewish. There was a stringy young guy, his face studded with acne, who approached him one morning when they were at breakfast.

"My name's Chris. I'm from Pinetree, Mississippi."

Jeffrey offered him a huge grin. "Hi. I'm Jeffrey from Brooklyn."

"I didn't see you at the church service yesterday," Chris said accusingly.

"I'm Jewish. I go on Saturday."

"Ohhh! I heard about Jews. Never saw one."

"Well, now you do."

Chris took a huge bite of buttered toast. He chewed it quickly, and then leaned his head toward Jeffrey. "Jews have horns, don't they?"

This yokel isn't real. "Yeah, we do."

"Does it hurt when you get a haircut?"

Jeffrey sipped his bitter coffee. "No. Not at all. I never feel a thing."

"How come?"

"It just doesn't hurt."

"Why not?"

"My horns are retractable." Jeffrey took the last sip of coffee and rose. "See ya around."

* * *

The sky was covered with fluffy clouds on the last day of September when Ricky visited her parents. She brought her ten-year-old son with her and he sat in the kitchen while Grandpa gave him a glass of milk and a piece of sponge cake. Nat was working, but teachers were dismissed at the end of the school day at 3 p.m. so she was off earlier than her husband.

Grandma and Ricky sat on the sofa bed in the living room. Her mother's eyes lit up as she reached into the pocket of her housedress and took out a letter.

"Jeffrey's in basic training. Is that letter from Jeffrey?" Ricky asked.

"Yes. I'll read it to you."

Dear Grandpa and Grandma,

Hi! How is everything with you? All here is fine yet we still work hard. By the time I get home I will probably be in the best physical shape I've ever been in. Possibly the best shape I'll ever be in.

Tonight starts Yom Kippur and I, of course, plan on fasting all day. This year I know it will be more difficult to do than ever before, but a lot of that is in the mind.

Her mother hesitated. "He should be home and not in the Army."

"I hope it's not too hard for him," Ricky said. "But I'm glad he's being a good Jew."

"Listen to what he writes next," her mother said.

"Sorry for interrupting."

Her mother continued, *Next week the platoon goes out on field maneuvers, including simulating combat situations. It all sounds very interesting.*

Have to close now, not much in the way of time here, you understand. Bye for now. Love, Jeffrey

Her mother smoothed down her gray hair. "I don't like that Jeffrey's in the Army. He could get hurt."

Ricky shook her head. "I think it's the best thing for him. It's teaching him discipline. But it's not the Army, it's the Army Reserve. In case of war, he won't get called up."

"So what's the Army Reserve for?" her mother asked innocently.

"It's to help, just in case there's a war."

"That sounds dangerous," Grandma said.

"It'll be okay," Ricky said. "He'll train twenty-four days a year and report only once a month every year.

That'll keep him in top physical condition." She got up to go. Nat would be coming home at 5:40 p.m. and she had to get dinner ready or he'd explode like a firecracker. All she wanted was peace in the house but she never knew how he would react.

Chapter 13

JEFFREY IN HIS EARLY teens had thrived in the private house where he lived with other boys. He did well in the Yeshiva they sent him to, but when he went to college there was a major problem.

He was summoned to the dean's office.

"Jeffrey, we found a gun in your locker. This is unacceptable."

How dare they look in my locker? They had no right to.

The dean, Mr. Salmon, a distinguished-looking man in his fifties, impeccably groomed in a dark-blue Saville Row suit, took a tissue from a box on his desk and wiped his glasses.

"I'm sorry. I didn't know I couldn't keep a gun in my locker. I have no intention to use it. It's just for protection."

"We'll give you another chance. You may have the gun back if you promise to keep it at home."

"I promise," Jeffrey said with conviction.

He didn't keep his false promise.

Soon, Jeffrey called his mother. "They expelled me from college," he said in an even tone.

"Why? You were doing so nicely."

"They're so stupid. Just because I had a gun in my locker is no reason to get kicked out."

Ricky thought, yes, it's a very good reason. *My poor boy still doesn't comply with rules. What's going to become of him?*

* * *

Jeffrey moved into an inexpensive furnished apartment in a private home in Bensonhurst. When the landlord complained about the noise from the late parties he was giving, Jeffrey moved into a three-room apartment. His adoring grandfather gave him money for furniture, but didn't have enough money to pay for the rent. Jeffrey understood that he would have to find a job to tide him over. He wasn't eligible for government aid and would have to fend for himself.

* * *

Jeffrey, a full-fledged liar, carried an umbrella to ward off the calamity of a Brooklyn downpour as he sloshed down Avenue U and noticed a sign in the window of a venetian blind store reading "Experienced Salesman Wanted." November's rent was overdue by ten days, and he desperately needed a job, any job that would tide him over until he could get one to match his extraordinary talents.

He closed his umbrella, shook off the water, and entered the store which was small, but neatly displayed with all kinds and colors of blinds. He knew he was dressed appropriately as his daily practice was to wear a three-piece suit. A white-haired man, with one high-heeled shoe, limped over to him.

"May I help you?" The man spoke with a Yiddish accent.

"I saw the sign in the window, and I'd like to apply for the position of salesman."

The elderly man removed his spectacles, and rubbed his nose. He took a tissue from the pocket of his woolen vest and carefully wiped each lens. "You look too young. You are how old? Experience you have?"

"I'm older than I look, but I can assure you that I'm twenty-four. My name is Jeffrey Jay Shulman, and I'm responsible and most dependable."

I made myself older, but it's all right. I have to protect myself.

"You look like a young college student."

"I'm not a college student. I just moved to Brooklyn from Philadelphia where I worked for three years as a salesman in the venetian blind department of Kaufman's department store." *I'm certain the old man won't go to the trouble of verifying this false information.*

"Very nice," the owner said in a weak voice. "I'm Menachem Mermelstein. My salesman just quit. To Long Island he moved. This is a small store. Why do you want to work here?"

"Your store is well-organized and makes a good impression. I'm sure I could increase your business. I would like an opportunity to try."

"Too educated you sound."

Jeffrey thought for a moment. He walked over to a plain white venetian blind and took a slat in his hand. "Pretend you are a customer. I'm your new salesman."

"Ya." The skin around the older man's weak blue eyes crinkled with anticipation.

"Sir, this is one of our latest featured models. Other

customers who have purchased this particular model have been highly satisfied. We install the blinds and make sure that they fit, and if you change your mind, for any reason, we will gladly return your money."

The owner clapped his hands. "Good! Good! A fine salesman you are. I pay a dollar more than the minimum and commission of ten percent of each sale. Okay?"

Jeffrey nodded his head that was covered with thick dark chocolate curls. He offered a big smile to the elderly man.

"Today can you start? Maybe after lunch?"

"Tomorrow is better. I hope this heavy rain doesn't get worse. Typhoon Irma just slammed into the Philippines. Almost two hundred people were killed. This weather is for the birds."

"Ya, you're right. At 10 a.m. I open the store."

"Then I'll be back tomorrow morning. Thanks for the job. You won't be sorry you hired me."

Jeffrey hurried down Avenue U and crossed Ocean Avenue. The blustery wind was strong, and he had to keep a steady hold on his black umbrella. He tramped a few avenue blocks until he came to the public library on the corner of Kings Highway, and approached the stooped librarian with thick-lensed glasses.

"Perhaps you can help me find detailed information about venetian blinds? I'm doing research for a company." He smiled graciously. His dark piercing intelligent eyes lit up.

After the librarian placed a book on the gouged wooden table, Jeffrey studied it, concentrating intently, not even aware of the pounding of the pouring rain against the window. He memorized the written word easily. He was proud to be smarter than most people.

The next day Jeffrey reported to his new job ten minutes before opening. The rain had stopped and the air smelled like a fresh cut lemon. A bright sun illuminated Avenue U where store after store were lined up like dominoes. Standing outside the store, he noticed a woman wheeling a baby stroller down the block, a man entering a clothing store, and an old lady squeezing tomatoes in a bin in front of a fruit market. When the young mother passed him, she smiled at him. *She's a pretty thing. She must think me handsome and wonder why I'm standing here.*

Exactly at 10 a.m. Mr. Mermelstein opened the front door and motioned Jeffrey to enter.

The first customer who came in was a rotund, middle-aged woman who had a puzzled expression as she looked around the assortment of venetian blinds.

"I need blinds for my living room," she said in a low-pitched voice. "Right now I have shades and drapes, but my next door neighbor has pretty pink venetians. I don't know what to buy."

Jeffrey nodded. A look of understanding came into his shrewd eyes. "I can show you slat blinds made of metal or vinyl that can be rotated 170 degrees, or vertical blinds consisting of slats of fabric, plastic, wood or metal."

"I see," the woman said. "What do you recommend?"

"What is the predominant color in your living room?"

"Well, now, let me think. The carpet is a brown and tan twist. The sofa is brown, and the chairs are also brown. Mainly the whole living room is brown."

"What is your favorite color?" Jeffrey asked as he bent forward, a look of intense interest on his face.

"I like yellow."

"May I make a suggestion?"

The woman nodded. "Please do."

"If you placed yellow pillows on your sofa, some daffodils in a vase, and had bright yellow vertical wooden blinds, you would perk up the look. Your living room would shine with attractiveness." Jeffrey spoke with confidence, pushing the more expensive line. "The vertical version uses a wider slat and has the added feature of being able to pull a cord to stack the slats together." *These blinds are much more expensive. Mr. Mermelstein will be pleased.*

Jeffrey sold expensive venetians for many months until he felt he never wanted to see another venetian blind in his life. *The only kind that would be acceptable would be a blind Venetian if I ever make it to Italy.*

Although a hot and humid summer arrived, Jeffrey came to work with his three-piece suit. Right after work he returned to the library to study books about investing and business. He was preparing to leave the store and go into business for himself.

One August day, Mr. Mermelstein rolled up his long white shirt sleeves and wiped the perspiration from his upper lip.

"It's a scorcher today," he said. "Take off your jacket, why don't you? Hot, you look." In an affectionate gesture, he put his arm around Jeffrey's shoulder.

"The heat doesn't bother me," Jeffrey said as he caught sight of the tattoo on Mr. Mermelstein's inner arm. "Were you in a concentration camp? You don't have to tell me if it makes you uncomfortable."

"It's okay. A long time ago that was. I was in Dachau. Lucky I am to be alive."

Jeffrey pursed his lips. "My father was in six concentration camps. He and my mother got an annulment right after I was born."

"So, Jeffrey, you are the son of a survivor."

"Yes, I am. I didn't see my father until I looked him up when I was seventeen. He's a Rabbi and he married three more women after he and my mother split. The Nazis did inhuman things. I don't understand how the German people stood for it."

"I wonder myself. I try to forget, but it ain't easy. I sure am lucky to be in this country and in business for myself. A blessing you are to me. I never did so good in business until you came." Mr. Mermelstein smiled warmly.

Jeffrey felt sad that he would soon be leaving this man who had been so kind to him, but he had to make his mark in the world. He took the examination for General Securities Registered Representative, passed it, and received his license. Now it was time to resign as a salesman.

The last week in August Jeffrey approached Mr. Mermelstein who was sitting at his desk in the back room making out an order form. "Ah, Jeffrey, do you think that twenty-five blinds, model 32784 is the right number? Or should I order more? Going fast, they've been."

Jeffrey eased himself into the chair next to the desk. "I think you shouldn't order more than ten."

"Why? You've been selling them like hot cakes. Faster I never saw my blinds disappear."

"I've liked working here. You've been a wonderful boss, but I'm leaving at the end of the week." Jeffrey looked at Mr. Mermelstein's face. Redness shot up from his chin and climbed to the top of his wrinkled forehead. His weak eyes filled with tears.

"Please, Mr. Mermelstein, don't take it so hard. You'll get another salesman who'll sell even more merchandise than I have."

"No, there's no one like you. You've been like a son to

me. My wife and me, we never had children, and you're the son I always wanted. Tell me why you're leaving?" Mr. Mermelstein paused and wiped his brow with an ironed handkerchief. "I know why you're going. When I hired you, I knew it. You're a smart fellow with a good *kup*, too smart to work as a venetian blind salesman."

"I like selling." Jeffrey loosened his tie. "I'm going to be selling financial products, stocks, bonds, mutual funds."

The older man clamped down on his handkerchief. "I wish you mazel. Will you visit me? I want to know how you're doing."

"I live near here and I'll drop in once in a while. You're a good man, Mr. Mermelstein, and I'll never forget you."

Chapter 14

PEOPLE ALL OVER THE world are acquainted with Brooklyn, one of the five boroughs of New York City, with its four million inhabitants. It's been touted in movies and plays and perhaps aliens in outer planets have also heard about its glories. Notable places are Coney Island with its amusement parks, and the world-class Brooklyn Museum of Art. Brooklyn's main library is named Grand Army Plaza. The majestic Brooklyn Bridge, built in 1883, unites Brooklyn with Manhattan, as does the Manhattan Bridge. And for music lovers there is the avant-garde Brooklyn Academy of Music. Famous people like Mel Brooks, Neil Simon, Jerry Lewis, and Barbra Streisand were born in Brooklyn. It has a small-town feel, with wide commercial avenues flanked by quiet residential streets.

On such a quiet street, lined with oak trees and bushes in front of apartment houses, Jeffrey's grandparents continued to live. Their small three-room apartment on the second floor in the back was in a four-story brick apartment house with no elevator. They had been lucky to find such an apartment in 1943 as apartments were scarce in the Midwood neighborhood because of the war. The rent of $45 a month was affordable for the post office employee. Furthermore, his wife had weak feet and couldn't climb more than one flight so it was just right.

The grandparents adored Jeffrey. He could do no wrong. He visited often and always brought a gift. Inside apartment 2D preparations were being made for Jeffrey's Sunday visit.

"Bernie, please set the card table next to the couch. Jeffrey will be here soon and I want to serve coffee and sponge cake."

Bernie, a man in his early eighties, took the card table from behind the living room door, opened the legs, and placed it in front of the sofa. Ida hurried in and put a patterned tablecloth on the table. She brought in silverware and napkins and set one place. Whenever Jeffrey paid them a visit, it was cause for a celebration. Ida made sure the rug was vacuumed and the crowded pieces of furniture were dusted. Bernie felt in his vest pocket for a silver Morgan dollar that he would bestow on his adored grandson.

Grandpa heard the clang of the doorbell and hurried to the tiny foyer that held a cabinet for groceries. When he opened the door, Jeffrey threw his arms around him. Then he went into the kitchen and bent down to kiss the tiny woman on her wrinkled cheek and presented her with a box of Barton's chocolates.

"How are you?" The old man grinned as he led his grandson to the cluttered living room.

"Just great, Grandpa. I quit my job at the venetian blind store."

The little woman carried in a tray with a cup of coffee and some goodies.

"What?" she uttered. "How will you make a living?"

"Don't worry, Ida. Jeffrey knows what he's doing." The older man sat on the couch next to his grandson.

"Sit down, Grandma. I'll tell you what I have in mind."

The little woman plopped down in an armchair. "Drink your coffee."

Jeffrey sipped and smiled. "I've been studying business. I took a course in New York University, and now I have a license to sell stocks. All I need is money to get listed in Dun & Bradstreet and incorporate, and my business will take off."

"Wonderful," the older man said. His loose dentures moved around in his mouth. "How much do you need?"

"I can incorporate a business in Maryland for $100."

Grandpa looked thoughtful. His cloudy amber eyes lit up. "Anything else?"

"I would call it Helena Investing, Inc. and you would be President."

"Really?" Grandpa offered a weak smile, not showing his dentures.

"You bet. I would be the CEO of the corporation, if that's all right with you."

"Why not?" Grandpa's dental plate had loosened when he dropped in weight, and he had trouble talking. "What do I have to do?"

"You need to pay $270 to TRW, the credit reporting service, so that we get a good rating."

"Okay." Grandpa pushed in his upper plate. "What would the corporation do?"

"We would be investment counselors. I know all about stocks, bonds, annuities, and every aspect of the financial market."

Grandma sat silently amazed by what she was hearing.

Grandpa grinned. "I'm proud of you, Jeffrey. Did I

ever tell you about the time I worked in a car rental agency when I was a young man?"

"No. What happened?" Jeffrey leaned forward, his eyes wide.

"Meyer Lansky, the criminal, came in with three men who wore trench coats. They asked for two cars and no paper work."

Jeffrey sipped his coffee. "What did you do? Were you scared?"

"Sure. My knees started shaking. I handed them two sets of keys."

"Then what?"

"The following day they returned both cars, only one car was riddled with bullets. Lansky peeled off $500 from a wad of bills and said, 'We were never here.' I was so frightened I quit the job and started selling advertising signs."

"Good for you, Grandpa. You did the right thing."

*   *   *

The first order of business for Jeffrey was to order stationery and business cards for Helena Investing. His deception had worked, and now he was a business man. His grandparents were proud of him and all he required was his grandfather's backing and a meager sum of money.

Jeffrey was flying on the wings of advancement. He applied to the Motor Vehicle Bureau for a prestige license plate. "Love Life," was his favorite saying and when he got the plate he fondly fastened it on his used car. One day he would have a new car, a Lincoln or a Cadillac.

In his pursuit of advancement, Jeffrey took a course to be an agent with a legitimate license in Life and Health

Insurance with the Metropolitan Life Insurance Company. He spent just forty-six hours learning Section 113 of the Insurance Law.

The same day that Jeffrey received his license, he had it framed and hung it on the wall in his office. He knew it would impress the clients he had the intention of attracting.

Jeffrey was a person who craved excitement, and soon he decided to contribute his service to the people in his precinct, the 62nd. He volunteered for the Auxiliary Police, an unpaid, unarmed reserve police force, a subdivision of the New York Police Department. This, he thought, might lead to his meeting some clients for his investment service. He'd be accomplishing two goals at the same time. Additionally, one of the attractions was the navy blue uniform he'd be wearing with the shield, baton, and handcuffs he'd be issued.

After filling out the application and waiting a month, Jeffrey was thrilled that he had been accepted into the Basic Training Course. He sailed through the physical as he was young and strong. After attending faithfully for sixteen weeks, the time came for the final written examination. There was an unusual woman in his class who looked the same age as his mother, but was plump and appeared to be no more than 4 foot 6 inches, decidedly not a midget, but definitely tiny. Jeffrey figured that no one would want such a small woman for a partner. She sat on his right during the exam and, before it was distributed, he engaged her in conversation.

"Hi," he said with a broad smile. "My name is Jeffrey. This is exciting, isn't it?"

"It sure is. I'm Sally. I've always wanted to be an auxiliary police officer."

"Me, too. I live on West 10th Street. Where do you live?"

"Shore Parkway in a large apartment house with an indoor garage and a pool."

Nice. This gutsy gal has money. She can be my first client. "I'm a financial adviser. What do you do?"

By this time the examiner was almost finished distributing the exam papers. Sally whispered, "I'm the director of the microbiology department in Coney Island Hospital."

"Nice." He nodded and smiled. *I'm going to cultivate this gal.* "Would you like to be my partner?"

"Sure. You seem like a reliable young man."

She was wrong. In no way was he reliable, but how was she to know this.

They passed the exam about penal law and self-defense with a straight baton. It was easy, and over coffee and cake they laughed about it.

People stared at Jeffrey and Sally as they patrolled 86th Street in their navy blue uniforms, each carrying a straight baton, handcuffs, and a shield on their shirts and caps. Indeed they made a strange couple, Jeffrey, 5'10", and Sally, a mere 4'6". One man laughed quietly behind his hand as he spied them, and a teenager just guffawed. Jeffrey thought that Sally looked really young for fifty-two and he admired her guts.

Jeffrey felt wonderful as he looked at the familiar stores lined up one after another, and heard the roar of the train from the overhead subway. The scenery reminded him of his favorite movie, Saturday Night Fever. He knew he resembled John Travolta, the actor he admired more than any other.

When they finished patrolling 86th Street, they moved

on to Bay Parkway, a wide residential street with both private homes and six-story apartment houses. He felt like a big shot as he strolled alongside his partner with his curly head covered with the auxiliary officer's cap. Sally looked up to him both literally and figuratively.

Two weeks later as they came to the corner of 84th Street, Jeffrey looked to his right and saw a teenager attempting to break into a car. He poked Sally on her shoulder. She nodded and cautiously they approached the guy, batons raised. The guy had succeeded in opening the hood and was trying to start the ignition. "Call for backup," Jeffrey whispered to Sally. She placed the call while Jeffrey approached the boy.

"What do you think you're doing?" Jeffrey blurted.

The punk with straight black hair down to his shoulders bounced up. In an insolent way he said, "I ain't answering you."

"Show us your ID," Sally commanded.

"You're not even real police," the boy answered with a leer.

"We're legally bound to assist the police," Jeffrey said. "You have to prove that this is your car, or else."

"It's my friend's car," he yelled.

A middle-aged man raced out of his home. "That's my car and this punk is stealing it. Thank you officers. What are your names? I'm gonna tell the cops what a great job you did."

Jeffrey cuffed the perp who looked to be about seventeen. Then the man grabbed Jeffrey's hand and pumped it in appreciation.

Two police cars screeched to a stop in back of the sedan. Police officers jumped out with guns drawn.

"It's okay officers," the man assured them. These guys apprehended this criminal who was about to steal my car."

A month later, the proud couple, the Mutt and Jeff (the mismatched cartoon characters) of the auxiliary police, received a commendation for work well done, and their colleagues stopped poking fun at the difference in their height.

The incident bonded Jeffrey and Sally. They celebrated by going out for ice cream sodas in Jahn's, a restaurant on 86th Street. Jeffrey treated Sally who was delighted to accompany a handsome young man to a popular eatery.

As they sat next to each other in a corner booth, Jeffrey told Sally about an opportunity for her to make money with a new investment.

"It's a mutual fund and it's solid. It's called Andromeda." He thought about how he told his mother his idea to start a new fund. He had asked her to help him name it, and she had come up with the name Andromeda, the nearest big galaxy to the Milky Way, approximately 2.5 million light years from Earth.

"Tell me more," Sally said looking up into his dark, intelligent eyes.

"You'll be getting in at the inception. I have other clients investing in it, and so far it's been paying 10 per cent." Jeffrey didn't have any clients, but how was Sally to know this? He spoke convincingly, a deception he had mastered.

Sally frowned. "How much money do I have to invest?"

"Not much. $10,000. You'll get monthly statements to see how you're doing."

"I don't know." Sally slowly sipped the chocolate soda through the straw.

Jeffrey spooned the vanilla ice cream. "The best part is that you can pull your money out any time you want."

"My money is tied up in CD's, stocks and bonds."

Jeffrey took a breath. This wasn't going to be as easy as he had thought. "Why don't you sell the stock that's paying you the least?"

Sally nodded. "I never thought of that. Okay, I'm in. Andromeda here I come."

Jeffrey breathed a sigh of relief. Now his corporation could take off. He was twenty-two and raring to go. The corporation needed exposure and expansion, and Standard & Poor's Register of Corporations, Directors and Executives listed well-known companies. Now that Jeffrey's grandfather had paid for the listing, all the officers of Jeffrey's corporation were composed of friends and his grandfather, with him really heading it as the CEO. The business was listed as a holding company, real estate, sales and management investment consultants. Meanwhile he kept studying business at the library. The address for the corporation was his apartment. Everything else was phony.

What was missing for complete exposure was Dun & Bradstreet, Inc. He had to falsify the assets of Helena Investing, so without any qualms he went all out. He arranged a listing on his pad.

Assets	$65,459
Liabilities	20,795
Working capital	44,864
Other assets	1,390,950
Worth	552,676
Cash on hand	12,286
Accounts receivable	18,123
Government bonds	32,250

Current fixtures, equipment	65,659
Real estate	1,250,000
Other investments	128,450
Total assets	$1,456,609

He listed himself as five years older and married, and his grandfather as twelve years younger and formerly employed by a brokerage house.

His accountant was a friend of his. He was honest, so Jeffrey was the one who put his name on the Dun & Bradstreet inquiry without informing him. He also added that he had 20 employees when in actuality he was the only one employed, but he had to make his way up the ladder of success without a college degree, and very few college credits. After he had been expelled from the university when they had discovered he kept a gun in his locker, he gave up on formal education. It was none of the college's business, and he felt they had been unfair. He didn't need a college degree to get ahead. He could always photostat his mother's, change the name, and hang it on his office wall.

Chapter 15

AFTER JEFFREY FINISHED BASIC training in the Army Reserve, he worked as the manager in charge of the movie house at Fort Hamilton in Brooklyn, adjacent to the Belt Parkway overlooking the Verrazano Bridge. He was also assigned to dispose of discarded material in the refuse area. He contacted various recycling plants to get price quotes. He had the brilliant idea to write to the Major in charge and suggested that the paper be shredded, and the money credited to the school. Unfortunately, they never took him up on his suggestion which he knew was their loss. He consoled himself by thinking about how people jeered at Galileo when they heard him declare that the planets revolved around the sun.

Since he realized it would take time for him to build up his investment firm, he decided to seek employment in a brokerage house in the Boro Park section of Brooklyn, a drive of only fifteen minutes from his apartment.

Rodney Maxwell, a dapper man in a gray business suit, interviewed him. He leaned back in his leather desk chair and asked, "Why do you want to work for Drake Securities?"

Jeffrey had researched the firm and was able to give him five reasons why Drake was a solid up-and-coming firm. Then he smiled and said, "I hate to waste my valuable time riding on a crowded subway train to Wall Street."

Mr. Maxwell laughed. "I like your candor. No other interviewee has given such an honest answer. You're hired. Be here tomorrow morning at 9 sharp."

Finally Jeffrey had found a job where his skills would be recognized. He reported on time faithfully every day, he learned about the market, and bought and sold stocks for customers. Completely satisfied with his position, he felt the absence of a relationship with a woman.

One morning when Jeffrey entered Jefferson Bank, he noticed a new teller who had long chestnut colored hair, bright dark eyes, and a waist he could encircle with his arms. With a jaunty bounce in his step, he walked to her window and made a business deposit. An ID that read Ann Palermo was fastened above her rounded breast.

"Hello, Ann. You're new here. Welcome to my favorite bank."

"Thank you, Mr. Shulman."

"Please call me Jeffrey. I wish you luck in your job. Take good care of my money."

"Don't worry, Jeffrey, I will."

Every time Jeffrey made a deposit he made sure to go to this attractive teller's window. When she didn't appear, he left the bank and waited to return at a time when she would be there. Finally, when Jeffrey saw her, he slid the deposit slip through the slot along with a short note.

Ann blushed when she read it. "My answer is yes. I'll meet you on Sunday at 1 p.m. outside the bank."

Jeffrey felt elated. On Sunday morning he visited his grandparents and told them about the success he was having both with his business and with his job as a stockbroker. However, he didn't mention that he was dating a pretty young thing since they wouldn't approve. Ann always wore a crucifix on a chain around her neck. What they didn't know wouldn't hurt them.

Ann and Jeffrey met on a warm Sunday in May. He had rented a new Cadillac and as Ann lowered herself on the soft leather seat she said, "Wow. I'm impressed. This car must have cost you a fortune."

Jeffrey glowed with pride. "It's an expensive set of wheels, but I can afford it. How does a sunny afternoon in Coney Island sound?"

"Great. I'd love to walk on the boardwalk. I'm stuck in a cage in the bank all week, and I sure would like to be outside. How clever of you to think of it."

Jeffrey drove the Caddie carefully. After all, it was a rental and he didn't want to return it damaged. They would charge him for even a scratch and he couldn't afford it. He was glad that Ann was impressed. His plan had worked wonders, but he wasn't surprised. Any girl would be thrilled to be riding in a new Caddie. There was no perfume like the scent of a car that just left the plant.

The young couple strolled on the boardwalk, looking out at the dark blue ocean with its soft waves, and listening to the shrill cry of the seagulls. After ten minutes, Jeffrey took Ann's hand in his. He felt relieved that she didn't pull back. The wide sandy beach wasn't yet filled up with bathers. That would come in the heat of July and August. They saw boys building sand castles, and babies asleep on blankets while their parents sunned themselves.

The boardwalk consisted of all types of stores one after another. In front of one storefront, a gypsy stood chewing a wad of gum, and wore gold earrings as big as half dollars, a bright kerchief on her long dark hair, and a wide beribboned skirt down to her ankles.

"Come in, lady. I tell fortune. Only three dollars. Esmeralda will read your palm. I very, very good."

Ann's dark eyes were wide with anticipation. She said nothing but stood very still. *How I wish I could have my fortune told. He can afford it.*

"Go ahead, Ann. This can be most interesting," Jeffrey said as he steered her into the parlor with his hand on her back.

The gypsy shook her head. "Only lady can come in. Not you. I get paid first."

Jeffrey removed his wallet and handed the gypsy the money. There was a wooden chair outside and he sat down and waited fifteen minutes.

Inside the dark room, hung with paisley curtains and lit with a few candles, the gypsy and Ann sat at a small table opposite each other. There was a crystal ball on the table, but the gypsy ignored it, instead taking Ann's hand in hers. The gypsy had rings on all her greasy fingers with the exception of her thumbs. She stared at Ann's palm, and sighed.

"What is it?" Ann cried. "What do you see?"

"A long life line you have. You will live to ninety-five and travel the world. Romania you will like best of all countries, and next England."

"Yes, yes," Ann said, looking anxiously at the gypsy. "What else?"

The mysterious woman held Ann's hand closer to her eyes. "I see a love affair with a dark man who is very rich. Beware of lies. You will marry him because you love this man."

"Oh, my," Ann said. "What else?"

"Marry you will, twice. Three children you will have.

One boy, two girls. You will have many grandchildren. That is all I see."

When Ann came out, she looked thoughtful. She wondered if Jeffrey was the man she would marry. *Is he for real? Does this silly woman know what she's talking about?*

"What did the gypsy tell you?" Jeffrey asked pleasantly.

"I will live long and prosper."

"Anything else?"

Ann shook her head. "It's all nonsense. She's only a woman who needs money, and she makes up a phony fortune. It was fun, but let's move on."

When Jeffrey spied a game arcade, he tugged at Ann's hand and led her to the Skeeball lanes. He had played for over a decade and succeeded in making high scores.

He told Ann how Skeeball is similar to bowling except it's played on an inclined lane. Jeffrey dropped the coin into the coin slot and nine baseball-sized balls of hardwood rolled down. The ramp was twelve feet long, and he sent the ball to the side of the lane. He knew it would end up in the hole with the highest points and he would get tickets through a slot. He didn't tell Ann how experienced he was. That would defeat his purpose of trying to impress her.

"Wow," Jeffrey cried. "I rolled the ball and it fell into the hole with 300 points. It was pure luck."

Ann clapped her hands.

He kept getting the highest score. The tickets kept adding up. When he had 2,000 points he stopped. "Now it's your turn."

Ann had never played before and her balls kept going into the gutter until Jeffrey showed her how to keep her wrist stiff and send the ball down the center of the lane. When she started to hit hundreds, she glowed with satisfaction.

"Let's put our tickets together. You pick out the prize you want," Jeffrey said as he walked to the display case.

Ann peered at all the cheap toys, the ceramic pigs, the dogs with rhinestone collars, and the ballerina dolls. Her eyes lit up when she saw a two-foot teddy bear on the top shelf. She pointed at it. "I'd like that very much."

"We have enough tickets for that," Jeffrey said as he handed a bunch of tickets to a short teenager with a T-shirt that read, 'I'm not short. I'm fun size.' The kid behind the counter put the tickets in a machine that counted them. He reached up for the teddy bear, the largest of the toys, and gave it to Ann who hugged the teddy bear to her heart.

"Let's go on the Cyclone," Jeffrey urged Ann as they continued strolling on the Boardwalk. Jeffrey loosened his tie as the sun beat down on them.

"I never did that. I'm scared," Ann said as she looked at the cars careening down.

"You should try it at least once. You'll get the thrill of your life." *She'll cling to me later and I'll comfort her.*

"I don't know. Listen to those riders screaming. I'm afraid."

"Afterwards they all get off and feel great. This wooden roller coaster is sixty-eight years old. It's the granddaddy of the amusement world. Come on, Ann, you won't be sorry."

"I'm sorry already."

Ann trembled as she sat next to Jeffrey holding tightly to the iron bar in front of her. Her hands whitened with the tight grip on the bar. She closed her eyes and wished she hadn't let Jeffrey get the upper hand. She tried to see herself comfortably asleep in her bed at home. Then she heard the creaky pulley's sending them up, climbing a mountain, bumping all the way to the top, and then she screamed as the cars felt like they were flying off the track, hurling her down into a living nightmare. Each embankment felt deadlier than the last.

When the ride finished and she stumbled out of the car, Ann said a little prayer, *Thank you God for letting me live.*

"Wasn't that fun?" Jeffrey asked innocently thinking that Ann had an experience she would never forget, and that she was happy about his suggestion that she try something new.

"It was awful. My whole body is sore, and my stomach is churning. It was terrifying. It was rickety and jarring and so uncomfortable that I'll never go on a roller coaster again. As soon as I got on, I wished it was over."

"I'm sorry. Let's sit down on a bench and you'll soon calm down."

"I won't calm down for a week. I may have to go to a chiropractor. My neck is killing me," Ann said, once they had found a bench facing the ocean.

"Let me rub it," Jeffrey said as he placed his hand on Ann's smooth skin.

"You should have told me that the hook to the right comes at the bottom of that first drop," Ann said in an accusing tone.

"I didn't want to frighten you," Jeffrey answered as he kept kneading Ann's neck. "I really thought you'd like the thrill the ride gives."

"I didn't like it at all. In fact, I hated it. I got that creepy feeling on top of the ups and downs, and then it had lots of side-to-side action that was miserable. Also, the ride keeps going when I thought it would be over. It was horrible."

"I'm so sorry," Jeffrey said. He wasn't used to apologizing but this *faux pas* needed an apology if he wanted to maintain a relationship with this lovely young woman.

Ann took a deep breath of fresh salt air. "Apology accepted. It was a ride of doom and I'm lucky I'm still alive. They should outlaw all roller coasters. They're dangerous to a person's health. How do you feel?"

"I'm fine, thanks. I like thrills. I have an idea that will surely calm your nerves. In fact, any time I'm uptight I go there."

"Where?"

Jeffrey smiled. "I recommend the New York Aquarium. Believe it or not, the Aquarium is right next door. Do you like fish?"

Ann nodded. "I do. I heard they have penguins that I'd love to see."

Jeffrey bought the tickets, and Ann gradually relaxed. They were in time to watch the attendant feed the penguins at 3:30 in the aqua theater. One penguin waddled in back of the others, not fast enough to catch the small fish that were thrown to the group. The attendant made sure that the dawdling penguin got his share of the food.

"He's so cute and laid back," Ann observed. "I'm so glad we came here."

Ann was fascinated when the sea lions performed. After the show, the young couple strolled indoors to view the exhibits. Ann clapped her hands when the electric eel lit up. Jeffrey was happy to explain that the powerful fish uses its electric shock to defend itself against predators.

"The first New York Aquarium was opened in lower Manhattan in 1896," Jeffrey explained. "My mother used to tell me that my grandmother would bring her there all the time. It was a round building and, in 1941, when she was eleven, it was closed, and she was terribly disappointed. This Aquarium opened in 1956 and my mother used to take me here when I was a child. Now, I understand that it's home to over 350 species of aquatic wildlife."

Ann smiled at Jeffrey's vast knowledge and wondered if he'd take her to dinner. By now her appetite had returned and her stomach was growling.

But Jeffrey seemed absorbed in going into the gift shop. As Ann looked at the stuffed animals, Jeffrey selected a present for her.

"What did you get?" Ann asked as she peered at the small box in Jeffrey's hand.

"It's for you."

Ann opened the box and she smiled at a pair of penguin earrings. "Oh, you shouldn't have, but I'm glad you did buy them. They're lovely. Thank you. I'll always remember the wonderful time I spent with you at the Aquarium."

"You're such a gentle person, and I hurt you by suggesting we go on the Cyclone. This costume jewelry will never make up for my rashness." And, as if he could read her mind, Jeffrey suggested that they drive to Sheepshead Bay.

Cautiously he drove the rented Cadillac to Palladino's Fish House, a charming, pricey restaurant with windows facing the bay.

The dining room was decorated with all kinds of fish paraphernalia, nets, shells, and a stuffed shark on the wall next to the booth where Jeffrey and Ann sat. The table, set with white linen, fine china and expensive crystal, looked stunning. Ann examined the menu. When she saw no prices listed, she frowned when she realized they were in a high-class restaurant.

"I'll have the halibut. Order whatever pleases you," Jeffrey said pleasantly.

"Thank you. I'd like jumbo shrimp scampi with pasta."

"Jumbo shrimp is an oxymoron," Jeffrey said with a slight smile.

"I don't know what that means, but you sound really intelligent."

Jeffrey gave the order to the waiter who had a thick, dark mustache. "What wine would you care to order with that, sir?" the tuxedo clad waiter asked.

White wine was appropriate for fish, Jeffrey knew but he didn't know which one would do. "What do you recommend?" he asked smoothly.

"Sir, I recommend our Italian wine, "Ecco Domani Pinot Grigio. It's refreshing, super light in color with lemon and apple flavors that lead into a somewhat of a slightly sweet and buttery finish, easy to drink and a good selection for a superb May day."

Jeffrey waited for the sales pitch to stop, but it didn't. The waiter continued selling the wine with a lengthy explanation which he had memorized for just such an occasion. "The blend is 95% Pinot Grigio, 6% Chardonnay. A low concentration of Surmaturo grapes gives the wine tropical fruit notes. It is truly refined elegance. My opinion is . . . ."

Exasperated, Jeffrey said, "Sounds good. Please bring us two glasses."

"Yes, sir. Immediately."

The meal was fabulous and, when Jeffrey drove Ann back, she leaned against the soft leather of the seat, looking satisfied with the most adventurous day of her young life.

"Please drop me off at my aunt's house on the corner of West 10th Street and Avenue P," Ann said. "I want to tell my family what a grand time I had."

"I'm glad you enjoyed our date, of course, with the exception of my insensitivity by taking you on the Cyclone." Jeffrey paused and smiled. "How about dating me every Sunday until we get tired of each other?"

Ann fingered her crucifix. "I'd like that very much."

After parking the car at the curb of an old frame house, Jeffrey leaned over and gave Ann a soft kiss on her lips. He made it quick and light, not wanting her to get the wrong idea. Ann, hugging the huge teddy bear, raced into her Aunt Jessica's home while Jeffrey sat admiringly watching her climb the stairs to the rickety porch, as he noted the sexy shape of her legs. Then he drove the Caddie to the car rental place on Coney Island Avenue and strode home, satisfied with Ann's positive response.

Chapter 16

ON THEIR SECOND DATE, Jeffrey and Ann went to the Central Park Zoo, and before their third date in June Jeffrey asked Ann where she wanted to go. "I love flowers and I'd like to visit the Brooklyn Botanic Gardens. The Japanese garden with its quaint wooden bridges, waterfall, and blossoming trees is so relaxing to look at." She smiled with her dark luminous eyes and her mouth with cupid lips.

"Then we'll go where you want," Jeffrey said obligingly. "Just don't expect to see the cherry trees in blossom. They bloom only until May."

"You know so much," Ann mused. *He always impresses me with his vast knowledge.*

The couple strolled hand in hand through the gardens when Ann spotted the hothouse. "Let's go in," Ann suggested. She pointed to the entrance looking quite enthusiastic.

Inside they examined the tropical plants, the cacti, the insect-eating plants, and the delicate orchids. Ann pointed to the tallest tree. "Look at that gigantic banana tree with clusters of bananas hanging down."

Jeffrey looked up. "Did you know that bananas are

slightly radioactive because of their high potassium content?"

Ann's eyes opened wide. "My goodness, did you read the whole encyclopedia when you were a child?"

"You bet." Jeffrey was pleased with Ann's high opinion.

Suddenly Ann's face turned white. "I don't feel well."

Jeffrey looked at the thermometer on the wall that read 110 degrees. He pulled Ann to the exit and through the door. Outside where the temperature was 80 degrees she started to pant. Jeffrey put his arm around her shoulder and led her to a bench where they both sat down. A few minutes later the color flooded back to Ann's face.

"Poor kid," Jeffrey said. "Your body couldn't adjust to the high temperature. Another minute in there and you would have fainted. Put your head on my shoulder, take some deep breaths, and relax. I'll take care of you."

One Sunday afternoon when Jeffrey dipped the oars of their rented rowboat into one of the lakes in Prospect Park, he turned to Ann. "Tell me about your life at home. I want to know all about you."

Ann blushed. "I'm the youngest and the only girl. I have two married brothers and my parents are protective of me, just like all Italian parents. I'm twenty, but they treat me like I'm fourteen. They know I'm seeing someone. They just don't know that you're Jewish."

"Does that bother you?" Jeffrey hoped that Ann would accept him, his Jewishness, his tendency to curve the truth to his advantage, and his present state of economy.

Ann leaned to her right and caressed the lake water with her fingers. "It annoys me that they're prejudiced, but it doesn't bother me that you're Jewish. After all, the Catholic religion is an outgrowth of Judaism."

"It's too bad about your folks. As for me, I live alone

and do as I please, but it's lonesome. My birthday is coming up on July 6th. Will you help me celebrate?"

"I'll be happy to." Ann looked him in the eye, smiled, and rejoiced that she had such a bright and generous boyfriend.

The first thing that Jeffrey did on the morning of his 23rd birthday was to sit down at his desk and draw up a personal financial plan. He began with a triangle and on the base he placed his bank accounts, IRA accounts, Israeli bonds, E & EE bonds, a total of 47%. The next 8% was corporate bonds, then mutual funds at 8%. Common stocks at 10%, then at 12% he listed silver bars. At the top of the triangle, he listed his stamp and coin collection, and OTC stocks at 15%. Then he leaned back with a wry smile, and thought about this as his future financial plan. He would work hard until he achieved his goal.

That night he and Ann went out to dinner and afterwards to the theater to see *Annie,* rated as one of the best Broadway shows. They sat in the sixteenth row in the orchestra and were able to admire Carol Burnett as Miss Hannigan who looked prettier than she did on TV. Ann said she liked Albert Finney as Daddy Warbucks, and Jeffrey agreed he did a fine job.

Driving back to Brooklyn across the Brooklyn Bridge, Ann, with her lilting alto voice, sang the popular song "Tomorrow." It was a great birthday and Jeffrey looked forward to spending many more with her. Being single was no pleasure, he acknowledged, and he needed love and companionship, but he wasn't willing to suffer through a traditional wedding with hundreds of guests. It was time to pop the question.

He took a deep breath.

"I love you, Ann. Let's get married."

Ann bit down on her lips. "I don't know. We've been going together such a short time. We hardly know each other."

"We'll learn about each other after we marry." Jeffrey took his hand off the steering wheel and covered her hand with his. "Let's get the license and the blood test and we can be married in City Hall. Why wait?"

"What about our parents? I don't think they'll approve."

"We won't tell them until afterwards. We'll continue to live separately until we can win them over."

It took a few more Sundays for Jeffrey to convince Ann to marry him, but in the end they went down to City Hall where they were married by a clerk with a diamond earring in his ear. They stood close together in front of the clerk. Ann wore a short white sheath and a matching silk hat with a veil, and she carried a posy of lily-of-the-valley. Jeffrey sported a cream-colored suit. They were so excited that they hardly heard the words that the clerk chanted. Before Jeffrey realized the short ceremony was over, he was nudged to place a plain gold band on Ann's ring finger. He lifted her veil and bent to kiss his bride with as much tenderness as he could muster. Not being a demonstrative person, he tried hard to appear as one.

Leaving City Hall, hand in hand, Jeffrey and Ann strolled to the subway. Jeffrey hadn't wanted to drive to Manhattan, and Ann had agreed that the traffic was heavy, and there wouldn't be a place to park.

"Where are we going on our honeymoon?" Ann asked as they bounced down the stairs and caught the Sea Beach train to Brooklyn. Some teenagers glanced at Ann dressed like a bride and chuckled.

"Pay no attention to them," Jeffrey said.

As they sat close together, Jeffrey whispered, "You know I have to be back to work on Monday. The same goes for you. We have only three days to celebrate. How about driving to Atlantic City? We could stay at the same hotel my grandparents honeymooned at."

Ann grinned. "Sure. You'll drive the Caddie and I'll sing. We'll take a real honeymoon when you get your vacation."

Jeffrey was a master at evasion. The rented car had been returned so he popped up with another pleasantly polite but insincere fabrication. "The Caddie needed some work on the carburetor, but I have my old car with the new prestige license plate, Dr. Drake. I registered it after Drake Securities where I work."

"Ohhh," Ann sighed. "I loved your Caddie. What a disappointment."

She'll be more disappointed when she never sees the Cadillac again. But if she really loves me, she'll adjust.

The enjoyable three-day honeymoon passed quickly, and when they returned to living in Brooklyn, they each went back to their respective homes.

The following Sunday they arranged for Jeffrey to meet Ann's parents for the first time. He set out to charm them with his sharp appearance, his humor, and his gift of gab. Ann lived in an old brick home with weeds and a rusted bicycle in the front yard. Her father had bushy black eyebrows and a beer belly, and Jeffrey thought her mother was a candidate for fat lady of the circus.

After a brief conversation, when they were all seated in the living room and had exhausted their talk about how pretty leaves looked when they changed color, Ann announced in a flat voice, "Jeffrey and I are married."

The fat lady screeched. Beer belly jumped up from

the faded green sofa, and eyed his daughter for several seconds before he shouted, "Did you have to get married?"

"No, Dad," Ann said in a quivering voice. "We got married because we fell in love."

Her father grunted. "Love is for fourteen-year-old kids like Romeo and Juliet. You should have known better."

"Why couldn't you wait until we could make a decent wedding for you, our only daughter?" With her chubby hands, Mrs. Palermo wiped the tears streaming down her cheeks.

"We kind of thought you and Jeffrey's parents wouldn't approve. He's Jewish and . . ."

Ann's mother groaned. Her father threw up his hands. They turned to look at each other with expressions of pain on their faces. They were strict Catholics and this would never do. They had sent Ann to parochial school and she had been raised in a religious household.

"What will Father Donovan say?" the fat lady whispered.

"Do your parents know?" Ann's father asked Jeffrey.

"Not yet." He wiped the perspiration from his forehead with a handkerchief he pulled out from the pocket of his jacket.

"I hate deception." Ann's father put his head in his hands.

Ann pulled herself together. "I don't care that Jeffrey's Jewish. He's good and kind. He wanted to get married without a fuss, and I agreed. He doesn't have a big family, just a stepfather, a half-brother, and his mother. I didn't want you to borrow money and get in debt for me."

"Will you convert?" Ann's father asked in an angry voice.

"No," Jeffrey answered quietly to show that he was in

control of his emotions. He smiled thinly. "But Ann and I will keep our own religions and we will live in peace."

"Ha," Ann's father sneered as he patted his huge stomach.

The fat lady sucked in a sharp breath. "We don't know anything else about the boy except that he's a Jew. What do you do for a living?"

Jeffrey, with a savage glitter in his brown eyes, knew he was in his element. With the confidence of a con man, he changed his expression to a charming one that he plastered on his handsome face. He would win them over without half trying. "I own my own financial business, and I work as a stockbroker for Drake Securities. I'm rated high, about a million and a half, in Dun & Bradstreet. You can check me out."

Ann's parents exchanged knowing looks.

Mr. Palermo raised his bushy eyebrows. "What did you see in my daughter?"

Jeffrey offered a full blown, devilish smile. "She's lovely, sweet, and innocent, and I think you did a good job bringing her up."

Ann's father and mother looked at each other in amazement. Jeffrey felt he had made a good impression, and was satisfied with his devious and masterful bit of manipulation. They would always be dissatisfied with his being Jewish, but there was nothing they could do about that.

A month later Ann moved into Jeffrey's apartment, and in the evening they approached Jeffrey's mother with the good news. Jeffrey's stepfather was out taking a walk with Jeffrey's half-brother.

Jeffrey's mother looked tired with shadows under her eyes, apparently caused by the stress of caring for her abusive, demanding husband, and young son while she still held down a full-time position as a junior high school teacher. Nevertheless, she warmly welcomed them into the two-bedroom apartment. In the living room, which was furnished tastefully in an eclectic manner, she served them Cokes and cookies.

The upright mahogany piano and a bookcase stacked with reference books and classic novels made an impression on Ann. *Jeffrey stems from a cultured and intellectual family.*

Jeffrey came right to the point. "Ann is Catholic and we got married in City Hall."

Jeffrey's mother looked surprised. For thirty seconds, she said nothing, looking at them helplessly. "Congratulations. I wish you a long and happy marriage." She rose from her seat to kiss the bride and groom. There were reservations she had about a marriage between her son, who had been taught the Jewish religion in both the home and the Yeshiva, and a girl who had been raised as a Catholic. But the deed was done and she had to accept it with grace. Jeffrey was always fragile and needed the love of a good woman.

When they returned to Jeffrey's apartment, where Ann had begun to set up housekeeping, she turned to him. "I was surprised your mother didn't give us a hard time. I like her."

"She's a good person. I feel bad that she's married to a man who abuses her physically and emotionally. When my kid brother was ten, she left Nat and moved in with me until she found her own basement apartment. My brother begged her to go back to his father, and she couldn't swing it financially so she returned to the brute. Someday she'll have enough guts to get out of a bad situation. Until then, I say nothing to persuade her to leave him. My grandparents also don't interfere."

"I feel sorry for her," Ann said as she rearranged the

closet space making more room for her clothes. "When will we move to a larger home?"

Jeffrey gave Ann a sardonic smile. "We'll move when we have a baby."

"I may be pregnant," she said softly as her heart pounded.

"That's impossible." Jeffrey stiffened with worry. They were in no financial position to support a baby. Pregnancy would stop Ann from working and complicate their whole monetary situation. "I thought you were on the pill," he said bluntly.

"I ran out of them." She draped her arms around his neck.

"How could you?" He pulled her arms away. His stomach started to churn.

Ann sucked in a sharp breath. "Why are you so upset? You told me you loved children."

"I do, but not yet. We should have good times before we settle down taking care of a baby." *I should have known you can't trust a woman.* Moving toward the front door, Jeffrey stormed out and slammed the door behind him.

Meanwhile Ann, appalled by his conduct, wondered what she should do. Perhaps she could win him over. When he returned two hours later, Ann had undressed and put on a thin, alluring nightgown. She sat on the bed and Jeffrey, relenting, bent to kiss her. Hesitantly he said, "You may not be pregnant, but I won't make love to you until you get more birth control pills."

Ann threw up her hands. "If that's the way you want it, okay, but it's like applying sunscreen after sitting in the sun all day."

Jeffrey moved to the closet to hang up his suit jacket. "I won't gamble on something so important. Sometimes it takes years for a woman to get pregnant." He spoke with confidence, trying to hide the worry underneath. He hadn't counted on a baby, as he wanted Ann to keep working while he built up his illegal Ponzi scheme.

A month later Ann announced over breakfast, "I feel pregnant. I'm nauseous and bloated."

Buttering his toast, Jeffrey said in a sneering tone, "You can't be pregnant."

Ann sucked in a sharp breath and flew into the bathroom. Jeffrey groaned as he heard heaving vomit-like sounds. He had trusted her and she had failed him. He felt confused and depressed. "How are you?" he called out in a flat voice.

She came back to the kitchen and rinsed her mouth with a glass of water. "I think I'm pregnant," she said in a thin, childlike voice.

When another week had passed, the pregnancy was confirmed. Jeffrey grew more and more uneasy. He wasn't sure how he could manage.

Ann was nauseous every day, and she was forced to quit her job. One rainy Sunday when they sat watching a movie on TV in the living room, she asked what happened to the Cadillac.

"I sold it," Jeffrey said sheepishly. "It was mine to sell, and I sold it. You can't work and we needed the money."

She looked at Jeffrey helplessly, unable to put her disappointment into words. Finally she murmured, "I loved that car."

"I think you loved the car more than you love me." Jeffrey moved closer and stuck his face right in hers.

"That's not true. You show me no sympathy for my constant nausea and still I love you."

Jeffrey's eyes blazed. "I'll tell you why I'm disgusted.

It's your fault that you got pregnant." The idea of her being pregnant was ludicrous.

"So what? We have enough money to have a child."

"Is that so? Nevertheless, I put my money into pork bellies and got ripped off. We have only enough to pay the rent on this apartment, pay for food, and barely enough to pay the doctor bills." Her being pregnant was appalling.

Ann's complexion turned as pale as a skeleton. "You told me you owned this house. Were you lying?"

"I was stupid, that's all," he snapped. "I never had a Caddie and I never owned property. All you are is greedy. You married me because you believed I was rich. Well, I'm not—not yet, anyway." He jumped up and walked to and fro with his hands clasped behind his back, finally settling into an arm chair.

Ann stepped into the kitchen and began to pace in quick, jerky steps. Jeffrey jumped up, followed her, and noticed how she grimaced. Suddenly she grabbed her stomach and ran into the bathroom.

While she remained in the bathroom, Jeffrey decided to eat. He slit a bagel, grabbed some lox and cream cheese, and made himself a sandwich. *She's being mule-headed. If only she wasn't pregnant, everything would be all right.*

A half-hour later, Ann came back to the kitchen. With a haughty lift of her chin, she said, "You don't have to worry any more. I'm not pregnant. I had a miscarriage."

Jeffrey's lips curled. "Are you sure?"

"Sure, I'm sure. Our baby has been flushed down the toilet. It's what you wanted, isn't it?" Ann held her stomach. She sat down on the oak kitchen chair, and gazed at Jeffrey with an accusing look in her eyes.

Relief poured into Jeffrey's cold heart. He rose and filled the kettle with water. "Do you want a glass of tea?"

Ann rose with difficulty and hobbled to the bedroom. She took off her jersey blouse and plaid skirt, and got into bed wearing her slip. She pulled the coverlet up to her chin and uttered a low moan. Jeffrey stepped into the bedroom. A muscle flicked in his jaw as he stared at Ann, a long painful moment thinking that it took the Lord to solve his problem. Without warning, Ann leaped to her feet, took the large teddy bear from the chair, and tossed it at Jeffrey hitting him on his neck. "I hate you."

"Can you get your job back?" he snorted, rubbing his neck while he ignored her sharp words.

"No. They hired someone else," she whispered past the huge lump lodged in her throat. "But one thing is clear. I can't stay married to a liar."

"What do you mean? I thought you loved me." A scowl knit his brow.

"I used to love you until I learned who you really are." She choked on the words. "I can't live like this. As soon as I feel better, I'm going to move back with my parents. Then I'll hire a lawyer and get an annulment."

"I can't understand you. I was good to you." His eyes blazed at her, dark in their torment. "You should love me whether or not I'm rich, and someday in the near future I'll be rolling in bills like a hippo in mud. You'll live to regret your decision. You're acting like a kid. It's time you grew up."

*　　*　　*

Jeffrey learned that it didn't take too long, after Ann got the annulment on the grounds that he hadn't told her the truth about his financial situation, she converted to Judaism and married a Jewish man.

Chapter 17

JEFFREY WASN'T VERY UPSET that he had to live alone again as he liked his independence. He forged ahead with his get-rich Ponzi scheme.

Carlo Ponzi was his idol and, even though he was dead, to Jeffrey he was his mentor, a genius who pointed the road to financial success. He had read about how Ponzi had hatched banking, land, and postage stamp scams by promising high returns and working it so that his early payouts were financed by funds from succeeding investors. Jeffrey found many investors—including Sally, his auxiliary police partner, who was paid off handsomely. She couldn't be more pleased and kept investing.

An opportunity presented itself for him to make even more money. Morris Newman approached him with a proposition that had great appeal. Jeffrey had taken the securities representative exam for him, and Morris had gotten his license and worked with him in Drake Securities. Morris wanted desperately to get a college degree and admired Jeffrey for his ability and brilliance.

Jeffrey had written Morris' essays for English 1, and he had to advance to English 2 and didn't have the interest or capability. He wanted Jeffrey to pose as him and pass the course which Jeffrey was happy to do. He loved the role of student and particularly of fooling the professor which was an exciting adventure; furthermore, he could make a good deal of money by charging Morris top dollar. It was ideal for him.

He registered for the night course in English 2 in Brooklyn College. Even though the college was smack in the city, it had a rural university feel to it. Truly it was one of the most beautiful campuses in the country. Jeffrey thought the quadrangle with Boylan and Ingersoll Halls opposite each other and the stately library in the center with its bells tolling the time was impressive, as was the lily pond adjacent to Ingersoll Hall. The location of the college, in the Flatbush/Midwood community, was calm in the residential neighborhood that offered the distinction of being part of the city, yet a refuge from it. On the bustling Flatbush side, there was dining, shopping, and the book store packed with students. The peaceful Midwood side had tree-lined streets with spacious private homes.

The first night Jeffrey was surprised to see that the professor, Dr. Brody, was a young beautiful blonde. He took the first seat in the middle row, so that he could make a good impression. He shivered with excitement as he realized she would never discover he was only pretending to be Morris. He determined to win her over with his thoughtful use of rhetorical discourse. It would be an adventure to remember, but not one to brag about, for only Morris and he would be aware of the deception, an adventure in which Jeffrey could revel in his dark side.

However, there was one time when Jeffrey almost got caught. He was walking alongside one of his classmates in English 2. It was twilight and they were crossing the quadrangle before class, and Pete, a short guy he was acquainted with, called out, "Hey, Jeffrey. What class are you taking?"

Jeffrey drew in a deep breath. "I'm Morris. Jeffrey's my twin."

"Since when do you have a twin?" he asked, raising an eyebrow.

"Since our mother expelled us at birth."

Pete turned on his heel and left. Jeffrey shrugged. It was a close call, but he pulled it off.

He titled his first essay, "*The Business of Criminal Rehabilitation.*" When it received an A-, he wasn't surprised. It was original and carefully thought out. It also inspired Jeffrey to apply to the prison at Rikers Island to teach the prisoners how to earn honest money in the stock market when they were released. Since his mother was a teacher, he asked her to help him prepare the lesson plans and she was happy to do it.

For the next paper Jeffrey wrote, "*The so-called 'macho-man' is gauged by the quantity of sexual conquests over the female. To be a man in this world we must act 'manly.' This includes exercising control over the weaker sex.*" Since Ann had acted like a weakling, he now thought of women as the weaker sex, weaker in strength, ambition, and emotion.

In class they were asked to write a practice essay and, as his ballpoint pen zoomed smoothly over the paper, he concentrated and calmly wrote that people are not entirely dependent on others' decisions unless they so choose to be. When Professor Brody gave him an A on his paper and wrote, "I would like you to read this to the class at the next meeting," he felt like a floating helium balloon. He knew that Morris was headed for the grade of A because of his brilliant mind and devious manipulation.

For the final essay in class, Jeffrey concentrated on the importance of marriage. Since his parents had separated when he was born and later the marriage was annulled, he knew firsthand about the effect of living with one parent. He wrote, *"Romance without marriage is the apex of the void."* The comments on Jeffrey's paper were sharp. "You've definitely made your point. But I submit you become somewhat anti-climactic near the end, in that you belabor the point. Watch these grammar and mechanics errors—they detract from your paper's overall effectiveness." She gave Morris a B+ for the paper and an A for the course.

Morris was thrilled and they both celebrated by going to dinner, naturally Morris' treat. They drove in Morris' Lincoln to an expensive kosher Chinese restaurant, Shang Chai, on Flatbush Avenue in Brooklyn. They sat and shared a smile over the deviousness of Jeffrey's achieving an A in Morris' name. Jeffrey was proud of his crafty methods. Everyone in his family was honest, but that wasn't the way to get ahead in this world.

"We formed a good alliance," he said as he jabbed at a piece of steak with his fork.

"You bet," Morris agreed. "How about taking my sociology class next September?"

"Sorry, I can't. I'm too busy. I've been accepted in the new program that I instituted on Rikers Island teaching investing to the prisoners. I'm still working as an auxiliary policeman, and now I've signed up to be a volunteer in Maimonides Hospital."

Morris sipped his wine, wiped his generous mouth with his napkin, and said, "But you don't even get paid for these jobs, and I'm willing to pay you like before, even more if you want."

"I'm making enough at Drake and in Andromeda Investments. You'll find someone else." With precision, Jeffrey cut a tasty morsel of steak satisfied with the upward road he was on.

"Never as good as you," Morris said with a frown.

*   *   *

One spring night when the stars sparkled and the air was sweet, Jeffrey visited his mother's apartment. Nat was out taking a walk and they could relax at the kitchen table nibbling on chickpeas. Jeffrey said with a smile, "Please tell me about an incident in your childhood."

Ricky thought for a few moments. "When I was three, we lived on the ground floor of a small walk-up apartment house that was close to a Chinese laundry where Grandma used to bring Grandpa's shirts to be washed and pressed. Wash and wear clothing hadn't been invented yet."

"Interesting," Jeffrey said. "Go on."

"Well, every time I went with Grandma to the store, the owner gave me two Lychee nuts. Grandma would open them for me and I would eat them with relish."

Jeffrey smiled broadly. "I never heard of Lychee nuts. What do they taste like?"

"They have a lumpy brown surface, very rough skinned, but easy to open, and when you open it the skin is white, sweet like sugar, and juicy. It looks like a peeled grape but in the center is a smooth brown seed. They're delicious but I can't find them in stores or I'd buy them all the time."

"That Chinese man was nice to you. He must have liked you."

"Oh, he did. One day he took me by the hand and

walked me around the corner to Woolworth's 5 & 10 cent store and bought me a ball."

"Unusual," Jeffrey remarked. "You never forgot his kindness even though you were a young child."

"I never knew his name but I'll always remember him."

*   *   *

Jeffrey always acknowledged his mother's birthday with a card, sometimes flowers, and sometimes a small gift. To celebrate this birthday, they went to a restaurant where he treated his mother, her husband, and Arthur to a fish dinner. As they were waiting for the check, Jeffrey took out a box with birthday wrapping and a bow and handed it to his mother.

"Happy birthday, Mom," he said with a grin.

"You didn't have to buy me anything, but I thank you for your thoughtfulness." Ricky tore off the wrapping and opened the box. To her delight she found a package of Lychee nuts.

"Oh, boy, I was pining for these. Where did you get them?"

"It was easy to find them in Chinatown."

Ricky kissed Jeffrey on his cheek. *My boy can be so kind and considerate. If only I could trust him, I'd be a happy mother.*

*   *   *

Arthur had come home from Yeshiva also with a birthday present, only it wasn't anything to eat. It was a kitten whose mother had rejected it. Ricky named the cat,

Houdini, as he always managed to get out of any box she placed him in.

* * *

Jeffrey's heart beat crazily as he dressed for his first time as the investment instructor on Rikers. Outside his bedroom window the rain beat steadily like it was saying *Go for it! Go for it!* He put on his white-on-white long-sleeved shirt with the French cuffs and pearl-on-gold cufflinks, his three-piece charcoal suit, and his silk crimson tie. He combed his rich brown curly hair, grabbed his leather briefcase and umbrella, and sailed out the door. He took the Sea Beach train and a couple of buses to Rikers, an island in the East River in Manhattan. All the while Jeffrey hoped he would get a friendly reception from the prisoners.

Impressing them was important to him; at the same time, he wanted the recognition, and, perhaps if the program was helpful, the publicity he craved. When he was seventeen he had located his father and started to visit him. He intended to tell his father, his wife and their three kids about his unusual pursuit. He'd also brag to his mother. This would be the first and only program of its kind in the U.S. and he would make sure that various publications were aware of it. He straightened his shoulders, feeling proud of himself.

Jeffrey sucked in his stomach as he went through the complicated security measures. Eventually he was lead to a classroom with peeling gray walls, no windows, and filled with prisoners in tan prison garb. They looked him in the eye with what he thought was savage glitter.

He wrote his full name on the blackboard, and hoped

that no one would throw an egg at his head, but there wasn't a chance of that since an armed guard was posted at each side of the room.

"You're all volunteers," he said in a loud commanding voice. "I'll teach you how to make money legitimately when you're discharged from prison, and possibly while you're still here. Is there anyone who doesn't want to learn this? If so, please raise your hand."

While Jeffrey gazed from one prisoner to another, no one raised his hand. He felt a loosening of his taut muscles. The creases on his forehead disappeared. Most of the prisoners were black or Hispanic, but there were a few Caucasian, all of whom had tattoos on their hairy arms. These were tough cookies and were not in prison because they were innocent.

"Does anyone know what stocks are?" Jeffrey asked looking around the room.

No one answered, so Jeffrey began to tell them about the history of the stock market. He continued, "When a person buys stocks, he owns part of a company and has a right to vote on who runs the company."

"You're joshing," said one of the black guys with a neck as big as a tree trunk.

A prisoner, with straight black hair and a scar over his eye and down his cheek, raised his hand. Jeffrey thought he had a face only a Mafia mother could love.

"Yes?"

"I'm gettin' out of this here place next month. Do ya think there's a stock I should buy?"

Jeffrey clenched his jaw and arched an eyebrow. He would have to make a recommendation so as not to lose face. "I've studied the market thoroughly and I've bought shares of Intel, a technology company that was founded in 1968. They make chips for computers. I think they're a solid company."

"They better be or you'll hear from me," Scarface said ominously. "How much a share?"

"You understand it goes up and down constantly, but right now it's selling for sixty cents, a really good buy. If you purchase 1,000 shares, you only have to pay $600 and you many clean up like a crook."

A small swell of panic filled Jeffrey's breast. He plunked his hand over his mouth. He realized he shouldn't have said such a stupid thing, and was surprised when the guys let out a bark of laughter. His lips curled as he eyed his students who probably were nice guys who got themselves in a jam.

It took months for the prisoners to see that Jeffrey wasn't out to hurt them. He felt he did a good turn and was proud of his creative endeavor.

When Scarface was released from Rikers he bought 1,000 shares of Intel and got word to one of the other men that he made good money. He sent a letter of appreciation that Jeffrey framed and hung on his office wall. He was now eager to embrace his future, one that recognized his brilliance. He bragged to anyone who listened that he put the gene in genius.

Since Jeffrey was so successful, he called local papers and told them the surprising news that he taught investing to prisoners. They interviewed him and wrote a column about the course. They had sent a photographer who took a picture of him exiting Rikers with a jaunty step, his chest swelling with pride while posing in his best three-piece suit as he carried his briefcase.

His father seemed proud of him although he didn't verbalize it. By now his father was no longer a Cantor, but had become a Rabbi and had his own congregation in Far Rockaway. His oldest daughter, Jeffrey's half-sister, was graduating from Yeshiva High School and he received an invitation that he accepted. The graduation was boring, but Jeffrey liked the exotic refreshments that his father's wife served at their home afterwards. His father had married his fourth wife, a young woman from Morocco. She treated Jeffrey with affection, actually more affection than his own father. She must have weighed at least three hundred and fifty pounds, a woman with so many chins they resembled a staircase. Jeffrey made fun of her, but not to her face.

Chapter 18

ONE DAY IN MARCH, when Jeffrey was twenty-three, an invitation came in the mail. He sat down at his desk that was overflowing with papers, and with an ivory paper opener slit the envelope. His half-brother, Arthur, was having his bar-mitzvah, first in the synagogue, and then a luncheon at the same kosher Chinese restaurant where he and Morris had eaten. He placed the palms of his hands on his desk, his eyes narrowed and he thought about his own miserable bar-mitzvah when he lived in a group home that made a bar-mitzvah for four boys at the same time. He wasn't a star, only one of a group.

He wondered why his mother had thrown him to the wolves when he was twelve. She had said it was because he was teaching Arthur to box. *Why couldn't she have separated us? I'll never accept this. I was so hurt and angry I never moved back home.*

The bar-mitzvah went smoothly and Jeffrey smiled when they took pictures, but kept his feelings to himself. Adding to his sadness was a chill of dread, since a few days ago Grandpa had entered Brookdale Hospital with bleeding ulcers. No other person on earth was closer to him than his grandfather who took the place of his absent father. He had this fierce love for him. When he was a child, Grandpa had plied him with toy guns, his favorite toy, and, when he served his time in the Army Reserve, Grandpa sold his Morgan silver dollars when they hit the top of the market, and gave the money to his precious grandchild. He bought the furniture for Jeffrey's apartment and never denied him anything. Without a second thought, he gave Jeffrey the money for the Andromeda fund, and emotionally and financially supported his business venture in Helena Investing. Grandpa placed him on a pedestal and worshipped at his marble feet. *Is it any wonder that I visit Grandpa daily in Brookdale Hospital?*

Not wanting to waste time looking for parking in a crowded parking lot, Jeffrey hung a stethoscope around the car mirror, and, with his license plate that read *Dr. Drake,* he parked in the space reserved for doctors. There was only one time when a guard asked for his ID.

In a confident tone, puffing out his cheeks, he said, "I'm a consulting cardiologist and if I don't reach the patient momentarily, he may die."

The guard backed off as he said, "Sorry, doctor. Go right ahead."

Grandpa was in Brookdale for six weeks. First he was treated for bleeding ulcers, next he needed a pacemaker, and then he had a prostate operation, torture for an eighty-three year old man. His mother looked for a decent nursing home for her father to recuperate.

Three days after he was in the nursing home, Jeffrey received a call from his mother asking him if he wanted to go with them to visit Grandpa.

"I was there yesterday but I want to see my grandfather every day that I can," Jeffrey said with compassion.

When Ricky put down the phone, Nat looked at her

with anger in his eyes. "I'm not going if the senile old lady is going. I don't want to be in her company." He grabbed Arthur by the hand and pulled him toward the door. "Come on, Arthur, we're going to a movie."

Arthur opened his blue eyes wide and kept silent. He wanted to see Grandpa but he couldn't oppose his father.

Ricky and Grandma drove to Jeffrey's house. He wasn't ready, as he had just stepped out of the shower.

When Jeffrey was dressed in his three-piece suit, Ricky drove them to the nursing home. When they stepped up to the desk, the nurse said in a soft, sympathetic voice, "We can't let you visit at this time."

Ricky's eyes clouded over when she realized her father had died. She plopped down on a chair, her head in her hands.

Enraged, Jeffrey said, "I don't care that you say we can't visit my grandfather. I want to see him and I want to see him now!"

The nurse relented. He was allowed to go up and found to his grief that his grandfather was gone. He flew into a rage and blamed the home for not saving Grandpa's life. He cried out in a shaky voice, "He was only eighty-three and should have lived longer. You should've done everything possible to stimulate his heart. Oh, my God, if only I hadn't taken a shower, I would have seen him, and could've saved his life."

Downstairs, the nurse appeared and quietly said to Jeffrey's mother, "I'm sorry to tell you that your father died just before you came. It was right after an orderly had told him he was going to have fish cakes for lunch. He offered a sweet smile and had been so pleased, but by the time the fish cakes arrived, he had passed on."

Jeffrey had visited him the day before, but the

guilt remained for not seeing him right before he died. Yesterday Grandpa had been so cheerful, smiling at Jeffrey without any teeth in his mouth. He was emaciated and didn't look at all like the man he knew, but to Jeffrey he was perfect. He remembered how Grandpa was so honest that he worked for a time as a messenger on Wall Street, carrying stocks and bonds, and was bonded for millions of dollars. *He was so trustworthy that he never suspected any of my sly ways.*

At his funeral, Jeffrey held back the tears that were in his tortured heart, his heart that held a special place for his beloved grandfather.

When they went back to Ricky's apartment, she had a strange intuition that prompted her to open the trunk of the car. Nat had left his briefcase in the trunk. She opened it, looked at one of the papers, and gasped. Her husband had an accounting of all his assets that he hadn't revealed. It was so much that she cried out, "I'm married to a liar and a thief. I don't know if I can live with him anymore."

Afterwards Jeffrey sat in mourning with his mother in her apartment while family and friends visited. His stepfather ordered pizza for dinner three days in a row. His mother couldn't cook as the Jewish religion forbade it. The mirrors were covered, and she sat on a hassock, all part of the mourning ritual.

On the third day Nat stood over Jeffrey who was seated on an armchair. He said in a gruff voice, "You've eaten in my home long enough. Now it's time for you to go."

Anger boiled in Jeffrey's chest. He raised his head and looked ready to explode, but to his credit he kept his cool, although his face reddened like a tomato. He was sorely tempted to make a fist and punch Nat until he doubled over from pain. A sinister atmosphere prevailed in the living room.

Arthur, always the peacemaker, strode over to his father. "Please Dad, I want to talk to you in the bedroom." Nat turned on his heel and stalked toward the bedroom. After they entered, he slammed the door behind him.

The taut silence that followed was relieved by the reappearance of Arthur and Nat after a few minutes.

"You can stay," Nat said with a frown. Jeffrey ignored him.

The next day Ricky said she could no longer take her husband's abuse, lying, secretiveness, crude, and selfish ways. She wanted a divorce. Jeffrey remained silent as this wasn't his business. His mother called a lawyer she knew and spoke at length to her.

The lawyer said there were only two grounds for divorce in New York State, adultery and physical cruelty. Jeffrey's mother knew there was no adultery, and Nat had stopped abusing her physically a couple of years back even though he kept up his emotional abuse. She determined to lie to protect herself. *I'm living like I'm half dead now, so I'll do anything it takes to get away from that underhanded man.*

"I can't let Nat in the apartment another minute. I'm calling in a locksmith," Jeffrey's mother said to him as she fisted her hands.

"Do what you have to do," he said. "Whatever you decide, I'll stick by you."

When Nat came home from work he tried the lock. It didn't open. He rang the bell and when there was no answer he pounded on the door. He knocked at the door like a butcher beating a tough steak. Inside Jeffrey and his mother tried to ignore the drumming on the door, their hearts racing. Jeffrey sat stiffly on the armchair in the living room. His mother, with her head in her hands, sat on the hassock as befitting a traditional Jewish person in mourning.

After five minutes the racket stopped. Jeffrey looked through the peephole and watched Nat stride away. "He'll be back."

An hour later the bell rang. Jeffrey went to the door and heard a cop say, "This man wants entry to his apartment. Open up."

Jeffrey's mother rose, opened the door and stared in wonderment at the two officers standing in front of her husband. She collected herself, trying to appear at ease and nonchalant, but didn't hit it off well. In a shaky voice she murmured, "My husband is abusive and I can't take it any longer. I'm getting a divorce."

The tall cop said softly, "I understand your position. Madam, you must let us in so that your husband can get whatever he needs. Later you can pack his stuff and leave it outside, and then you'll have to go to court to straighten this out."

"Okay, but I want to see what he takes."

Jeffrey's mother followed them and narrowed her eyes as Nat took wads of money from the pockets of his suits. He had told her they could no longer eat in restaurants, not even once a week, since he couldn't afford it, and all along she had been footing the bill. Now was the time to use profanity, but she wasn't used to it. Even when they had taken the trip to London and Paris, she had paid for it. He was loaded, but cheap. She and Jeffrey would be glad to see him go.

When Jeffrey moved into his first apartment, he asked

Nat for his painting. Nat sneered. "You can't have it. It's now part of our furnishings."

Jeffrey hated the guy and, since he was now out of the home, Jeffrey had his picture back. It was ironic—Nat out, picture in.

Chapter 19

A FEW MONTHS AFTER his grandfather died, Jeffrey sat at his desk rummaging through a pile of mail. He peered at one letter with interest, split open the envelope and, with a fast beating heart and a torrent of perspiration, learned that the credit card he had taken out for Helena Investing had $100,000 credited to Grandpa's account. He realized that either they made a mistake or the Dun & Bradstreet rating resulted in such high credit.

Why shouldn't I benefit from this? It's my inheritance.

He went wild, bought three hundred dollar suits, expensive shirts, and shoes. Then he visited overseas countries. The travel agent on East 16th Street had an adrenalin rush with all the business Jeffrey gave him. Every weekend he flew to England on the British Airways Concorde. He always requested a window seat so he could look down at the puffy clouds as they flew at 60,000 feet.

The first time, he was so excited that his pulse pounded, but he hadn't eaten breakfast or lunch and was starving. He turned to the flight attendant in the form-fitting blue uniform and ordered the mousse of salmon and trout that was enveloped in thinly sliced smoked Scottish salmon, served with pinwheels of buttered brown bread. His mouth watered. It was delicious. He was never a drinker, so he skipped a cocktail and substituted a large glass of freshly squeezed orange juice. He thought it was fascinating that he had a gourmet dinner while flying through the sky faster than a rifle bullet.

Jeffrey was charged up when the plane landed a few hours before it left, the trip lasting less than three hours. He felt like a time traveler in a science fiction novel. He thought about how most people would think that, as the sound barrier was broken, there would be a booming sound in the cabin, but there was only an increase in engine thrust. He had looked out the window and enjoyed a view of the curvature of the earth. There had been tiny dots about five miles below which were 747's and jumbo jets flying slowly across the Atlantic. The whole experience was awesome, and without his sly scam he never would have lived through this adventure.

When he landed in England he had a rental car waiting for him at Avis Rent-A-Car.

"I made a reservation for a car with an automatic transmission," Jeffrey said.

"I'm sorry, sir," the clerk explained as he shook his head. "We don't have a car with automatic transmission."

"But I made the reservation," Jeffrey wailed. He knew he was an obnoxious New Yorker and he was determined to get the best they had.

"We can give you a brand new Volvo Estate Wagon and a profuse apology."

Jeffrey settled for the Volvo and got in the usual way. He found the steering wheel on the other side and with his face turning red he squeezed over and pulled out of Heathrow.

Boom, he was in the center of London and his driving was opposite from what he was used to. He struggled for ten minutes and passed a truck with a galvanized pipe sticking out. The pipe grabbed the end of the car and tore off the whole side of the car.

Jeffrey emerged, perspiration running down his face. He entered a hardware store and approached the salesman.

"I need a cop," he said to a pale thin man. "I hit a truck."

The salesman went to the door and gazed at the car. He answered, "You hit a lorry. You need a bobby. Jolly good job. You ruined a brand new estate wagon."

The bobby showed up fifteen minutes later. He examined the car. "Where is your passport?" he asked.

"I don't have a passport, but I do have military I.D."

The bobby examined it and asked, "How long have you been in England?"

"Twenty-five minutes."

The bobby frowned. "If you've been in England for only twenty-five minutes, then in three days you'll ruin this country."

*   *   *

What Jeffrey missed most was Grandpa who never went any place in his life except for the Catskill Mountains and Atlantic City, but, if he were alive, his grandfather was so honest he wouldn't have spent the $100,000 on his credit card. But it didn't bother Jeffrey in the least.

Jeffrey returned to Avis and came out with a Rolls Royce. By now he managed to drive to England's farmland and gazed with uncommon interest at a herd of cattle as he kept driving on the left side of the road. The peaceful scene was completely contradictory to the hustle and bustle of life in Brooklyn. Without warning, a cow bolted out in front of the car. He swerved, but it was too late. The cow was hurt, the car demolished, and Jeffrey received a few bumps and bruises. He made his way across the field to the farmhouse, apologized to the farmer, and used his phone to call the rental agency.

"Hello, this is Mr. Jeffrey Shulman. A cow ran into the Rolls. I'm sorry but it's totaled."

"Mr. Shulman, you're in England less than two hours and already you wrecked a Volvo Estate Wagon and a Rolls."

"I said I was sorry." *The agent should have been sympathetic and not so flippant.*

Luckily Jeffrey had taken out a large insurance policy that covered the cars. He didn't give the disaster another thought and enjoyed the rest of his stay.

The next trip took him to the rain forest in Brazil which was even more exciting than flying the Concorde. On a canoe going down the Amazon, he spied an Anaconda, one of the world's largest snakes. The Anaconda pushed against the canoe until Jeffrey's heart pounded like a kettle drum. He thought the boat would capsize, his corpse would be shipped to Brooklyn, and he would never have children.

The green snake with its menacing eyes looked ferocious, and Jeffrey started to shake like an earthquake just hit. The guide in his Portuguese accent said, "Be not scared. These big snakes do not hunt people." Jeffrey was not reassured until the snake slithered away.

When Jeffrey returned home he brought back many pictures and gifts. He presented his mother and Arthur each a stuffed Piranha, an omnivorous freshwater fish with sharp teeth and a voracious appetite for meat, whether four-legged or two-legged.

In December, when Jeffrey's mother had her vacation, he said, "Grandpa's credit card is paying for trips." Jeffrey didn't say how much money was on the card, but he convinced her to take a trip to Hawaii, and said that the card would pay for the airlines and hotels, but she would have to pay for meals. She agreed. The card was almost maxed out but Jeffrey was confident that he would think of another way of making money.

They flew to Los Angeles and stayed at the classy famous Beverly Hills Hotel. His mother was impressed with the seat in the elevator and the phone in the bathroom. They couldn't eat a meal in a pricey restaurant in Beverly Hills because of the cost, but Jeffrey's mother treated them to dessert. When it started to rain, Jeffrey yanked a man's broken umbrella from a metal trash container. The umbrellas were selling for $125 so Jeffrey thought he did well, especially since the umbrella had little wrong with it.

Ricky insisted on going into a women's clothing store. Jeffrey tried to dissuade her because he realized the dresses cost hundreds, if not thousands, of dollars, but his mother ignored his warning and strode in. A saleslady dressed like a countess walked over to assist.

"May I help you, Madam?" the countess said while Jeffrey's complexion turned the color of salmon.

"Yes, thank you," Ricky said, calm as the Dead Sea. By this time Jeffrey's stomach was churning. He wondered what his mother was up to.

"I'd like to see a navy dress."

"Yes, Madam, what size?"

"Sixteen."

"I'm sorry, Madam, our dresses are only up to size eight."

Jeffrey let out a breath of relief.

Outside the store Jeffrey turned to his mother. "You knew all along they only carry small sizes, didn't you?"

"Of course," his mother replied. "I'm a size fourteen but I wasn't going to take a chance."

That evening they discovered an inexpensive diner and, while they shared a large salad, Jeffrey suggested they go to Disneyland.

"Hmm," Ricky said. "Why not?"

Jeffrey drove the rented Cadillac to Anaheim as Ricky looked out the passenger window at the sights along the way. At Disneyland Ricky paid for their tickets. In this play land they would create a happy memory never to be forgotten. Jeffrey had his camera with him and began taking pictures when they stepped into the first area at Disneyland, the enchanting Main Street, U.S.A., reminiscent of the Victorian Period. In the town square, young women in long dresses, bonnets, and parasols strolled about so guests could take their picture. Jeffrey kept clicking his camera as the horse-drawn street car passed by. The crowded streets were filled with men, women, and children conversing and laughing, clearly enjoying themselves. One young couple stopped to share a lingering kiss.

They stopped off at the candy store and bought taffy, then went on to the store that sells Disney collectable items where Ricky bought a plastic figure of Donald Duck. Outside, a figure dressed in a Mickey Mouse outfit approached them and shook hands.

When they strolled toward Sleeping Beauty's Castle, Jeffrey pointed to the buildings they passed. "Did you know that the design of the buildings creates an illusion of height? The buildings are built at ¾ scale on the ground floor, then smaller on the second story, and even smaller on the third."

"How do you know this?" Ricky asked.

"I researched it," Jeffrey said proudly.

In the Country Bear Jamboree, Jeffrey guffawed as the bears told jokes. It became his favorite site, while Ricky was thrilled with the dancing dolls in 'It's A Small World.' She admired the costumes on the dolls that were dressed in native styles like the green clothes on the Irish and the white fur on the Eskimos. As they rode on the water, they passed different sites, all the while the music kept playing the same lilting song, *It's A Small World*. Ricky prayed that soon it would be a small peaceful world filled with happy people.

"Let's take a ride in the Haunted Mansion," Jeffrey suggested and Ricky agreed.

They were guided into one of the buggies and were told the ride would take four-and-a-half minutes. During the ride in the darkness they were treated to theatrical effects with hovering ghosts and skeletons of all sizes and shapes and weird music.

The vehicle stopped next to a haunted room with couples dancing.

"What's wrong?" Ricky asked.

"Don't worry. It'll start again."

"We're not moving. We're stuck," Ricky said.

"They'll fix it," Jeffrey said. "Meanwhile, let's keep our minds occupied by talking."

"Okay. I'm glad you're no longer married to Ann. I liked her but she wasn't Jewish."

"She was going to convert."

"I don't believe in conversion for love. Next time you

marry, I hope it will be to a Jewish girl. I'd like to have Jewish grandchildren."

"We'll see," Jeffrey said.

The vehicle remained in the dark tunnel for twenty minutes while the couples in the display kept revolving with their arms entwined.

The following day Jeffrey and Ricky flew from LAX to Honolulu where they stayed in a hotel where the corridors were lined with bold wallpaper decorated with palm trees. They ate breakfast on the balcony, and admired the Pacific. Jeffrey rented a car, and they drove to Pearl Harbor.

"My goodness," his mother cried, "just look at the bullet holes in the steel buildings that are left over from December 7th, 1941. War is hell."

"Yes, I know. But just look around at all the ocean going vessels. See how large our Navy is. It's looking like a line-up of redwoods in the forest. Let's stay on the Navy base."

"Can we?"

"Sure." Jeffrey had forged an ID that made him a captain, so that the suite they stayed in cost only $7 a night. *They're so stupid, they didn't even check. Ma never suspected that I never made captain when all I had advanced to was private first class.*

At 6 a.m. they were awakened to the sound of banging. Rushing to the living room window, they saw sailors loading a missile onto a long, thin sub.

"That's a Triton missile," Jeffrey announced.

"I can hardly see the sub in the water." His mother scratched her head.

"That's because they use special black paint that doesn't reflect light or sonar waves. The Triton is a fiber-optic anti-helicopter land-attack missile."

"You know everything," Ricky said. She didn't realize that Jeffrey was smart and devious enough to use the $100,000 on her father's credit card and pose as a captain in the Army Reserve.

"Aren't you glad you came on this trip?" Jeffrey remarked.

His mother nodded. It was a trip she'd never forget.

From there they flew to the island of Kauai where Jeffrey rented a Lincoln. The orange globe of the setting sun had dipped making the road dark and ominous when he drove to the Kauai-Sheraton Coconut Beach Hotel. Without warning, Jeffrey's mother began to shriek.

"What's wrong?" Jeffrey stepped on the brake and the car jerked.

"This car is infested with roaches as big as mice. Return it and get another one."

Jeffrey shook his head. "Open your door so the light goes on. They won't hurt you. I can't return this car. It was the only Lincoln they had. I can't make an impression with a Ford."

The next day Jeffrey's mother forgave him for adding more gray hairs to her head. She bought him scuba equipment, and he descended into the clear blue water to gaze in fascination at the fabulous colorful tropical fish. When he emerged from the water, he said, "This was one of the best times in my whole life."

When Jeffrey returned home, he opened his mail and found an invoice for Grandpa's credit card. Since he didn't want a messy investigation, he took the only path open to him.

He declared bankruptcy.

This meant that Helena Investing was kaput. He had to make money another way, so he figured, if he wrote large checks for hundreds of thousands, he would make the interest and live on it. He'd put a stop on the checks and no one would be the wiser. He also continued to work at Drake Securities and kept on with his Ponzi scheme with Andromeda. It was clear sailing with not a cloud in sight.

Chapter 20

IN JULY, WHEN THE air was steamy and the clouds looked like soap suds, Jeffrey paid his mother a visit. He shook hands with Arthur and hugged his ninety-one-year-old grandmother.

Ricky couldn't remember when he had last kissed her, but she was satisfied that he was speaking to her since there were many times his anger boiled over and he stopped talking. They sat in the living room that had a window air-conditioner and she served Jeffrey's favorite drink, orange juice, and a dessert he loved, brownies.

"What's new?" Jeffrey asked after he downed the drink.

"I can hardly believe it, but I'm taking Arthur and Grandma to Israel next week."

"What a delightful surprise. I went there twice on Grandpa's credit card and it's wonderful. I wish I could go, too."

"I can't afford to take you, but, if you agree, you could cash in a bond that I bought for you and use the money for your trip. I'll pay for the hotel and the meals."

Jeffrey flashed a warm smile. "Thanks," he shot back. "I love traveling, and Israel, a homeland for Jews, is my favorite country."

"I already booked a tour through Brooklyn College and we have a flight, but you can take another plane and meet us there."

When Ricky saw the DC-8 from Arista airline, her mouth went dry as she figured it was a small plane for such a long journey. Maybe there would be a crash, so she subsequently took out trip insurance and made Jeffrey the beneficiary.

After boarding the plane, it didn't look as small as she had thought. There was room for 199 people and it was completely booked. Jeffrey had booked his flight with TWA.

Arthur, at fourteen, was thrilled with the fact he would see Israel. He took a window seat, stared at the planes on the tarmac, and later the clouds. Grandma fell asleep except for the meal that she ate with gusto.

After many hours in the air when Ricky stretched in her seat and couldn't fall asleep, the plane finally landed in Greece and the trip from there to Tel Aviv took only one-and-a-half hours. Mother and son were exhausted when they deplaned, but Grandma had slept and she was wide awake.

Ricky had dreamed of bending down and kissing the Holy Land, but the arthritis in her back prevented her. Instead, she leaned over, touched the ground, and put her hands to her lips. It was a kiss she never thought she'd experience in her life.

The tour bus was waiting for them and they drove through busy streets to the Dan Hotel.

"This hotel looks like a palace," Grandma said when she stepped out of the bus.

"Unbelievable," Arthur agreed. Unbelievable was one of his favorite words and he used it often.

"What did you say?" Ricky asked. Her ears hurt her from the steep landing of the plane which affected her hearing.

"Never mind," Arthur shouted.

They were all sleepy, so Ricky and her mother lay down on the twin beds while Arthur slept on a cot next to the terrace. And after they woke up refreshed, Jeffrey knocked at the door at 6 p.m.

"Hi, Jeffrey," Arthur said. "How was your flight?"

"Great. We stopped in France. I rented a car and we can eat dinner now if you're up to it."

"I'm starved," Arthur said. "I could eat a horse if it was kosher."

"There's a restaurant in the lobby that has a gorgeous fountain," Jeffrey said with a gleam in his eye.

They stepped into the elevator and emerged into the sumptuous lobby that had a white baby grand piano on an island.

"This is some hotel," Ricky said, "It must have cost millions of shekels."

"You better believe it," Jeffrey remarked.

When they were finished with the meal, Ricky said, "I ate an awesome melon. I don't know what kind it was but it looked like a grapefruit on the outside, and tasted like a combination of a Persian melon and a coconut."

"You'll soon discover that Israel has the most delicious fruits in the entire world," Jeffrey said.

After dinner Ricky had a headache. Jeffrey handed her two aspirin and suggested they take a walk. First they accompanied Grandma to the room, and took off for an exploration of Tel Aviv.

There was only a sliver of a moon and a bright star that Jeffrey pointed out was the planet Venus.

"It's hot here even at night," Ricky said.

Jeffrey nodded. "I heard it's a record heat."

Arthur wiped the perspiration from his upper lip. "Boy, am I hot."

"Just look at that sea," Jeffrey observed. "There's crystal clear fresh blue water that I'd love to swim in."

"Why don't you and Arthur go swimming?" Ricky encouraged.

They agreed and went back to the hotel for their trunks while Ricky remained in the room writing in her journal about their trip.

*   *   *

A few days later they moved on to the port of Haifa where they stayed at the Dan Carmel Hotel in a huge suite that was dubbed the Chagall Suite after the famous artist.

"Sit down, Grandma," Jeffrey said. "Take a load off your feet."

She listened to her cherished grandson and in a couple of minutes fell asleep sitting up.

The following week they registered at the famous King David Hotel in Jerusalem. Ricky spied a store in the lobby that she was immediately attracted to.

After they checked in and had unpacked their suitcases, Ricky said to Jeffrey and Arthur, "I spied an interesting store in the lobby. Let's have a look."

It didn't take long for her to buy an olive wood camel that stood a foot high.

Jeffrey announced, "Look what I got, a golden Menorah with modern figures in different athletic positions."

"Unbelievable," Arthur said. "Both you and Grandma have the same hobby. Shopping. Shopping. Shopping."

"I'm taking you on a tour of the shuk," Jeffrey said. "You'll love it. It's an Arab market with a line of stores on both sides. The shop owners expect you to bargain, so don't pay the first price they ask."

In one of the shops, Ricky spied a hand carved olive wood chess set for which the owner asked an extravagant price.

Ricky opened her purse and pulled out a fresh $2 bill. "This is a bill straight from the U.S. Treasury. It's never been in circulation and it's worth much more than $2."

The owner wrapped up the chess set and Ricky was overjoyed with her purchase.

"Great buy," Jeffrey said winking. "You know, I'm friendly with a guard at the Treasury building in Manhattan who puts aside newly minted two dollar bills and I pay the stipulated price. I sold you some and I never believed you could buy a beautiful chess set for only one bill."

"Just lucky, I guess," his mother said grinning.

In Jeffrey's rented car, he drove the family around the tiny country. He spoke Hebrew since he had graduated from Yeshiva High School and somewhere he had learned Arabic, too. Every place he went, he displayed his intellectual ability.

One sunny day Jeffrey said, "Let's visit a Kibbutz. It's Tisha B'Av, the day of mourning, and, since we're all fasting except for Grandma, we should keep busy so we won't notice hunger pangs."

On the drive to the Kibbutz, Jeffrey stopped whenever he saw a soldier struggling with his rifle and duffle bag as he marched along the highway. He called out in Hebrew asking if the soldier wanted a lift. He picked up the soldier and then left him off, and the same thing happened with two more. Ricky felt a swell of pride in her chest. There were times he surprised her with his compassion. She wished there were more times like these.

On the tour bus that they all took to Masada, Jeffrey was chattering and extremely animated as he had never been there. They left Grandma in the bus at the base of the desert fortress, and boarded the cable car to the top of the 1300 foot barren cliffs. Jeffrey gazed at the Dead Sea beyond the eastern edge of the Judean Desert, and he compared it to the times he had been in Coney Island. No way did it look the same. Coney Island reflected amusement, and Masada, bravery and tragedy.

The tour guide was a dark-haired beauty, soft-spoken with a pleasant Hebrew accent and a cameo skin. She wore a blue skirt and a white blouse, the national colors of Israel. Jeffrey followed the group and listened to her every word. He was so enchanted with her beauty he could have followed her around the world.

When they toured the zealot's living quarters, he looked into her limpid caramel eyes that were edged with long, sultry lashes. His pulse raced.

When she led the group to the storerooms, Jeffrey noticed her arched eyebrows and striking eyelashes, and his pulse leaped more than a pole vault.

At the bathhouse, he focused on her sexy crimson lipstick, and a trickle of perspiration snaked down his spine as she related the history of Masada, and then how Josephus, a first-century Jewish Roman historian, recorded what had happened. The guide gazed at Jeffrey with her luminous eyes, and he started to sweat even more. Between the white jeans he wore, the burning July sun, and the beauty of the Israeli guide, he began to feel faint.

He tore his eyes away from hers and looked out at the Mediterranean where he imagined the Roman galleons were sailing. He seemed to see the war ships steered by two rows of oars. On the front of the ships, the imperial standard of Caesar flew in the breeze.

When they went to the synagogue, the guide spoke about how the Jewish rebels tried to overcome the Romans who were intent on conquest. Josephus recorded how the 960 men, women, and children led by Eleazar ben Ya'ir decided to burn the fortress and end their own lives, rather than be taken alive. The Zealots cast lots to choose ten men to kill the remainder. They then chose one man who would kill the survivors. The last Jew killed himself.

Jeffrey imagined himself as the leader of the Jews in Judea, Eleazar ben Ya'ir. The date was early 73 when he had to make the decision about what to do with his people. The Roman governor, the pig, Lucius Flavius Silva, marched against Masada with the Roman legion and laid siege to the fortress. They tried many times to breach the wall unsuccessfully. Jeffrey thought of himself as he led the Jews, telling them to throw down fire and rocks. He imagined what a brilliant leader he was.

Finally the Romans built a rampart against the western face of the plateau. For three months they used beaten earth and thousands of tons of stone to build the rampart, and then they breached the wall with a battering ram.

When they entered, they discovered that all the buildings, except the food storerooms, were ablaze and everyone had committed mass suicide to avoid facing slavery or execution.

When Jeffrey, his mother, and Arthur left Masada, instead of using the cable car, Jeffrey, who was in great physical shape, raced down the mountain, his heart pounding, and he reached the bottom before they did. He had a memorable time. They all received a certificate congratulating them on being at Masada.

Meanwhile, outside the bus, Ricky met with six lively Arab women dressed in flowing abayas. She attempted to talk with them but there was a language barrier. They pointed north where they lived and seemed to ask where Ricky was from. She took out a piece of paper, drew a map of the United States, and a circle around New York City. She pointed to her mother who looked out from the window of the bus. Then with her finger she indicated to them that the lady was her mother and would they like to meet her. They nodded, but when they attempted to board the bus, the driver said they couldn't. One of the young women grabbed hold of Ricky's hand and pulled her into the circle they made. Singing loudly they all danced in a frenzy. When they finished, Ricky was exhausted but happy.

The following day the bus took the family to Safed where they visited an ancient synagogue. They noted that the Joseph Caro Sephardic Synagogue was furnished with cushions instead of chairs.

"I wouldn't want to sit on a cushion," Ricky said, "not with my aching back. I'm glad my synagogue has comfortable chairs."

"It's best that Grandma stayed in the bus," Arthur said. "She's enchanted with Amnon, the bus driver."

"She's single," Jeffrey joked. "Maybe we should get them together."

"Unbelievable," Arthur said.

The bus went on to the Syrian border where they took pictures of the Israeli border guards. The tour guide,

George, a muscular guy with a big smile, spoke to the passengers. "The side of the road is full of mines that are too much work to dismantle."

Ricky shivered.

He continued, "Look out the window. The mines are marked with red triangles. Every once in a while a cow steps on one and it goes off."

"My Lord," Ricky whispered.

"Don't worry, Mom," Jeffrey said. "Nothing is going to happen to us."

"I don't feel too well," his mother said as her stomach felt tied up in knots. "The road is twisting and the mountains are high. You know I have motion sickness and it's gotten to me."

The following evening Ricky felt much better. The family took a cruise on a boat on the Sea of Galilee. This suited Ricky more than the bouncy bus ride of the day before. Jeffrey was in a jovial mood.

"Mom," he said, "Do you know that Israeli cows don't say 'Moo'; they say, 'Nu?'"

Ricky looked at him seriously for a moment before she burst out in laughter.

The tour bus took them to the city of Tiberias where they boarded a boat that took them around the Sea of Galilee.

Jeffrey gazed with admiration at the peaceful blue water. "The son of King Herod founded Tiberias in the year 20 C.E. In the middle of the second century, after the Bar Kochba Revolt, the city became fit for scholars."

"How can you remember so much?" Arthur asked with a puzzled expression.

"Some people have it, and some people don't," Jeffrey answered.

The tour guide led them to a fish restaurant on shore.

"I never ate or even heard of St. Peter's fish, but it's delicious," Ricky said.

Arthur pointed to a sign. "Look at what that says, Mom. 'Tipping is not a city in China.' I guess that means they're looking for a hefty tip."

Ricky took the last bite of the fish. "They'll get 10% and that's it."

The site of the Kotel, or Wailing Wall as it is known, is considered by the Jews the holiest place on earth. Both Temples were located there when sacrifices were offered, and people came from far and wide to view its magnificence and pray to the one God.

Grandma couldn't walk the length of the courtyard so Ricky left her in the busy lobby of the King David hotel. She accompanied her sons to the Kotel where they split up, the boys going to the left side and Ricky, her hair completely covered with a kerchief, went to the right. With her hand holding her prayer book, she walked slowly to the Wall, but was annoyed when women stopped her asking for charity. It's too holy a place to be bothered with money. She saw women touching the Wall, praying loudly, some only mouthing their prayers. She stood back a dozen feet. *I'm not holy enough to place my hand on the stones of the Wall.*

Twice she went with her sons and twice she kept her distance from the Kotel.

The third time when she went she was alone. The sun beat down and the day was hot. *How do I know that those women are holier than me? I've done some good things in my life. I will touch the Kotel, pray, and put a message for peace in the world in one of the crevices just like other people have done.*

When Ricky touched the Wailing Wall, something miraculous happened. With her eyes open she had a vision. She closed them, opened them again, and sure enough there was the same vision. *I see an empty well with orange stones going up to the sky and at the top is a man with a beard looking down at me. I don't know who the man is, maybe Abraham, Isaac, Jacob, or Moses, or perhaps an angel who will look after me. I'm in awe. My breathing has stopped but I'm not frightened.*

Ricky told her sons about the vision and they also didn't know what to make of it. When she was home, she asked a Rabbi but he wouldn't comment. She never forgot the only vision she ever had in her life.

Another trip they took to Mount Zion was to visit King David's tomb. This time Grandma came along. The large raised tomb was in a corner of a room situated on the ground floor. The tour guide told them, "This site is the traditional site of the tomb of King David and is one of the holiest places for Jews, Christians and Muslims. It is truly one of the few sites in the entire world that is shared by the three religions."

Grandma looked at the sepulcher of King David and was in awe. It was one of the outstanding times in her life. She had helped raise money in the First World War, and had been awarded a certificate, but standing near King David's tomb thrilled her even more.

Ricky and her sons also felt much moved by the spiritual experience. They looked at the blue velvet cloth with Hebrew writing placed over the sarcophagus, and quietly wiped their eyes with their fingers not wishing to be embarrassed by their emotion.

Ricky returned the last time to the Kotel to collect the stones that were scattered around the courtyard. They would be returning soon and she needed them to put on her father's grave, her grandmother's and her great-grandmother's grave. Jews don't put flowers on graves, but stones. They show others who come to pray at the graves that someone else was there.

Chapter 21

IT WAS A DISMAL day in September with torrential rain, and wind that howled like a pack of wolves. There was a sharp crack of lightning and a moment later a blast of thunder when the phone rang in Jeffrey's office.

When he answered, Morris said, "I need to come over and speak with you right now."

"Come tomorrow. The storm will be over and it'll be safer."

"Tomorrow is too late. It's important and I want to come today."

"Suit yourself."

A half-hour later the bell rang and Morris stepped in, dripping water, soaked to his underwear, his umbrella turned inside out. Jeffrey handed him a thick Turkish towel as they entered the kitchen. Morris removed his jacket, placed it on the table, and wiped his face and stringy black hair.

"It must really be important for you to come over in such a storm," Jeffrey said as he wiped the kitchen floor with paper towels.

Morris plunked down on a chair. "It means the whole world to me. I need another favor. I'm still enrolled in Brooklyn College, and I need you to take another course and you have to register tomorrow. I'll pay whatever you want."

Jeffrey's eyes widened. "What course this time?"

"Physics 101." Morris looked at Jeffrey like a dog begging for a bone.

"I never studied Physics. Milk of Magnesia isn't my cup of tea. I'd rather pass on this," Jeffrey said as Morris kept dripping and Jeffrey kept wiping.

"It's a required subject for a Bachelor of Science." Morris smoothed down his soaked hair. "Please, Jeffrey, I'm desperate."

"Not this time." Jeffrey looked him in the eye like he meant business.

Finally, Morris set a sum that he couldn't resist. Jeffrey could buy a new gently used car with the money.

"Okay." He steppled his hands. "But Physics isn't as easy as English."

"You're bankrupting me, but I'll pay it."

Jeffrey knew he wasn't bankrupting the guy whose father owned a huge lumber yard and they lived in a million dollar home on Bedford Avenue near Brooklyn College. He had no pity for Morris, the jerk. The pity he felt was for himself. If he was caught, he'd be arrested, fined a huge amount of money for misrepresentation, and probably land in jail. It didn't bother his conscience, but he didn't relish being caught.

And that's how he took Physics.

This time he didn't have a beautiful young teacher. Dr. Hooper was a wispy-haired, stick-thin man with blotchy skin. He never smiled. Jeffrey decided to sit in the last seat in the row next to the window where he could look out at the stars when he got bored. When the professor spoke about Einstein's elusive Theory of Everything, Jeffrey finally paid attention, and fantasized that he could come up with the answer.

If he wrote the term paper on what he learned in the Hayden Planetarium, Jeffrey knew it would be easier for him. Sure enough, it proved to be a cinch. He got an A on the paper and the course, and in addition he enjoyed the Planetarium.

Morris was thrilled with his phony grade, and once again they went out to celebrate.

Over a steak dinner Morris said, "You're a dynamic guy with great self-confidence."

Jeffrey thought of himself as a daredevil. "Thank you, Morris. I'm just a free spirit who drinks deeply of life."

For a few weeks Jeffrey played with an idea in his mind. He had learned a great deal about the financial market and he wanted to capitalize on his knowledge. He decided to approach the local paper with his idea of answering people's financial questions. The editor said he'd try him out and then if it panned out, he'd pay him a weekly salary.

Jeffrey had a way with words and his self-confidence paid off. He was soon running a weekly column with his picture at the top. The name of the column was *Wall Street Watch*. It was a huge success, but Jeffrey had a plan to turn it into more cash for himself. He'd syndicate the column with papers throughout the country. It worked, and finally he was drowning in money and he loved the feel of it.

He had to toot his own horn so he drove over to his mother's apartment one evening and brought along a column.

"What do you think about this?" he asked Ricky as he offered her a grin.

She looked at it. "Why, that's wonderful. I especially

like your picture, your confident smile, your black jacket, and striped tie."

"Read it," Jeffrey urged.

Ricky read aloud, "*I have said that Treasury securities are the safest way to hold dollars. But you can't use Treasury securities to pay your bills each month, and unless, you are dealing in very large amounts, Treasury securities aren't practical for handling the day-to-day and week-to week flow of cash.*"

"What do you think so far?" Jeffrey asked as he sat on the sofa and leaned toward her.

"Sounds interesting. And you don't have any spelling mistakes."

"That's because my column is edited. But what about the content?"

"I'll read some more. "*Money market funds provide a way of handling cash that is almost as convenient and flexible as a bank checking account. And some funds provide almost as much safety and interest as Treasury bills.*" I never knew that," Ricky said with enthusiasm. "I'll have to look into this. Writing this column is a good service you're doing for people. I'm proud of you," Ricky said as she put her hand on Jeffrey's shoulder.

*   *   *

After the relaxation of the trip to Israel, Jeffrey dashed about frenetically going from work at Drake Securities to managing Andromeda, the mutual fund he built up with more clients. He also went to his volunteer job as an auxiliary police officer and continued writing his column.

*   *   *

Ricky continued to live in the corner apartment house. Arthur was now in the dormitory in a Yeshiva, so she and Grandma occupied the four-room apartment except when Arthur came home weekends. One windy day she heard a loud banging outside and went to find out what was causing it. Around the corner she looked in amazement at the heavy machinery that was ripping apart the underground pipes. New ones were piled up set to be installed. Working on Avenue O were big-muscled men in hard hats using jackhammers to tear up the street. They were replacing antiquated conduits and, when they were finished, they'd have to repave the street. Meanwhile the noise was worse than the crackle of thunder.

Back home in the living room Ricky said to her mother, "I hope you don't mind the racket."

"What racket are you talking about?" Grandma said.

"They're putting in new pipes around the corner."

"I didn't hear anything."

Ricky realized that her mother always had a hearing problem since the time she had diphtheria when she was a young girl. Now it was to her advantage not to suffer from the loud noise.

"I'm taking my laundry to the basement and I'll be back soon," Ricky said. "Is there anything you want washed?"

Grandma wrinkled her brow. "My corset. My underwear." She hesitated. "And one of my dresses."

The basement had washing machines and dryers for the benefit of the tenants. It was easier for Ricky to take the laundry downstairs than go to a commercial laundry. She just had to keep a supply of quarters on hand.

After Ricky placed the wash in the machine, she noticed a squirrel in the basement. He scampered away and she thought nothing of it. Squirrels were cute in her estimation and never caused any problems. As she walked through the lobby, she met one of her neighbors. Mr. Harper, a retired teacher, with horn-rimmed glasses that slipped near the end of his nose.

"Good afternoon, Mr. Harper," Ricky said. "You know I just saw a squirrel in the basement."

Mr. Harper frowned. "Did you notice that it didn't have a bushy tail?"

"No. Now that you mention it, you're absolutely right."

Mr. Harper fisted his hands. "Since they started to tear up the street, the rats became displaced. That was a rat you saw. Don't do the wash anymore in the basement. They're dangerous."

"Oh, my goodness. As soon as everything is washed, I'll grab the laundry and dry it indoors. Do you think the landlord will get an exterminator?"

"Our lousy landlord? No way."

More rats occupied the warm basement and now no one went down there. Ricky trembled with the thought that, since her apartment was on the ground floor, sooner or later they'd invade.

Arthur came home Friday afternoon and she and Grandma were happy to see him. They sat around the marble table in the foyer that was used as a dining room. Suddenly Arthur called out, "A rat!"

Grandma got nervous and stood up. In an instant she fell to the hard wooden floor as the rat ran in front of her and she tripped over it. She screamed, "Mama, Mama." Her mother had been dead for fifty-five years but she turned to her mother for comfort when she was in excruciating pain.

Ricky felt her eyes well up. She bent over her mother and grimaced.

"Call 911," she shouted to Arthur.

The ambulance took Grandma to the hospital where they diagnosed a broken hip. Ricky wanted only the best orthopedic surgeon she knew to operate on her ninety-two-year old mother. However, he was at a conference in Los Angeles and wouldn't be back for four days.

She instructed the doctor, "Keep my mother in bed and medicate her for the pain. We'll wait until the doctor returns."

When he came back and stood at her bedside Grandma said, "Doctor, I want to go home. I don't need an operation."

"But Mama," Ricky said, "you're hip is broken. An operation will fix it."

The doctor held up his hand signaling that Grandma was the boss and could do whatever she wanted. Calmly he said, "All right, you may go home."

Slowly Grandma moved her legs to the side of the bed, unsuccessfully tried to stand, and cried, "Oy vey."

The doctor said, "After I operate, you'll be able to walk again."

Grandma was operated on early the following morning.

Thankfully, the operation was a success and, after three weeks, Grandma was discharged even though the doctor said it would be better for her to go to a rehabilitation center. But the old woman was stubborn and refused. Instead they sent her home with a commode.

At home, next to her bed, Ricky placed the commode which was supposed to be easier for Grandma to use instead of walking to the bathroom. Ricky was in the bedroom when Grandma called her.

"I have to go," Grandma said.

She stood on weakened feet next to the commode. Ricky attempted to put her on the commode but Grandma weighed a hundred pounds and she dropped her. Ricky tried desperately to lift her but she couldn't. She attempted to explain to her mother the need for her to go for a short time for rehabilitation.

Grandma cried, "No, no, no."

Ricky called the ambulance and Grandma was so infuriated she wouldn't talk to her. Her mother's anger felt like a dagger in her heart. She also blamed herself for not being strong enough to lift her mother.

After two weeks in rehab, Grandma was walking. When Ricky visited, she saw her mother standing on a chair, a rolled up magazine in her hand with which she struck the wall.

"Come down, Mama," she called out. "What are you doing?"

Her mother grinned. "I just killed a roach," she bragged.

Ricky spoke to a middle-aged nurse who told her that her mother was climbing up on chairs if she saw a roach on the wall. She managed to kill some pests but she was endangering herself. There was nothing they could do to stop her and they certainly couldn't tie her up. They had the place sprayed and set roach traps.

"Your mother is a feisty lady," the nurse said. "If she breaks her hip again, we're not responsible. But it's too early for her to be discharged. The doctor will probably discharge her in another few weeks."

As soon as Ricky went home, she called Jeffrey and

told him what was happening with Grandma. Suddenly she heard something move in the cabinet under the sink. In a shaky voice she said she believed a rat was in her apartment. Jeffrey emitted a whistle and concluded it was up to him to take action. Five minutes later the doorbell rang, followed by loud pounding.

Opening the door Ricky was shocked to see two cops with drawn guns. "Come in, officers," she said as she led them through the apartment as they searched for rats.

After no rats showed themselves, one of the cops who had a ruddy complexion said, "Madam, I think you shouldn't be here. Rats are dangerous. We'll wait till you pack a suitcase."

"Thanks, but I have all my stuff here. I can't leave. I have to go to work tomorrow and I'll make other arrangements."

After the police left, Ricky decided she needed protection. She drove to an animal shelter and picked out the largest cat in the place. He must have weighed at least twenty-five pounds. She called him "Morris," and bought him a bed to sleep in, a litter box, and cat food. Morris would make sure there wouldn't be any rats in her apartment.

That night Ricky, with her stomach in knots, slept in the bedroom with the lights on. When she got up she found Morris parked on top of the piano. He yawned and looked like he would never move from there. He couldn't protect her. She picked him up and brought him back to the animal shelter.

Early the next morning Ricky packed a suitcase with clothes for a week, cosmetics, and important papers. She went to work, and at 3 p.m. registered at a motel in Sheepshead Bay in Brooklyn. When she got hungry, she drove to a diner and sat at the counter looking at all the people who had their own beds in their own homes. *Everyone will go home but not me.*

She stayed in the motel for three days and found she couldn't sleep from the noise in the adjoining rooms. Doors were banging. People had loud parties. The TVs were blasting.

There was a speech teacher she was working with. When she confided to her, Doris kindly offered to have her stay in her house. She had a guest room.

Doris' husband was still in bad shape from an accident when a bus hit him. She had six children from two to ten. Ricky tried to help with chores. Washing the dishes for nine people exhausted her. She wondered how Doris did everything by herself.

I don't want to ask Jeffrey to put me up. After all, I am responsible for putting him in the group home. But maybe he forgave me enough to let me stay with him.

Jeffrey had forgiven her and he proved to be a gracious host. Ricky slept on the couch but the canary that Jeffrey let out of the cage kept flying over her head. She said nothing about it. A canary is peaceful—a rat is not.

Jeffrey never ate breakfast so Ricky went without it. Lunch was a salad, and every night for three weeks Ricky treated Jeffrey to a meal in a kosher restaurant. She had her favorite roast beef sandwich and lost ten pounds.

After work, she began a vigorous search for another apartment. She was paying $145 a month for a two-bedroom apartment. Rent-control had kept the price reasonable, but she couldn't get another apartment and keep within her budget.

"What should I do, Jeffrey?" she asked her son as they sat in a booth in the restaurant. Jeffrey was cutting off a sliver of steak while Ricky paid no attention to the roast beef sandwich in front of her.

"I have an idea that may work. It'll cost you but, if it works, it's worth it."

"I'm so aggravated, I'll try anything."

Jeffrey poured a dollop of ketchup on his steak. "Hire your own exterminator and see if he can get rid of the rats."

The following day an exterminator examined the apartment. He was a rotund, cheerful fellow, with a German accent.

"Missus," he said. "I found a hole in the small bedroom and another hole under the sink in the kitchen. Sealed them up, I did. I also found a dead rat. No more rats will come in."

Ricky breathed a long sigh of relief. "Thank you. You're worth every penny."

"You're velcome."

"Please write on the bill that you found a rat."

"Sure, missus, I do."

* * *

Grandma was discharged and came home to an apartment that was clear of rats. A month later the bill came in for $69,525 for her hospital and rehab care. Thankfully Medicare and Grandma's medical insurance, which Ricky had taken out for her, took care of the entire bill as Grandma had no savings of her own except for her monthly income of half of Grandpa's post office pension and another half of Grandpa's social security. Ricky couldn't afford the cost of Arthur's Yeshiva. Part of

Grandma's allowance was paying for it and mother and son were both grateful about that.

Ricky sat at the kitchen table with the exorbitant bill. She held it close to her eyes and then laid it down, picked up her reading glasses, and looked at it for a full minute while an idea raced through her mind. Grandma had tripped over the rat that the landlord had done nothing about even after many tenant complaints and even though the Health Department had warned him. As a result, a woman of ninety-two had suffered severe injury and pain. Even her mind had deteriorated, her short-term memory affected. Ricky decided then and there a telephone call to a lawyer she knew might turn into a legal suit. It wouldn't hurt to try. She dialed the phone and asked for Mr. Miller.

Ricky took off the earring and held the phone to her right ear. "Mr. Miller, I'm unsure if this is a legal case or not."

"Tell me about it."

The end result was that the attorney took the case on a contingency basis. Nothing had to be paid up front. Papers were signed and the case moved forward.

Mr. Miller called Ricky. "We have to have a deposition. I know your mother is elderly and infirm and I'll be coming to your apartment with a stenographer. Is next Monday at 4 p.m. a good time for you?"

Ricky agreed but wondered if her mother would be able to answer questions. They sat on the sofa. Heavy rain was pelting the window. Ricky spoke loudly knowing her mother's hearing was getting worse.

"Mama, why were you in the hospital?"

"That's a silly question."

"Okay, it's silly. But please answer me. Why were you in the hospital?"

"I broke my hip."

"That's right. Now tell me why you broke your hip."

"I fell down." Grandma pointed to the spot where she had fallen.

"Yes, that's where you fell. Now tell me why you fell?"

"I just fell, just like that."

"Do you remember the rat?"

"No. What rat?"

"The rat that ran in front of you? You stood up and tripped over him."

"Yes, that was a bad rat."

My mother will forget that she tripped over a rat. I have to remind her right before the lawyer comes.

After work Ricky drove to Toys-R-Us and looked at all the stuffed animals. There wasn't one rat among them. She settled for a cat that was about the size of the rat that did the damage.

She waited to talk with her mother until fifteen minutes before the lawyer was expected. She hoped her mother's mind would be clear enough to remember what she told her.

"Mama, a man will ask you your name and address. Then he will ask you how come you fell. Take this stuffed toy in your arms. See how big it is. It's the same size as the rat you tripped over."

Grandma listened as Ricky smiled encouragingly.

The bell rang and Mr. Miller and a short, stocky woman with a run in her stocking came in and sat down at the dining room table.

"How are you?" Mr. Miller asked Grandma.

"Good. How are you?"

"Fine, thank you. For the record please state your name."

Grandma smiled and gave her full name.

The stenographer's hands flew over the keys of the stenotype machine.

"What is your address?"

"Here, I live here with my daughter."

Mr. Miller turned to the steno typist. "Insert this address."

"Did you break your hip?" Mr. Miller supplied the date.

"Yes. In the hospital they fixed it and now I can walk."

"How did you happen to break your hip?"

"A big rat ran by. My grandson screamed, 'Rat.' I got scared and stood up and tripped over the rat. I fell down and it hurt a lot."

"How big was the rat?"

"Big."

"How big?"

Grandma pursed her lips. She raised her hands and held them out.

Mr. Miller said, "Client indicates a twelve-inch rat."

When the interview was over, Ricky told her mother that she did well.

Grandma said, "The questions were easy."

A month later, Ricky's phone rang. Mr. Miller informed her of the good news. The landlord's insurance company had settled the case. It was less than he hoped for, but they took into consideration her mother's advanced age which brought it down considerably. After all the legal costs, Grandma would be getting a check for $75,000.

Ricky's eyes were moist. Her heart beat rapidly. She couldn't believe the astounding news. She knew immediately where the money would be spent. Grandma deserved to live in a home, a place where no landlord would be so cruel as to ignore the problem of rats in his apartment house. And she, too, would benefit from living in a home. She hoped Arthur would like the idea.

She called Jeffrey and told him about the settlement. "I can't believe it," he said. "That's wonderful."

"Tomorrow I'm driving to Staten Island to look for a house. The $75,000 will be the down payment and I'll take out a mortgage to pay for the rest."

"Good idea," Jeffrey agreed. His mother was stepping up in the world and he was glad for her.

Chapter 22

A MONTH AFTER JEFFREY was born, construction began for the Verrazano-Narrows Bridge. It was built to connect the boroughs of Staten Island and Brooklyn, a magnificent suspension bridge with an upper and lower level, each with six lanes.

Today, Ricky drove to the bridge, put her foot on the brake, stopped at the toll booth, and paid the seventy-five cent toll. She wasn't sure where she was going in Staten Island as she hadn't visited it for years. When she was a child, her parents took her to the park in Staten Island and they went by way of the ferry. Later, when Jeffrey and Arthur were youngsters, she drove to the small zoo that they all enjoyed. Jeffrey loved the Cassowary bird with the big feet.

As Ricky drove along the highway, she had a feeling that it was time to take the next exit. In a few blocks it led to an area where there were identical homes that looked small and seemed like they were fairly new. She parked the car in front of one house, got out, and walked to the front door.

I'll take a chance. I'll ring the bell and see if someone can help me. I'd better do it before I lose my nerve.

A man wearing dungarees and a T-shirt with holes in one shoulder answered the door.

"Excuse me," Ricky said with a smile. "I'm looking to buy a house. This looks like a nice area."

"It is," the man said. "If you drive down the next block, there's a young couple looking to sell their house. You'll see it because there's a sign outside. It's a beautiful house because it was the model for this neighborhood. Most of the people here are civil servants. You know cops, teachers, clerks, and such."

Ricky drove to a house with pretty bushes in the front and a "For-Sale" sign on the grass. The owners were a young Italian couple with a three-year-old toddler. Graciously, they showed her around the house which was furnished in modern style with furniture that looked brand new. The living room had a huge fish tank with colorful tropical fish swimming gracefully around. Adjacent to the living room, off a tiny foyer, was a bathroom with a shower. *Grandma could sleep in the living room and the bathroom would be right near her.*

The kitchen was huge with granite counters, and the stove and refrigerator also looked new. *Oh boy, a dishwasher.*

A door in the kitchen led to a small patio with a garden with red and yellow flowers surrounding it. *Grandma would love to sit in this patio on a pleasant day in the summer.*

Upstairs Ricky looked with interest and approval at the master bedroom and two other smaller bedrooms. The bathroom was done in chocolate brown tile and looked fashionable. Her apartment had worn, broken white tile that had grayed with age. This bathroom was fit for a movie star.

There was a staircase to the attic that was completely finished. She'd decorate it for Arthur using an aquatic theme. *It's time for me to ask what they want for this house.*

"What's your asking price?"

The short man looked serious. "We're asking $125,000."

"My son is a mortgage analyst. I'll speak to him and get back to you."

As soon as Ricky returned to Brooklyn, she drove to Jeffrey's apartment. "There's a house I saw in Staten Island that I'd like to buy. I can't negotiate the price. Will you please help me?"

"Sure. We'll go tomorrow morning."

The next day Jeffrey stood with a metal tape measure, a clip board, a ruler, and a pencil. He moved from room to room taking measurements and drew the accurate outline of the entire house. Ricky was amazed at his skill.

Ricky and Jeffrey sat on the large sofa in the living room. The couple sat on the smaller sofa. "My mother likes this house but I believe it's overpriced."

They went back and forth with the price, each bargaining with zeal. Finally it came down to $110,000 including the furniture in the living room and the fish tank with the filter and fish. Ricky couldn't resist.

There weren't enough words of thanks that she could come up with. Mother and son went to a restaurant to celebrate. It was one of their best times.

It didn't take long until everything was packed and, following the moving van, they arrived at their new home. When Grandma walked into the house, she looked around. "This is a nice house," she said. "When do we go home?"

It took a while to convince Grandma that they weren't going back to Brooklyn. She was now a resident of Staten Island. Ricky had placed a tall bureau in front of Grandma's bed in the living room giving her privacy. She showed her where she'd be sleeping and a few steps away she could use her own bathroom.

One day Houdini, the cat, disappeared. Arthur was convinced after three days that he would never come back.

"Please, Mom," Arthur begged, "Let's go to New Jersey and buy a SharPei puppy."

"It's a rare breed and they're expensive," Ricky said.

"You can afford it," Arthur said. "Pretty please. Grandma would love to have a dog in the house."

Ricky gave in and bought a little bundle with wrinkles on its face.

"What do you want to call him?" Arthur asked.

"Zaide. In Yiddish it means grandfather and he looks like an old man."

The following day Houdini showed up and found a new pet in the house.

Ricky sat at the dining room table when Houdini put his paw on her leg. He never did that and she surmised something was up. She followed him upstairs where he entered the bathroom and jumped in the tub, his head cocked to one side, looking up at the faucet. *What a smart cat you are. In Brooklyn the bathtub faucet dripped, but here it doesn't. You're telling me you want fresh flowing water.* Ricky turned the handle of the faucet and let a small stream of water out. There was peace in the house.

In the summer Grandma stood at the glass door and looked out at the patio where there was a round table and chairs.

"Don't you want to go sit outside, Mama?"

"No. It's too cold outside."

The temperature was a pleasant eighty degrees, but

Grandma was obstinate and she never took advantage of the warm weather. *I'm disappointed, but my mother has a mind of her own.*

*   *   *

A few months later Ricky called Jeffrey.

"Hi, Mom," he said. I was just practicing blowing the shofar I bought in Israel. It's not easy but I'm improving. What's new?"

"I don't have good news. I was at work and the aide I hired to take care of Grandma said she fell in the kitchen and broke the same hip. The surgeon operated and she's in the hospital."

"Take it easy. I'm driving over to see how she is."

Jeffrey and his mother spoke to the social worker after looking in at Grandma who seemed comfortable with the pain medication they had given her.

"It seems that the best plan for your mother would be for her to go straight to a nursing home since the doctor believes she'll never be able to walk again," the social worker said.

It was with deep regret on Jeffrey's and Ricky's part that, when Grandma was discharged, she went straight to a nursing home in Staten Island. They thought she might be distressed, but instead she seemed resigned to go to the nursing home. Her memory was progressively worsening, but her spirit was good.

Chapter 23

At 10 p.m. one night in December, Ricky called Jeffrey. "Arthur and I went to the movies and we met two young ladies, one of whom I knew from my job, and the other one, Lena, kept questioning me about you as I gave them a lift home. She's very interested in meeting you."

Maybe I shouldn't have told Lena about Jeffrey. Her questions made me uncomfortable. There's something about her that's weird but let Jeffrey decide for himself; after all, he's an adult.

"Is she pretty?" Jeffrey asked, hoping that she was.

"I think so," his mother replied. "She has long auburn hair with bangs over her forehead and dainty features. If you meet her, you'll judge for yourself."

Even though it was late, Lena called Jeffrey and, although they spoke for two hours, it turned out to be a far from auspicious introduction.

They met the next Saturday night and Jeffrey was impressed with her good looks and her intelligence. She said she had just graduated from college with a major in chemistry, but she wasn't working. She had borrowed $10,000 from friends and family, and she had the intention of paying it back as soon as she got a job. She attributed her trim figure to her membership at an exclusive Manhattan gym where she worked out.

It didn't take long before she asked Jeffrey for a favor. "I can't afford the cost of the gym. Is there any way you can help me break the contract?" she asked with a Delilah look.

"That's easy," Jeffrey said. "I can make up stationery with my name as a doctor and write that my patient, Lena Powell, is too ill to continue with her exercise routine."

Lena threw her arms around Jeffrey's neck and kissed him.

She made Jeffrey feel important. At the same time, she kept calling, and he felt like she had him in her clasp like an octopus.

It didn't take long before Lena persuaded Jeffrey to hand over his credit card, but, before he knew it, she had bought two pair of $300 shoes, and loads of other clothes. When she cuddled up to him, he didn't protest.

Most of the time when they dated they went to various restaurants. Jeffrey noticed that Lena loved to eat and was so intent on her meal she had no time to converse. After she stopped exercising, she began to put on weight.

Before Jeffrey realized what was happening, they got engaged. Lena insisted on a professional photographer to take their picture, and she wanted Jeffrey to wear his captain's uniform. He still hadn't told her that he was really a private.

Jeffrey started a new corporation and put Lena on as an employee. She didn't seem to mind if she had to work minimum hours. He felt victorious as if he had found a soul mate, a woman who molded reality to her own whims. Lena prodded him into a new field, that of mortgage analyst.

He designed a false Master's Degree in Finance, framed it, and hung it on the wall in his office alongside the other phony degrees. Then he worked with homeowners who wanted to refinance their mortgages or pay off the loans before the maturity date when portfolio values fluctuated wildly, which added a degree of uncertainty that he accounted for as a mortgage-backed securities analyst.

Math came easily to Jeffrey and he liked working with numbers. His customers never questioned the legality and he was happy to make money and save them money at the same time. The methodology he used was similar to the financial model used in analyzing bond portfolios with which he had had experience in Drake Securities. One field led smoothly into another. His strong intellectual curiosity and an interest in research stood him in good stead.

Additionally, Lena investigated worthwhile properties. Jeffrey enjoyed visiting homes, drawing diagrams, and deciding the worth of each property. He remembered how he had helped his mother bargain for the home in Staten Island.

He kept working with Sally as his auxiliary police partner. She kept investing in Andromeda Mutual Funds and, since it was based on a Ponzi scheme, the value of her fund kept increasing. Sally and Jeffrey became good friends and he sensed an unreasonable jealousy on Lena's part. She made stinging remarks like, "How's that midget you're working with?" or, "If you had some real trouble, would Sally hide under your coat?" He just ignored Lena and changed the subject reverting to the state of the weather. He had surging energy in his life which, in what he considered this jaded age of fatigue, condensed forty-hour weeks, and unconditional surrender to television and the passive life that led to laziness. It made him seem like a charged battery. Jeffrey slept few hours, was always on the run, and was making more and more money which Lena helped him spend.

Lena moved in with Jeffrey saying that she couldn't afford the rent on her apartment. They became intimate and it seemed natural to Jeffrey in this day and age. She was using a diaphragm and he relied on her for protection. When she approached him one day saying, "Jeffrey, I think I'm pregnant," you could've thrown him down with the point of a carrot.

Since Sally headed the laboratory in the Brooklyn hospital, they decided to ask her to do a pregnancy test. Jeffrey drove with trepidation to the hospital, parked in the doctor's lot, and hoped with all his heart that the test would be negative. He wanted a baby but only when he was married. He wasn't ready to get married at that point since he was still in the beginning stage as a mortgage analyst. Furthermore, he couldn't trust Lena.

In the hospital Lena provided a urine specimen, and Sally came back with a frown. "You're pregnant," she announced in a harsh tone. "Where was your diaphragm?"

Lena grinned sheepishly. "It was in my purse."

Sally nodded. "Then that's where you should have had sex."

As Jeffrey steered Lena toward the exit, his palms were damp. *What am I going to do now?*

"What do you suggest we do?" Lena asked calmly.

"I don't believe in abortions," Jeffrey said as he led her back to the car.

"I don't either."

Jeffrey bit down on his lips. "I don't believe in giving babies out for adoption."

"Neither do I!"

Jeffrey's stomach was a cement roller. "There's no other option but marriage."

Lena offered a devilish grin. "I'll make you a good wife. I promise. And in a few months you'll not only have a wife, but a child. Isn't this exciting?"

Jeffrey breathed deeply. He was more nervous than excited. Never in a billion years had he expected this. A vulture had swooped down and hit him in the head.

"We need a larger apartment," Lena said as she placed her hands on her abdomen.

"I suppose so. I need a private office with a door, some place away from the baby's room."

"I'll start looking. Maybe we'll find an apartment in the quiet Midwood neighborhood, some place near Bedford Avenue."

"Whatever."

"We need to plan a nice wedding," Lena said as they entered the car.

Jeffrey grasped the steering wheel tighter. "Let's fly to Las Vegas and get married. No fuss. No family. We shouldn't waste money when we need it for the new apartment and the baby."

Lena's pitch raised a decibel. "I want a real wedding with a Rabbi and a caterer."

"Okay. We'll rent a hall."

"I want a military wedding in the Officer's Club on Governor's Island. I'll wear a white wedding gown and you'll wear your uniform with all the ribbons."

"It sounds like you have everything figured out." Perspiration dripped down Jeffrey's back.

"Yeah, I've been thinking about this. I kind of thought I was pregnant, and what else to do except get married."

Oh, my God, what have I gotten myself into?

In a bossy tone, Lena said, "Let's not go home. I want to go to Avenue J to a specialty store where they have wedding gowns."

"Isn't it too early to look for a gown? You'll be getting bigger before the wedding can be held."

"That's all right. I'll buy a gown that's a size larger."

Jeffrey raised his shoulders and clenched his teeth. Lena was pregnant and he didn't want to upset her so he drove her to Mollie's Bridal shop. Lena kept trying on gowns in the dressing room as he sat on a beach chair in the store. Every ten minutes she emerged from the dressing room and asked what he thought of the gown.

"It looks too tight."

Lena tried on more until Jeffrey's patience was wearing thin and eventually there was one that fit her like a potato sack. "This is the one I like," he said. "It makes you look like a pretty bride." Jeffrey paid a small fortune for the dress that wasn't worth the price of a pair of socks.

When they returned to the apartment, Lena nagged Jeffrey to make a reservation for the Officer's Club. He postponed it lying about the office being closed at lunch time. If he made a reservation under Captain Shulman, they might check and learn he wasn't a captain and he would end up in the brig for impersonating an officer.

By now Jeffrey had a headache the size of Central Park, but Lena wouldn't let up. After lunch she insisted they go to a real estate agent to locate an apartment. Everything was moving like a subway train, so fast that Jeffrey's stomach churned. He wanted to return to work, but Lena said they had to take care of the wedding. She would take care of finding the Rabbi to perform the ceremony.

The real estate agent showed them six different

apartments. After a while they all appeared the same to Jeffrey. The kitchens had the same refrigerators, stoves, and sinks, and most were newly painted with cream walls, and the rents were atrociously high.

At long last they settled on an apartment on Avenue L off of Bedford Avenue on a residential street in the Midwood section. What Jeffrey liked about it was that the office and the child's bedroom were separated by a dining room. He believed he wouldn't hear any crying, but was later proved wrong.

Chapter 24

LENA SAT NEXT TO Jeffrey on the modern sofa in the living room of Ricky's home.

"We're having a military wedding on Governor's Island and we expect you to pay for one-third," Lena said bluntly.

Jeffrey had called his mother prior to this visit. She had commented to him how sudden this was and he had agreed. It was Lena who insisted on a military wedding. His mother had asked if she was pregnant and in a brash way he had denied it. She had told him that, just in case he wasn't telling the truth, and Lena was pregnant, he didn't have to marry her, but he did have to support the child and act as a father. Again Jeffrey denied the pregnancy and Ricky kept silent.

"Well, are you paying?" Lena asked again.

"I guess it's customary," Ricky had answered.

"You have to wear a formal gown," Lena ordered.

"Okay. What else?"

"That's all for now. Let's go Jeffrey." Lena stood up and walked to the door, Jeffrey meekly following.

*   *   *

The invitation came two weeks later. Ricky winced as she read it. Her name wasn't on it. It was as if she didn't exist, as if she wasn't paying for one-third of the wedding, as if Jeffrey didn't have a mother.

It named Jeffrey's father and his stepmother as a couple, and Lena's parents. How did Jeffrey allow Lena to get away with this outrage? Ricky knew that Lena would be the boss in this marriage and Jeffrey would put up with her bullying.

*   *   *

The day of the wedding Lena wore a white wedding dress that bulged. It was obvious she was pregnant. Jeffrey wore his blue officer's uniform. Dejection was painted on his face.

Ricky screwed up her face before the ceremony. Her mind was in a fog and she wished she was anyplace but there.

Jeffrey felt the walls in the ballroom were closing in. Lena was stout in her white, lace-trimmed wedding gown. Not only didn't she have a waist but she looked like a three-tier wedding cake, round at the bottom with her red hair covered with a veil at the top. She smiled when she greeted each guest, about 150 people, most of whom Jeffrey did not know. He had to remind himself to smile when the photographer snapped pictures as he felt like bawling.

By now Lena was suffering from nausea from the pregnancy, so they postponed the honeymoon and that was fine with Jeffrey.

Right after the wedding in the early afternoon, Lena

went to a wig store where they cut off her long hair and replaced it with a wig that looked exactly like her hair.

"Why are you doing this?" Jeffrey asked.

"I was brought up in a Jewish home without rules and I became a druggie. Then two years ago I turned orthodox. I expect you to keep the Sabbath, no turning on lights, no television on the Sabbath, only kosher food."

"Do I have to get a wig, too?"

"Don't be ridiculous."

Jeffrey hadn't bargained for such a strict interpretation of Jewish rules, but, if he had to put up with it, he would. He figured that this really wasn't a mixed marriage but was confused since he asked himself, if Lena was so religious, why did she have relations with him before marriage.

After they moved into the apartment, they began searching for a dining room set. They attended an auction and found an antique set for one-tenth the original price. Jeffrey would have wanted a modern set, but Lena ignored his taste, and he had no inclination to argue the point.

When Lena was seven months pregnant, looking like a barrel of pickles, no makeup, face, arms and legs bloated, Jeffrey took refuge in his office. The walls were paneled in walnut veneer and his diplomas were hung neatly surrounded by his false Bachelor's degree, Master's degree, and his phony mortgage analyst license. He felt like a qualified professional.

It was 11 a.m. on a rainy day in December and the raindrops plunked on the window of Jeffrey's office. The couple occupied the second floor of a private brick home. Jeffrey had washed the windows as he liked a clear view of the bare trees and people dressed in their winter coats passing in the street below. Lena refused to do any work. Lunch consisted of a bologna sandwich or a bowl of canned tomato soup with crackers. Jeffrey's marriage was like a seesaw, sometimes with fun, like when they went to furniture auctions, or walked on the boardwalk on a cold winter day, but other times it was horrible when Lena pushed her way into his privacy.

Jeffrey sat on his leather office chair with its high back and padded arms. He gazed at the paper on his desk attempting to figure the current mortgage. He heard a sharp knock at the door of his office, and he was irritated that Lena would have the nerve to interrupt him.

He didn't say, come in, but Lena barged in anyway and slowly lowered her bulk to the chair next to the desk. The chair made a sound like an angry bull.

"I have something for you," she said in her strident voice. It's 'Lena's House Rules.' I believe that to have peace in this house you should follow these simple rules." Lena put the paper on the desk.

Jeffrey clenched his jaw. "What about my rules?"

Lena frowned, looking like the MGM lion. "You can make up your own rules, and I'll try and follow them if I can."

Jeffrey took the paper in his hand. "What the hell is this? 'No putting down, belittling remarks, no cursing, no violent expressions.'"

Lena wrinkled her forehead which was breaking out in pimples. "You just cursed, and you tell me I'm putting on too much weight."

"Okay, no cursing, but you are putting on too much weight. Didn't the doctor put you on a diet?"

"I'm pregnant and I'm eating for two."

"Two what? Two horses?"

Lena stuck out her tongue. "After I give birth, I'll take

off the weight. I'm not listening to a male doctor who can't imagine how hungry a pregnant woman gets."

"And what about this? 'You must clean up after yourself, no newspapers, clothes, or dishes left around the house.'"

"That's only fair," Lena said tossing her head. "I'm not your maid."

"Okay, I'll buy that. And what about this rule? 'No silent treatment.'"

"Silent treatment is hostile. There are hours you don't talk to me."

Jeffrey fisted his hands. "If I feel like cursing, isn't it better if I'm silent?"

"No. Just stop cursing."

"That's hard. And what about your demand, 'All money coming into the house must be discussed before spending'?"

"It's only fair."

Jeffrey threw up his hands. "This means that if I need to eat a bite in a luncheonette, I have to ask you?"

Lena nodded. "We should each have a personal allowance."

"How much?"

"I'm not sure. I'll think about it. Actually I meant big expenses. And Jeffrey, what about my last rule, 'No social plans made with others before discussing first'?"

"That's ridiculous. Sometimes Sally and I go out for a bite. And sometimes Morris and I go out for pizza. Every time we do, it's stupid for us to ask you for permission."

Lena placed her hands on her growing growling stomach. It was before lunch and her stomach always growled when she was hungry. "I'm your wife and I have a right to know."

Jeffrey jumped up and walked around the desk. He leaned down over Lena's head and shouted, "If there's time to tell you, I'll let you know, otherwise, I can't abide by these confining rules. Now I need time to write my own rules."

Lena pushed down on the arms of the chair, awkwardly raised herself, and waddled out of the room.

Sitting at his IBM Selectric, Jeffrey typed his rules, and then brought them into the kitchen where Lena was digging into a bag of potato chips. He handed the paper to her, and she frowned as she glanced at them.

Lena read the first rule. "Do not go through Jeffrey's papers or diary or files."

Jeffrey read the rule again. "I want to impress upon you the importance of my privacy."

"Don't be a pompous ass. Did you include this rule because you're writing about other women, women who are thin and appealing?"

"No, I'm not writing about women, but I demand my privacy." Jeffrey hated her uncalled-for jealousy, but there might come a time when he would write about other women and he didn't want her snooping.

"I don't like the next rule, Jeffrey. 'Do not enter office area 9 a.m. to 5 p.m., Monday through Friday, while Jeffrey is working unless officially invited.' It sounds like you want to keep away from me."

Jeffrey bit down on his pen. "I'll be working. Just imagine if I worked out of the home, you wouldn't have access to me then. I can't be interrupted when I work."

Lena grabbed more potato chips and gnawed on them. "This is an unfair rule and I can't abide by it."

"You're making it difficult to work," Jeffrey said staring at Lena as she crossed her swollen legs at the ankle. "I mean the next rule because I need complete privacy. 'Do not listen into telephone conversations, interrupt phone calls, or pick up an extension under any circumstances.'"

"I never do this."

"Oh, yes you do, and you have, and this will have to stop."

"You're aggravating me in my delicate condition. I especially don't like the next rule, 'Do maintain reasonable cleanliness habits. This includes not leaving mountains of dishes in the sink overnight; not leaving food stuffs in the kitchen where it attracts bugs; throwing away the garbage.' A man is supposed to dispose of the garbage, especially when his wife is pregnant."

Jeffrey went to the refrigerator, opened the door, looked in for a minute, didn't see anything of interest, and banged the door shut. "All right, you can cross that rule out. I'll take out the garbage, but you have to collect it." By now he was boiling under the collar. He detested these rules as much as the taste of spinach. They shouldn't have been necessary, but he had to get his major point across. "What about my last rule, 'Do not track Jeffrey down regarding his whereabouts; quiz him on his every move; or keep him on a leash.'?"

Lena rolled her tongue around her lips that were dry and cracking. After the wedding she had given up all makeup including lipstick. "I need to know where you are. Suppose I go into labor and I need you? I don't keep you on a leash. You're not a dog."

Then why do I feel like a dog? Jeffrey decided not to aggravate Lena any more. He was anxious to have a healthy baby, one to whom he could pour out the love in him that he couldn't give to the demanding, manipulating, bossy, selfish Lena. He apologized.

When Lena stalked out of the room to take a shower, Jeffrey felt an indescribable feeling of depression. The ringing of the phone cut through his dark thoughts. It was his mother asking if he could drive Arthur and her to the airport in an hour.

"I can take car service but instead of paying them I thought you might need the money," his mother said.

Jeffrey needed a change of atmosphere and readily agreed. He'd leave a note for Lena that he had to go out.

The drive on the Belt Parkway was uneventful. After Jeffrey dropped off his mother and half-brother, on the way back his thoughts dwelled on his pathetic life. He was a bug captured in a glass jar.

From out of nowhere he rammed into a truck in front of him. He lost consciousness, and the next time he opened his eyes he was in a hospital bed with bandages on his head and left arm. An hour later, he reached for the hospital phone and left a message on his mother's machine that he had been in a car accident and was in the hospital.

Four days later when Ricky returned home, she listened to the message, her heart pounding. Immediately she called Jeffrey's home. Lena answered.

"I heard about Jeffrey's hospitalization. Where is he? How is he?"

Lena's voice was sugary when she said, "It is not necessary for you to know anything about Jeffrey." She banged down the phone.

Ricky's eyes filled with tears.

Chapter 25

ON A DAY IN February at 2 a.m., when snowflakes hurled about at a dizzying pace, Lena went into labor screaming like a hyena in chains.

Jeffrey grabbed his camera before they went to Maimonides Hospital. They allowed him access to the delivery room when he said he was a cardiologist. Snapping pictures of Lena when she was in heavy labor kept him busy. Her face was distorted with pain, but he wanted the pictures as a souvenir. He fancied himself as a distinguished photographer.

The baby, a girl, had swallowed her bowel movement when she was in the birth canal, and the infant was in danger of suffocating. She needed a transfusion but Jeffrey's blood didn't match hers. Hurriedly he called his mother to rush to the hospital for the transfusion. Meanwhile Jeffrey prayed like he had never prayed before.

By the time his mother arrived, the doctor said the newborn was all right.

Jeffrey was relieved. The praying had worked. He believed in God, but now his faith was strengthened.

Lena and Jeffrey named the baby Grace after Jeffrey's great-great-grandmother, a woman he had been told by his mother was a holy person who lived to 102. She was so orthodox she wouldn't eat meat in the United States since she wasn't sure it was kosher.

Jeffrey was exhilarated, the way he was when he flew on the Concorde. Never in his life had he felt such pride. He flopped down on a metal chair next to Lena's bed. Tears stung in his eyes and he reached for a tissue from the box on the table next to Lena's bed. He wiped the moisture away before they fell, embarrassed by his show of emotion.

*   *   *

Jeffrey wasn't sure how his fatso wife got pregnant again a few months after his daughter was born. He had a habit of turning reality into fantasy. By then, he was working like a draft horse, and was so tired he didn't know what happened. That was his version and he stuck to it.

When Grace was four months old, Jeffrey and Lena stopped off to see his mother who sometimes believed his lies but was always skeptical. He left her perplexed, never knowing when he was truthful. Jeffrey raced around her like a bear around a gopher.

A visit was unusual once he married, but this time Jeffrey came with a Mother's Day card.

Lena decided to stay in the car with Grace. Jealous Lena hated her mother-in-law, most likely because of Jeffrey's attachment to her. Jeffrey couldn't understand why his wife felt such antipathy, since his mother had always shown her kindness, been generous with gifts like paying part of the wedding, buying Grace's layette and the most expensive carriage that Lena demanded. She had given Grace a stuffed kitten that she had made and had never criticized her daughter-in-law.

After Jeffrey greeted his mother and gave her the

card, he excused himself to go to the bathroom. When he emerged he asked to use the phone on the wall in the kitchen to call his brokerage company for an update. He dialed and was talking when Lena banged heavily on the front door.

Startled, Ricky opened the door. Lena stood there, her eyes burning with anger.

"What's taking Jeffrey so long?" she shrieked.

"He's on the phone with his brokerage company."

"I don't believe that."

Lena stalked into the kitchen. "I can't trust you. You're calling a woman."

Without provocation, Lena struck Jeffrey in the stomach with a closed fist, and with her pudgy hands on his back she pushed him out of the house. Jeffrey tripped and almost fell. Ricky followed and heard Lena berating her husband for leaving her alone and calling some woman. The front door of the car had been left open by her, and the baby lay in a car crib in the back seat crying her eyes out.

Jeffrey felt violated, in a quandary, not knowing what to do, grumbling, nursing his boiling resentment, but abandoning all veto power.

Ricky watched this demonstration while her stomach knotted in pain. There was nothing she could do to help her son.

On a day in August when fierce gusts rattled the window in Jeffrey's study and sheets of rain splattered the glass, Lena wandered into the room demanding that Jeffrey stop working. He slumped back into his desk chair, as he clamped down on his pen.

"I want you to go to the drug store. We're out of shampoo for the baby and you have to get it right now."

Irritation crept into Jeffrey's voice. "Right now? I washed Grace's hair two days ago. I'm busy working."

"I don't care how busy you say you are. Just go and bring back Johnson's Baby Shampoo."

Rain pelted Jeffrey's head as he raced two blocks to the pharmacy. Inside he grabbed the first bottle of shampoo feeling a grim sense of duty mixed with revulsion at his wife's bossiness. Hurriedly he paid, ran back, dashed up the staircase, and handed the shampoo to Lena.

"Now you can wash Grace's hair," Jeffrey said.

"I'll do it later when I get a chance." Lena put her hands on her wide hips and glared at him.

Finally when Lena washed the baby's hair, Grace screamed, her head reddened, and she developed severe scalp irritation.

Devastated, Jeffrey diapered Grace, covered her with a light blanket, and bolted with her out of the apartment, the shampoo bottle in his pocket. Laced with guilt, he put the bawling baby in her crib bed in the car and drove to the office of the pediatrician.

Dr. Rose, a tanned and athletic man in his fifties, wore a white linen coat. The obligatory stethoscope dangled from his throat. He carefully examined the six-month old baby, prescribed an ointment, and winced when he held the bottle of shampoo up to the light.

He cleared his throat. "This is a counterfeit product," he declared.

Jeffrey was shocked. He pondered what action to take. It seemed that publicity would be effective so he called the local Brooklyn paper and told them about the crooked company and the hazard of using their product. The paper sent a photographer to the home. Mr. John Parker, a lanky man who wore filthy sneakers, posed Grace playing with some bottles of the counterfeit shampoo and shot one picture after another.

The photograph that was published in the paper showed a pretty little girl. Lena toyed with the idea of Grace's becoming a baby model. When Jeffrey heard Lena's plan, his face turned the color of a setting sun. He didn't want Grace exposed to the hardships of modeling but once again he abandoned veto power. Lena enrolled Grace in an agency that charged a hefty sum for taking professional pictures of her, but the baby was never used, and both Jeffrey and his mother were relieved.

After complaining to Johnson & Johnson, Jeffrey learned that the false company had already been notified by the FBI, the FDA, and the U.S. Customs Service. "I hate greed and crookedness," Jeffrey thought. "Those people should be punished."

*   *   *

When Grace was eight months old, Jeffrey was doing business with a millionaire many times over, a man who was as sharp as the point of a dagger. Lionel Morgan, one of the nouveau riche, had invited them to stay overnight at his mansion. Jeffrey was thrilled but Lena was jealous of the relationship between the men and refused to go. It took much persuasion on Jeffrey's part, including promising her a diamond bracelet, for her to accede to his wishes.

As Jeffrey drove through Connecticut, he rolled down the window of the car and breathed in the fresh air, admiring the lovely landscape of rolling hills, meadows, and lakes. After a few hours, they arrived at Morgan's Hope, a garish estate that Lionel Morgan had purchased two years before for the paltry sum of four million. They drove in silence which gave Jeffrey the time to contemplate how lucky he was to be affiliated with Lionel.

He pulled up to the closed gate, imposing with its scrolled black iron bars, and located a speaker next to the driver's window. After Jeffrey pushed the call button, a rough man's voice answered. Jeffrey identified himself and the gate swung open. The car bounced over cobblestones and he accelerated down the lane bordered by extensive lawns.

As they approached the fifteen-room house surrounded by a high wall of hedges pruned into tortured curlicues, Lena frowned. She had packed her suitcase with one change of clothes, and the smaller one with Grace's baby items, all the while arguing against the trip. She was dressed in an unattractive gray dress that resembled the Great Pyramid while Jeffrey was well-dressed in tan slacks and a brown blazer, for once abandoning his traditional three-piece suit.

As they continued down the winding driveway, they passed a tennis court partially hidden by evergreens. A large gazebo was visible on the back lawn as well as an Olympic-sized pool. A golden retriever turned in wild circles as they approached the carved gray stone mansion covered in ivy, gargoyles leering from the ledges that gave the place a threatening atmosphere.

"It looks like Dracula's castle," Lena said feeling uneasy, her plump body shivering with distaste. "I have a bad feeling about this place. Let's not stay here. Turn the car around. We'll go home."

"Your imagination is racing like a locomotive. I need to stay."

"I don't like or trust Lionel with all that money he's

rolling in like trash. I'm sure he's with the Mafia." Lena glared at Jeffrey, gripping her seat belt.

Jeffrey ground his teeth, anxious to enter the house, disgusted with Lena's prejudice, her irrationality, and her bossiness. "He's Jewish, not part of the Mafia, not a criminal, just a good business man."

A servant, an elderly stooped man with a broad nose, opened the front heavily carved oak door. After he lumbered down the steps and stood next to the car, Jeffrey lowered the window and smiled ingratiatingly.

"What is it you want?" Jeffrey asked.

"May I park your car, sir?" the so-called valet asked in a voice that was smooth but sounded threatening like Vincent Price, the curmudgeon of dark movies. A fleeting thought raced through Jeffrey's mind. *What if Lionel is a criminal, perhaps dealing in drugs, perhaps part of a cartel? Forget it! Calm down. Breathe the fresh country air.*

"Yes, of course." Jeffrey stepped out of the car, helped Lena out, then took Grace from her car seat and carried her up the marble steps into the house, all the time noting the angry expression in his wife's eyes, doing his best to ignore her fiery rage.

A young maid in a black dress and starched white apron led them through a vestibule lined with potted palms, flowering plants, and nude Greek statuary. Lionel stood at the entrance of a cozy library with floor-to-ceiling bookshelves. He smiled pleasantly as he patted Grace on her head and welcomed Jeffrey and Lena to his home. He was a mild-looking man with even features and tortoise shell glasses that made him look like a college professor, wearing tennis whites as if he had just come from the tennis court. He offered drinks that Jeffrey declined, but Lena accepted. She plopped down on a maroon leather wingback chair and handed Grace's milk bottle to Jeffrey who sat opposite her. Holding his daughter in his lap, Jeffrey fed her the bottle as if he was used to doing this task daily, which he was.

Sometimes Jeffrey had to conduct mortgage business with Lionel in Connecticut and he left Lena alone with the baby. Since they lived in a private home, Jeffrey felt that any crazy person could break in and he wanted Lena to be able to defend herself. There were many registered guns in the house and Lena could be trained how to use them.

So Jeffrey sent her for training, the worst mistake of his young life.

Soon she learned how they all worked, even a .357 magnum for which she obtained her own license. Lena was proud of the accomplishment that gave her an added sense of power.

*   *   *

With the coming advent of Succoth, the Jewish holiday of booths that commemorated the Biblical time that the Jews wandered for forty years in the desert, Ricky was faced with the problem of setting up the sukkah outside her bedroom window. She wasn't strong enough to attach the poles and Arthur was living in the Yeshiva and couldn't help. Jeffrey had always helped with the construction of the temporary booth.

When Ricky called, Lena answered.

"I'd like to invite you to eat dinner in my sukkah," Ricky said, "but I can't put it up by myself. Jeffrey has always helped me."

"He can't help you this year," Lena said, "He's busy. Goodbye." Ricky's gut wrenched. Lena wouldn't let Jeffrey help his mother with her sukkah. Poor Jeffrey was married to a shrew.

*   *   *

Fourteen months after Grace was born, a son was born to the unhappy couple. Jeffrey loved being a father, but hated the role of husband with a ring through his shapely nose. Mostly he tolerated it by keeping his mouth shut. Still and all, he was so proud of fatherhood that he sent his mother a telegram that read, "Happy Mother's Day. Your gift. Baby boy. May 10 at 4:58 p.m. 7 lbs. 5 oz."

Eight days after Danny was born, the circumcision took place in Jeffrey and Lena's apartment. Ricky and Arthur were among the invited guests. The maple trees were in bloom and the bright sun shone down on the residential neighborhood. It was a perfect spring day in May, a day when an individual happily celebrated the birth of spring and a new life.

Ricky wore a new yellow suit with a white ruffled blouse, and carried two gifts for her grandchildren. She was thrilled to have her first grandson and she hoped she'd have many more. She and Arthur climbed the staircase of the private home to the second floor where people were milling around. Lena proudly held her son on her lap. They sat on the sofa and other people stood talking while others sat on the dining room chairs.

"What do you think of my baby?" Jeffrey asked his mother.

Ricky looked hard at the newborn and was astonished to see the eight-day-old move his head and look with intelligent dark eyes at every person in the room, inspecting everyone.

Reva Spiro Luxenberg

"He's the most unusual baby I have ever seen. May the good Lord always bless him."

Suddenly Lena's mother appeared at the door. She had an angry expression like she could bury the world. She stood with her hands on her hips glaring at Lena.

In a loud voice that blasted like dynamite through the apartment, she shouted, "You had the gall to name the baby after someone in your husband's family."

"I like the name Daniel," Lena said in a soft voice. "It's a name from the Bible of a religious and heroic figure. The parents name their child, not the grandparents."

"You're an ungrateful daughter and don't deserve to have a baby like this." Lena's mother jerked the baby away from her arms and she began to descend the staircase carrying him.

Lena shrieked.

Jeffrey raced to the staircase and pulled Dan away from his mother-in-law who continued down the stairs and left in a huff.

Lena sat on the sofa and cried like her heart was breaking. Her mother had always been harsh with her. Because she was so critical, Lena had left home at eighteen and gone to live in Israel to get away from her. She always had ambivalent feelings toward her mother, and especially now that she had become orthodox, which her mother hated.

*   *   *

Jeffrey had a problem, coping with the loss of another job. For years he had been in charge of the movie theater at Fort Hamilton. Without a seven-day notice, he was discharged for payroll fraud.

He sat at his desk with his head in his hands. *I was always of the opinion that nothing's perfect, not me, not anybody, not even the Liberty Bell that has a crack.*

He wrote an official protest of termination explaining that he was ill one day and left early, and if something was wrong with the payroll it definitely had nothing to do with him. Whoever reported him claimed it was confidential information and in protest he wrote, "Is it not every person's right to know his accuser?" He desperately needed this job to get away from the craziness at home. This was a major disappointment he would never live down.

At home Jeffrey changed diapers, gave the kids their bottles and baths, while Lena made it her hobby to eat like a hippo. Dan was a good baby, cried only when he was hungry, and smiled all the time. Jeffrey didn't know what he was smiling at since the atmosphere in the home was black and depressing.

In April, 1985 Jeffrey had written a note to Congressman Stephen Solarz protesting the President's visit to the Federal Republic of Germany to pay homage to the Nazi murderers at the German War Cemetery. He wrote, "I do know that when the West German Chancellor visits America he does not go to Arlington National to visit the brave Americans who defeated the previous regime. I ask that you very, very, very strongly oppose Ronald Reagan on his visit."

He signed the letter as Captain, United States Army without a twinge of conscience even though he wasn't a captain, but he wished to make as big an impression as he thought necessary.

Congressman Solarz answered, "Thank you for your very thoughtful and moving letter concerning the

President's visit to the German War Cemetery in Bitburg."
The Congressman agreed with Jeffrey, speaking forcefully
in the Rotunda of the Capitol. Jeffrey felt pride in his letter
that he had written from his heart.

One day, seated in his office, trying to make sense
of complicated financial projections, Lena broke his
concentration by coming in carrying Dan on her hip.
"You have no time to volunteer. I want you to give up
being an auxiliary police officer. You're a father of two
now, and you have to devote yourself to bringing money
into the household."

"I need some time off," he protested.

"No you don't," Lena screamed. The baby began to
cry, Grace woke up, and also cried, two babies bawling
like flowing fountains.

As always, Jeffrey surrendered to Lena's strong will
and her yelling. "Okay, I'll stay home." The two of them
had brought enough baggage to the marriage to start an
airline. He was devastated, needing to get away, needing to
have time to himself for recuperation. There was manifest
cunning in their apartment which had become a bleak
business. In his gut he felt something would materialize,
and it did.

Sometimes in life serendipity plays a role that is
unpredictable, and, after Ricky bought a home in Staten
Island and moved out of her apartment, she let Arthur
and two of his friends use the apartment. Jeffrey called
Arthur about renting the apartment. Arthur had already
decided to go to college in Staten Island and move back to
his mother's home, so he agreed.

"What will Lena say?" Arthur asked.

"I don't care. She can't let me alone long enough
for me to do any work, and she listens in to my phone

conversations. She monitors my every move, leading me around like a dog, but she still wants me to bring in good money. I think the idea of an outside office is good."

"It's your life, Jeffrey. Use the apartment and pay the rent if you think it'll help you, but I hope you know what you're doing."

Jeffrey should have known something calamitous was going to happen, but he didn't. His judgment was often impaired and when he didn't want to see reality, he just blocked it out with a pair of dark sunglasses. He went about his merry path moving in a desk and a chair and some files. He began to let in some attractive girls and they had a party of sorts. He was tired of Lena and her domineering ways, her huge bulk, the loss of the femininity she used to have. If she was a different wife, he wouldn't have turned to young women for fulfillment. He took pictures of the girls and, not thinking put them into his briefcase wanting a reminder of good times. He had concluded that there was no way out of his dilemma but to try to lead an outside life. He'd never divorce his wife because he always believed children should be brought up by two parents.

*   *   *

One morning as Jeffrey sat at his desk he heard a key being inserted in the lock. He grabbed his gun from the drawer and, as a person entered the foyer he pointed the gun at the individual. No one was going to invade his domain and get away with it.

His mother stood there wide-eyed. "What are you doing?"

"Why are you here?" Jeffrey said as he put the gun back in the desk drawer.

"I was in the neighborhood and I needed to go to the bathroom." Ricky's knees felt like jelly as she strode to the bathroom.

*   *   *

Paying bills on time, and donating charity every month was Jeffrey's modus operandi. He believed that for every dollar one gives in charity, one gets back a reward. Ever since he worked, he had always given charity. In June, 1986 he wrote a check for $500 for Israel, $72 for the Hebrew Institute for the Deaf, $18 for Kolel America, and July 1st $1,000 for the Hebrew Institute for the Deaf. These were his favorite charities and, as he wrote these checks, he had the intuition that something bad was going to happen, but with these donations perhaps the good would balance out the bad.

Chapter 26

When Dan was three months old, Jeffrey left to go to work with Lionel in his office in the city. They worked like beavers for many hours and Jeffrey came home late to suffer the arrows of Lena's wrath.

After Jeffrey washed his hands and sat down at the table, Lena banged down the dish in front of him. In the microwave she had heated a steak and a potato. Jeffrey was hungry and gobbled down the heavy meal that was hard for him to digest, doubly hard due to aggravation from his nasty spouse.

After a refreshing shower, he put on his striped pajamas, climbed into bed, and clutched the oversized pillow while he slept. Deep in REM, pleasant dreams filled his relaxed mind. The aggravation of the day, the hustle of work, the intrusions and harassment of Lena were all replaced by escape to dreamland.

Dan, three months, and Grace, eighteen months, occupied the next room. They had been asleep when Jeffrey entered the darkened house at 9:30 on this fateful night. He stood over their cribs, peering down on what he had helped create. He watched them for over five minutes, thinking, relaxing, and experiencing a loving warm feeling toward his two beautiful children. Ah, he thought, my little babies, how much I enjoy observing them grow a little bit bigger every day.

He thought about the moments of looking at them sleeping in their childhood innocence and how those moments were able to be stolen only when their mother was asleep. Should she awaken, he would be hurriedly ushered out of their room. It was against her house rules for Jeffrey to enter their room when they were sleeping, and he could do it only when she wasn't aware of the crime.

Lena would say, "Grace shouldn't see you before she goes to bed because she loves you too much and wants to stay up with you."

The logic of his daughter's excessive love always confounded him.

The ride on the "M" train home had been a most unpleasant ending to an unrewarding, long, arduous day. The sleep he experienced was truly the best part of the day.

Suddenly Jeffrey's cherished sleep was shattered by a shout and a flash of light.

"WAKE UP," was the command he received. Opening one eye, he immediately recognized the round shape of the boisterous monster.

"WAKE UP: GET UP," came the command again from Lena, the drill sergeant.

This time he turned his head and muttered, " . . . please, I'm tired; whatever it is, let it wait for morning."

"Who is this woman?" Lena shouted. Now, somewhat awake, Jeffrey realized she had broken into his locked briefcase, violated its sanctity, and had removed a photo of Janice.

"You took these pictures and then you slept with her. Right?" she shrieked.

Jeffrey knew that by the tone of Lena's voice there was no way he would be able to explain the truth to her. Actually, an explanation at this time would be tantamount to condoning her invasion of his private briefcase. He chose to neither admonish her, nor give her clarification. The most important issue was to get back to sleep, to escape the harsh reality of the 250-pound, 75-decibel, 100%, obnoxious creature. But sleep was not to be at that moment. Sleep would come, but not until much later in the evening.

The path Jeffrey picked was simple. Lena hated, more than anything, his not sleeping by her side. Knowing this weakness, he employed it to what he thought would be his advantage. He pulled out the brown leather suitcase from the closet, threw it on the bed, and chucked in some odds and ends. He immediately grabbed the first shirt and pair of pants, put them on, and stood in front of Lena.

"If you won't let me sleep, I'm going to leave and sleep elsewhere." This was the ultimate threat, though he didn't realize it at the time.

Lena was holding the photograph while Jeffrey threatened to sleep elsewhere. He didn't connect the two aspects.

The aggravated and enraged woman left the room momentarily. A brief pause of solace was at hand.

She returned, all too soon, for what he anticipated to be additional yelling, but when he looked at her, jawboning is not what he saw.

He was greeted with the sight of the monster holding two items. In her right hand, she clutched a pistol. In her left hand, was the brown envelope that contained Janice's photos that had been in Jeffrey's locked briefcase.

He stood still, perplexed and angered. His anger was

not about the innocent photos, but her irresponsibility of daring to remove a firearm from its appointed place. Lena was aware of safety and range rules; how dare she threaten him with a gun. He still couldn't fathom what she might do with this weapon.

As Lena walked around the room to her side of the bed near the window, Jeffrey stood close to the door silently waiting for her next move.

Suddenly something changed; something happened, everything was not the same. Lena dropped the envelope of photos. Her leopard eyes squinted, the red eyebrows tensed. She clutched the weapon with both hands. Slowly she raised the sights. Jeffrey stood mesmerized, not recognizing her plans. The sights were aimed at the middle of his chest. He could see the bullets in the cylinder on either side of the barrel. She held on tight; he stood wondering.

Thunder filled the night together with a flash of light. A strange new sensation sprung up. A bullet burst from the barrel of the enemy's gun blasting through Jeffrey's chest, as a hot rush raced through his body. It came through his back like a sledgehammer through rotting wood. He was a stick of butter violated by a flaming knife. The impact lifted him off the ground and immediately threw him back to the floor. As he sprawled on the floor, he grabbed his satin comforter from the side of the bed, little comfort did it provide as he held it tight and watched with horror as it filled with his blood.

Somehow the horror passed and he was not afraid. He knew that he had been shot in the heart by a madwoman using a .357 magnum at near point-blank range. He had been killed with a hollow-point bullet. He knew that. It was only a matter of seconds until his lungs breathed their final breath.

How sad! His wife killed him; his lovely children were left fatherless. The thoughts dashing through his head were, *I'm sure the bullet pierced my aorta. Pity my babies, O Lord, our God, and forgive my transgressions.*

Hear O Israel, the Lord Our God, the Lord is One, he said in his mind as he lay dying. He believed in his heart that he must leave this world with the Lord's praise on his lips.

Blood continued to surge, his clothes dyed a new shade of red. His attention was not on his life's blood draining away, but on his daughter who climbed out of her crib, entered the bedroom, and looked down at the floor where her daddy lay moaning, moving from side to side, the red liquid spurting out of his chest pooling on the floor, spurting onto the walls and onto his daughter.

Grace gazed at this unusual sight taking it in with a perplexed and drowsy expression.

Jeffrey imagined her thinking, *Why is my funny Daddy, my loving Daddy, acting so weird? What's wrong with my Daddy?*

Fleeting thoughts raced through Jeffrey's mind. *I must control the sounds I make; I must cease all this moaning and groaning. I'm scaring my sweetheart and I must die quietly before I scare my little bubby.*

There was no fear, no apprehension, no anger for the crime. Vengeance would come in the form of justice and take its process in time. And even if Lena could persuade a jury that it was an accident, self-inflicted, or self-defense, God on high witnessed all and would be the true judge.

Less than a minute had passed. It was now 11:06 p.m. The cute round face, the brown eyes, and the soft curls urged Daddy to "come and pick me up." The pain in Daddy's body was minimal compared to the pain in Daddy's heart.

Don't be scared, my little bubby, Daddy loves you so much.

But now his children were about to be made into orphans. *Daddy will die, Mommy will go to jail. Who will escort Grace down the aisle at her wedding? Who will go to Dan's law school graduation? Daddy must live.*

And with this thought in mind, Jeffrey amassed all his energy and dragged himself onto the marital bed. His adrenal glands had not been shot out. He held on tight, unsure if he could accomplish his task, taking one final last look at the loving and perplexed face of his daughter. He picked up the phone but couldn't talk.

The pain. The agony. The pain. So intense. So overwhelming. He knew he had to be stronger than the bullet. He determined to win out over the certainty of death for the children's sake. In his mind he cried, *Help me win, God. I need to win. The Angel of Death can come get me later, but now I need to win.*

Jeffrey hoisted himself to a standing position but standing upright was not possible, walking in a hunchback position was possible. Forward, forward to the outside. *Will someone be there to help me? God of my fathers, save this father for the sake of his children.*

He stumbled and crawled as he tried to get outside, but in vain. Another thought raced through his tortured head. *Lena's waiting outside. She reloaded the gun and will fire six more rounds. It will put me out of my misery, but it will surely deprive the children of their loving Daddy.*

Jeffrey collapsed at the top of the stairs. He could go

no further. *What will happen now? Am I destined to die at the top of the stairs?* He tried to scream.

"*Help! Help! Help!*"

Then he began to plead, "*Please help me, help me for my children. They need you to help me. Please.*"

The screen door opened a crack and then wider. Lena had returned to finish the job that was taking too long to complete.

NO! He was wrong. It was a man. He was unarmed.

He said, "I'm a doctor." He ran up the stairs toward Jeffrey.

But where does a doctor come from at night at 11:10? Was he really a doctor, or was he going to finish me off? Am I paranoid?

Minutes before, I had stared down the barrel of a .357 magnum that was held by the person I trusted with my life. Yet she had taken my life. Who then should I trust now?

"Listen, sir, I'm a doctor. You've been shot, but it's not that bad. Let me look at it. Okay, lie still, try not to move. An ambulance will be here soon. Listen to me. If you had to be shot, this is not such a bad place for the bullet to go. I work in the Emergency Room of Maimonides Hospital. I've seen lots of gunshot wounds, and this is not that bad. Just lie still, the police and ambulance are on their way. Just lie still."

Such bullshit I never heard. I dare not say that to the doctor, for if I insult him, he will leave me on the floor to die. But not for a second did I believe this was not a serious injury and that I had been shot in a good place.

"*Please give me pain medication,*" Jeffrey pleaded in his mind, not being able to talk. *Of course, it was to no avail, for the doctor had no medical bag with him, and, had he* had supplies on hand, I doubted he would've administered anything.

Jeffrey heard shouting downstairs. His ears searched for Lena's voice among the crowd. If she was still upset enough, the ordeal might just be starting. She might have reloaded, was building up the courage to reenter the house. Would she shoot the doctor, also, because he was a witness? He must warn him to leave; yet again he couldn't form a sentence. His mind was playing tricks with him.

I wanted to live because I knew I was needed. My children spoke to me. "Daddy, you just gotta live. We love you and we need you."

But if the lunatic came back upstairs to finish the job, I couldn't let her kill the doctor also. I must warn the doctor of impending death. But my thoughts remained locked in my mind. I was unable to translate them into words.

I rolled a little toward the doctor, as again the doctor uttered those familiar words, "Lie still just a little longer."

"Ohhh, the pain is so great. Please I beg you, put me out or allow me to pass out! THE PAIN. THE PAIN.

Indeed, pain seethed throughout my body. I leaked front and back. Never in my life had I felt anything like this. If I live, never again will I complain of mild pain.

My fears about Lena were unfounded. I heard police radios and the deep voices of the policemen engaged in their appalling work. From the sound of their voices, I could sense the adrenaline flowing.

"Where's the gun? Who has the gun?" That question must have been repeated a dozen times. Expeditiously, the house filled with policemen, the echo of their chattering radios identifying their location.

A cop stepped over my body, heading toward Dan and Grace's room. I thanked God that help was getting to them.

I hoped that the officer, whose legs were all I saw, was a father also, so he would care for and comfort my precious babies.

A different officer bent over me saying, "It's all right. You're going to be okay."

Why do they bullshit so much? It must be their training.

"What happened?" he continued.

I couldn't talk. Wife shot me. Photos. Photos.

I heard two officers in the kitchen. I listened intently as they spoke and in my mind's eye I could see them. They had recovered the weapon of tragedy, and were unloading it.

"Oh shit, this baby's a .357 magnum, Sarge."

"Okay, let's see what's spent."

"One spent, Sarge. The bullets are hollow points."

The gravity of the danger struck me. Still I feared not, but now it was less conceivable that I should live. A .357 magnum loaded with hollow point bullets, fired at near point-blank range, into a chest. No way, José! I'm lucky for these few minutes.

The doctor began to yell at another cop, insisting that he call Hatzolah, a community private ambulance service.

"Tell the dispatcher to call on her phone," the doctor yelled. The admonished policeman meekly obeyed.

"Central, what's the ETA of that bus?"

The answer seemed garbled. Again the doctor, still hovering over Jeffrey's body, persisted. "Call Hatzolah. They can be here soon. EMS takes forever."

And once again the cop insisted that the radio operator use her landline to call.

My blood continued to pour. The difference in ambulance service was inconsequential. I was dying and I didn't want to die on the floor. Every minute seemed like hours. Every few minutes seemed like days. This experience was the culmination of a lifetime. How horrible to die this way. Maybe I could get up and go into Grace's room and die holding Grace and looking at sweet little Dan. What a waste to simply die on the extension of the living room floor—besides, look at the irony of dying in a room called living.

They finally arrived, two EMS ambulances with paramedics. They instantly asserted their authority, taking over the scene, as the cops picked up Grace and Dan preparing to take them to the station.

I'm getting weaker and disoriented. The blood loss is massive. It feels strange to have the pressure suit wrapped around me. It's as if I am one of the Challenger shuttle astronauts, doomed to perish. Why couldn't I die more comfortably, without a bulky pressure suit?

The sirens wailed, the ambulance raced, the clock ticked final seconds. The EMS drivers joked as the ambulance jolted over the potholed streets. The blood flow continued.

The bus, the euphemism for ambulance, slowed, went into reverse, and docked at the receiving bay. People raced, shouts were heard, but still Jeffrey bled.

Save me from the pain and agony! Save me!

As the stretcher was placed on the ground, its wheels extended, I braced for another ride. From the corner of my eye, I noticed a tall, thin, black man in his mid-forties. He gazed down on me expressionless. I wondered who the man was, but what I really wished to ask him, if I could, which I couldn't, was about the way he looked at me. In my mind, a person bleeding to death with organs hanging out would arouse some curiosity. But it didn't seem to bother this man. It was as if he had seen the same thing happening night after night, which he probably did.

Several minutes later I discovered that the mystery man, who appeared callous, maybe apathetic, was the X-ray technician. He followed me into the emergency room where he would perform his internal photography.

I'd only been in the E.R. for three minutes before the tall, black man lifted me and placed a black and silver plate under the small of my back. The X-ray machine then loomed above as all in the room stood back. The funny clicking noise that X-ray machines make caused me to feel violated by the destructiveness of the radioactive particles passing through. Just minutes after they were taken, the X-ray films were studied by the medical team far off to the right of the E.R.

It didn't take long for the doctors to decide that immediate surgery was the only route if Jeffrey were to be saved.

I'd never had surgery before, but it certainly seemed preferable to death.

The resident walked to Jeffrey's stretcher as he concealed the plastic tube in his hand.

"Swallow," he commanded. "Swallow and it won't hurt so much."

He lubricated the plastic nasal gastric tube and then inserted it up Jeffrey's nose.

As it hit the back of my throat, I once again felt violated. I was not in control and these unknown doctors were doing with my body as they wished. The NG tube was uncomfortable, but not really painful. It made the act of swallowing something I would rather not do.

My thoughts were irrational and I knew it. Please let all these people leave me alone. All I need is rest, aspirin, fluid, and a Band-Aid, and I'll heal fine. I must get home and put the kids to sleep.

But right after thinking that, I thought . . . hey, Jeffrey, are you nuts?

Two interns stood at the foot of the bed. One turned to the other and queried, "What's the story here?"

"This guy was shot by a cop. I think he was running away from a burglary."

"We really treat the scum of society here, don't we?" the other responded.

I wanted very much to correct their misconception, but all I was capable of was moaning.

More doctors entered the room. The X-rays, statistics, and lines occupied their time.

"Well, we have at least a definite spleenectomy here," one of the masked and gowned physicians proclaimed. "Prep him for emergency surgery. Indicate spleenectomy."

A figure hovered over me. "Just relax. I need to shave your belly and your chest." *I was not built like an ape so that was a rather simple, expeditious procedure, a dry shave, no soapy lathers, no water, no lubricant.*

The anesthesiologist approached to ask some standard pre-operative questions. There was certain information that was important for him to know. *More of my adrenaline began to flow.*

"I need some history. I must ask you some questions."

I knew what his questions were going to be, so why wait for the list as more of my life's blood trickled away. I summoned up every vestige of strength and every ounce of adrenaline so I could utter more than one syllable words.

"No medical history. No previous surgery. Allergic to sulfa and penicillin."

My eyes were shut tight. It was very difficult to get all those words out. The doctor's eyes opened wide. He hadn't expected such a soliloquy. Quickly, he jotted down what I had said and then scampered away.

Suddenly I was alone for what seemed an eternity. I stared at the ceiling and counted the imperfections in the plaster, the only thing I could do besides groan.

Once again I was being attended to. Several people grabbed the stretcher for a short ride to the operating room. The O.R. was different from the way I had pictured it. I had been in delivery rooms twice, but the delivery room seemed warmer, softer, and pleasanter. Perhaps it was the circumstances. Giving birth to a child is less emotionally traumatic than being impregnated with a bullet.

The O.R. team was assembled in green uniforms, like a baseball team without bats and spiked shoes, much buzzing in the background, nothing definitely audible, but the tone was unmistakable: hurry, hurry, rush, rush. "He doesn't have that much longer to live."

I expired at 12:05 a.m. on the operating table, exactly one hour after being shot, the E.K.G. flat, no more spurting blood, no more pumping blood, no kids to care for, no money to be earned, no vacations to be enjoyed, no good deeds to perform, no arguments to have. I would be judged based on the merits and demerits of the past.

AND SO HE DIED

And God looked down from His heavenly throne. And God proclaimed that the Angel of Death shall this day be deprived of this admission. And after four minutes of not beating, my heart once again pumped the small quantity of blood remaining. And I lived. And I was reborn.

In the seconds before I went under, I looked up and saw two brown eyes with bushy eyebrows above them, covered hair, mouth and nose masked. The man's body was encased in a womb of sterile coverings. All that was visible were the two warm brown eyes that looked down. Then a confident, reassuring voice echoed from behind the face mask.

"We're going to start now," Dr. Shelly said.

Please take good care of me. My kids need me.

"Don't worry. You'll be fine. Just relax. You're going to go to sleep now."

During the operation I saw men with beards discussing whether or not I should live. They weighed my fate and the one who won out for sparing my life did so, not because I was a good person, but because I had donated charity right before I was shot. The Angel of Death was defeated.

Chapter 27

ON A BLISTERING SUMMER day on a street in Staten Island lined with row homes where all the three-bedroom houses looked alike and most were occupied by civil service employees, Jeffrey's mother sat at her desk, the air-conditioner turned to high. Ricky sat stiffly, uncomfortably, on a gel cushion as her coccyx had been broken by a fall and there was nothing to do but absorb the pain in silence. Arthur was away in camp as a junior counselor, and the cat had died. The phone rang. Maybe it was Jeffrey calling, but maybe not, either he was too busy to phone or his bossy, jealous wife wouldn't let him.

"This is Richard Morris, your son, Jeffrey Shulman's attorney. I'm sorry but I have bad news for you. Jeffrey was shot by his wife three days ago. He's in Kings County Hospital. The children are with their maternal grandmother. Mrs. Shulman was in jail for twenty-four hours, but is now out on bail."

"Oh, my God, I just knew something bad was going to happen. His crazy wife was at his throat. Something had to give."

Ricky raced down the stairs ignoring the pain in her lower back, anxious to drive to the hospital as fast as her Dodge Dart could take her.

In the Intensive Care Unit, under heavy anesthesia, tubes like slithering snakes ran from machines into Jeffrey's body. Ricky shivered with fright and patted her son's leg with love trying to soothe the victim. The sounds of the machines were hammers hitting into her head.

The surgeon walked over. "I operated on your son. The bullet caused considerable damage. It penetrated his chest, came within an inch of his heart, and left through his back. We transfused twenty-seven units of blood which is more than the human body has. It's a miracle that he's still alive."

"Do you think he'll make it, doctor?"

"I don't know. What's not good is that he had a heavy meal prior to the shooting, and infection may set in. I couldn't close his chest. It has to heal from the inside out. I'm sorry to tell you that you should be prepared for the worst."

Somehow Jeffrey hung on to life and later was transferred to a crowded, noisy ward in Kings County Hospital. Patients were playing boom boxes at the highest possible decibels, their families shouting to be heard.

Jeffrey spoke to his mother in a voice so weak she could hardly make out his words. "I don't want to die here. Please move me across the street to Downstate Medical Center."

"In your condition you shouldn't be moved," Ricky answered.

"I'll chance it. Also please go to the apartment and get my furniture, clothes, and personal papers. Put it all in storage until I get my own apartment. Don't take the dining room set."

Ricky nodded. "The dining room set is worth a lot of money. Are you sure you want me to leave it for her?"

"Yes, I'm sure. I can't talk anymore."

*   *   *

Ricky sat at the ambulance entrance waiting for Jeffrey's stretcher, her mouth dry as sand, her hand clutching a tissue until it fell into shreds. Her thoughts revolved around prayers for her son's life. *Please God don't let him die in the ambulance like my grandmother did. He may be mixed up and do bad things, but basically he's a good person. Don't let him die. He's only twenty-seven years old.*

When the stretcher didn't arrive in twenty minutes, which felt like twenty hours, Ricky rose and stumbled to another entrance where she was told that Jeffrey had come in ten minutes ago.

It was midnight before the truck came for Jeffrey's furniture. His mother's knees buckled and she almost fainted when she entered the apartment and saw her son's blood not only on the floor, and the quilt, but scattered all over the walls. She dropped onto a chair, took a deep breath, and pushed herself to get up and gather Jeffrey's possessions.

A sound at the foot of the staircase startled her. Imagining Lena coming back to take whatever she could salvage pierced her heart like a ball of fiery anger. She raced to the staircase prepared to throw Lena down the stairs, not even considering the enormous weight of the murderer, or that she was much younger and stronger. It made no difference to her. She would push Lena's shoulders until she landed at the bottom and lay like the heap of trash she was.

But it wasn't Lena, lucky for her; it was only Arthur asking how much longer before they went home.

*   *   *

The doctors kept Jeffrey in the hospital for a month. He had a spleenectomy, distal pancreatectomy, repair of stomach, debridement, and resection of a portion of the left lobe of the liver, transverse colectomy, colostomy, and mucous fistula, big words for many internal operations. He did develop a peri pancreatic abscess which required re-exploration, drainage, and prolonged wound care, more cutting, more anesthesia, more pain pills, and more pain.

Every day Ricky and Arthur stayed for eight hours at Jeffrey's bedside praying for his recovery. Their conversation consisted only of the state of the victim's health. Their anxiety level was as high as Mt. Everest, and their depression was as low as the Dead Sea.

After three-and-a-half weeks, Ricky turned to Arthur. "We need a break. We have to go to Atlantic City for a night and relax or we'll break down and not be able to help Jeffrey."

The next day Ricky drove to Atlantic City and stayed at a hotel. They walked and talked on the Boardwalk, not looking at the hotels and shops that lined the famous Boardwalk, but discussing Jeffrey's plight. Ricky said, "We need to make a pact not to talk about Jeffrey while we're here. We have to gamble in the casinos, go to a show at night, and act like we're having a good time."

Arthur, who was seventeen and devastated by the fate of his brother, agreed. Putting quarters into the slot machines and pulling the handles did change their concentration. At night they went to a show, and watched Harry Belafonte sing love songs with his mellow voice, and the next day they were at Jeffrey's bedside.

A month later, Jeffrey was discharged to his mother's home for convalescing. His abdominal wound, which had to heal from the inside out, needed constant application of saline solution. Ricky just couldn't look at the site that had the appearance of a split tomato, and it fell to Arthur to pour saline on the open wound. Because of his experience with nursing his brother, Arthur later became an Emergency Medical Technician, and saved lives during the first bombing of the World Trade Center by leading people thirty stories down a smoke-filled, darkened staircase, including a woman in an advanced state of pregnancy.

The second month, Jeffrey went back to the hospital for ten days where he had the colostomy closed. He asked that no one visit him, so family and friends stayed away.

The pain was excruciating, and, in an effort to give Jeffrey some relief, a surgeon prescribed Stadol, an anesthetic that's used in the operating room. Jeffrey moved from his mother's house to another apartment in Brooklyn and soon became addicted to Stadol.

In another month, Jeffrey returned to Downstate for another operation which dealt with the excision of scar and multiple sutures in sinuses and repair of incisional hernia. He lost 5 CC of blood and postop was stable and sent to the recovery room. Again he asked for no visitors. All he wanted was to see his children.

After he was in his apartment, Sally, dressed in her Auxiliary Police uniform, visited him and they spoke in the living room that was furnished with used furniture from the Salvation Army and the marital bed where he had lain bleeding with a bullet in his chest.

Lena had emptied the bank accounts, and Jeffrey was living on public assistance and Social Security Disability.

"How are you doing?" Sally asked as she sat on a lumpy couch, her short feet dangling over the edge, not touching the filthy carpet.

"I'm over the earth, not under it, but only barely. Lena fired a hollow point bullet at me and there are pieces of it in my chest that can never be removed. I can't work and I miss my children. Originally she was indicted on Attempted Murder, 2 counts First Degree Assault and Criminal Possession of a weapon, but this was dropped because she pled to a lesser charge of Battered Wife Syndrome. Very soon she will be sentenced and I'll be allowed to speak before the Judge. Can you believe she was in jail for only twenty-four hours?"

"I'm so sorry," Sally said with tears welling up in her eyes.

"Do you know the first thing she told the police after the shooting was that Grace pulled the trigger?"

"Unbelievable."

"I wrote to Smith & Wesson, the manufacturer of the double action .375 magnum. I'll read you what they answered." Jeffrey leaned over a small table next to his armchair, a look of pain on his screwed up face, and took a paper in his hands.

The minimum single action trigger pull for a Smith & Wesson revolver when it leaves the factory is 2½ pounds. The resultant double action trigger pull is between 10 and 12 pounds.

"Of course, her attorney advised her to change the plea of not guilty by way of Grace's shooting me, to guilty according to Battered Wife Syndrome. The murderer has also been receiving my Blue Cross checks. She changed my address to that of her parents, and is cashing all the checks, and she's free to do whatever her evil heart tells her. I have to fight for everything, my health, my finances, my children. I'm tired of fighting, but there is no other way. My enemy is smart and ruthless."

Sally bit down on her lips.

Jeffrey continued as Sally watched him with pity in her eyes. "When this matter first came before Judge Marcus for conference, a plea bargain was offered by the District Attorney for a sentence of three years to nine. Judge Marcus insisted that such a sentence was too lenient considering the heinous nature of the crime. He said that four to twelve was a decent minimum if Mrs. Shulman would plead guilty. Now the Judge is willing to accept one day in jail as sufficient, a travesty of justice. I can't understand this turn around."

"This is unbelievable." Sally's eyes darkened.

"Some journalist wrote about the pervasive pattern in the criminal justice system of gender-based leniency toward women. Women consistently get light sentences, and the disparities are especially striking in family members. I read about the battered women's clemency movement that has obtained pardons for female murderers who had flimsy claims of abuse and probably had been driven by jealousy motives like Lena who claimed that I beat her."

After Sally left, Jeffrey sat down at his desk to carefully prepare his impact statement before the case came to the Supreme Court, Criminal Term.

The following week he appeared in court with the Assistant District Attorney of Kings County, a nice, clean cut fellow. He assured Jeffrey that he would receive the justice he was looking for. By now Jeffrey doubted it because he felt the only justice he would get would be in the afterlife.

It was unbelievable, but Lena pleaded guilty to assault in the second degree. Jeffrey could hardly believe that she didn't plead guilty to at least a felony. She argued that she was suffering from post-partum depression and had been an abused wife which Jeffrey knew was poppycock. She was to be sentenced and he hoped it would send her to jail for a long time.

The judge had ruled a sentence of one day in jail was fair and for shooting Jeffrey she was given five years' probation. Before he heard counsel, the judge declared he was prepared to hear the plaintiff.

The courtroom was empty except for Lena, the court reporter, the bailiff, the Assistant District Attorney, the Attorney for the Defendant who wore an expensive charcoal suit with a gold tie, Judge Mallory, and Jeffrey, dressed in one of his three-piece suits. The courtroom was like every other courtroom Jeffrey had been in or seen on TV with the Judge seated on a bench looking down with authority at all present. Jeffrey studied his eyes which he concluded were as cold and lifeless as an eel's. He felt deflated, thinking he could never plead his case and win him over.

Slowly, painfully, Jeffrey rose and spoke his piece. "The innocence of Mrs. Shulman has been rendered and is a moot issue by virtue of her affirmation of guilt. Her claim of Battered Wife Syndrome is false, and in fact, a self-serving fraud.

"There are many victims of the criminal actions of Mrs. Shulman. While I was the person shot, I am by no means the sole victim when Mrs. Shulman crouched into a combat stance and carefully aimed her .357 Magnum pistol at the middle of my chest, squeezed the trigger, and inflicted severe injury to me.

"For the record, I want to state that the injuries I sustained were the loss of my entire spleen, my entire transverse colon, half of my pancreas, the left half of my liver, a portion of my stomach, and several loops of small intestine, damage to my left kidney, and a shattered rib upon the bullet's exit."

Jeffrey couldn't have spoken so long and clearly if it weren't for the Stadol that eased the pain. He had administered it by injection, a drug that is ten times stronger than morphine with the effects lasting from four to seven hours. He had never smoked or used alcohol in his life, but had become a full-fledged addict due to the shooting. He knew a doctor who prescribed it for him and Jeffrey always managed to have a supply on hand.

Leaning against a wooden bench, Jeffrey continued, "Decorum prohibits me from expounding upon the pain and suffering I endured as a result of the thunderous blast, but I assure this Court the gravity of pain, the loss of all those organs, as well as the suffering from the numerous surgical procedures that followed, is so horrific that I cannot find an adjective to describe such enormity.

"My mother, my father, my brother felt enormous anxiety upon seeing me in the hospital so that they were also victims of this shooting. Additionally, my two children are victims of this crime.

"I am not a lawyer, nor a judge. I have little understanding of what is appropriate punishment. I can only say there is no way for Mrs. Shulman to undo the damage that she has done. No amount of time in jail, or on probation, or monetary compensation can ever come close to allowing her to pay for such a grave sin."

Jeffrey watched the Judge for any sign of compassion, but he showed no emotion. It was as if he were a log. Jeffrey took a breath and continued.

"While Mrs. Shulman advises this Court of her guilt, she has never apologized to her victim. She struts in and out of court with impunity, and outside of this room she reaffirms her innocence to what she pleads guilty to before you.

"This attitude makes Mrs. Shulman a victim as well, a victim of herself, since she cannot recognize what wrong she has done.

"Perhaps Mrs. Shulman is so pathetic that the Court may show leniency towards her, but the Court should also recognize how rewarded Mrs. Shulman has been by the Criminal Justice System.

"Mrs. Shulman has retained sole custody of our children, to their detriment, I might add, up until now.

"Your Honor, please consider all the victims about whom I have elaborated. Please take into account the layman's perception of the punishment process as seen through my eyes and the letters you received and the interest of the media. Please be just to the Defendant, but even more, just to the innocent.

"Please note special consideration due to our children and the way they have suffered, and will continue to suffer.

"Think about how you may establish terms for probation that will be fair to all. Please consider an appropriate sentence.

"I ask you, Judge Mallory, not to pronounce sentence on Lena Shulman, but to pronounce justice."

Perspiration dotted Jeffrey's brow, feeling cold and

clammy he wiped his forehead with his handkerchief, and plastered a phony smile on his face. Lena, a hidden octopus, had taken the children and disappeared into the dark forbidden ocean somewhere in New York State.

Jeffrey applied to Family Court and was awarded custody of Grace and Dan, but as hard as he tried he couldn't see them. Many times when he went to court the children were never brought in. The black widow spider showed up sometimes and always gave a false address. Jeffrey could see she had no intention of ever letting him near them which cut him to the core. He thought about the uselessness of a piece of paper that gives custody without substance. He lost faith in the justice of the courts, but wrote to the Deputy Inspector General of the New York City Resources Administration in a futile attempt to see his children, thinking all the time how Lena was cruel, slick, and manipulative, always getting her way. Jeffrey felt helpless and the Stadol had side effects making him even more depressed and anxious.

The Bureau of Child Welfare received a letter from Jeffrey stating that Lena forcibly separated the children from their father, demonstrating her non-compliance with court orders and the judicial process pertaining to family visitation. He questioned her mental stability as she attempted to murder him. All he had written was to no avail, getting him no place.

Special Services for Children answered him citing "confidentiality" as a justifiable reason for stonewalling their investigation.

Jeffrey wrote to the Kings County District Attorney that Lena lied when she gave her address as that of the apartment of her grandparents. He knew that the children were someplace else; the woman was committing perjury when she stated that they are there.

When Jeffrey wrote to the Office of the City Clerk asking for his marriage certificate in an attempt to obtain a divorce, he discovered a cover-up. Their records showed that a license was issued and returned incomplete as the marriage was performed by a student rabbi. He was shocked, relying on Lena to get a rabbi and all she came up with was a student. In a way he was glad that they weren't married, but he still attempted to get a divorce and was granted one. The question of the legality of the marriage went through the courts and was ruled differently by various judges. Jeffrey considered it one of the least problems he was plagued with.

Every night after he fell asleep he woke up heavily perspiring, dreaming of being shot. The doctor called it post-traumatic stress disorder or PTSD which develops after exposure to a terrifying event. Being shot, Jeffrey said, qualifies as a terrifying event. He had flashback episodes, especially nightmares. They were so frightening he did everything to prevent himself from falling asleep. He read, watched TV, studied law books, studied medical books, and walked the lonely apartment. He was also subject to depression, anxiety, emotional numbness, and irritability.

It was 3 a.m. and Jeffrey hadn't fallen asleep. The wail of an ambulance passed his house and made him shiver. He thought about all his possessions that Lena had and the angry thoughts brought the blood to his cheeks. He rose from bed, the bed where he had been shot, the mattress still filled with blood, and he sat down at his desk. He listed everything that belonged to him that his mother hadn't taken, and decided to take Lena, her parents, and her grandparents to Civil Court for a modicum of justice.

He wrote on the summons "Defendants acting in concert with one another did enter the home of the plaintiff without authority or permission and seized valuables owned by plaintiff in the amount of $25,000." The valuables he treasured the most were the photographs he took on his travels that had no monetary value, but were dear to his heart.

In court Jeffrey was represented by counsel who billed him for $750. The attorney told him, "The evidence elicited at the traverse hearing appeared to be in your favor, but judges are known for reluctance to sustain a default judgment except under exceptional circumstances." Jeffrey concluded that that baloney meant he paid out money, but received nothing.

He moved to an apartment in Far Rockaway and his mother felt there was an improvement in his life. She visited him one windy day when the howling of the wind seemed to say to her, *Jeffrey it's time you got better, hang in there, hang in there.*

"Jeffrey," his mother said as they sat in the messy kitchen, "why don't you change the old mattress?"

"Too expensive," he said as he downed a glass of Sunny D, a sweet drink packed with sugar, something he shouldn't have. Since the shooting and the loss of his pancreas, he had diabetes and needed to avoid sugar, but he ignored doctor's orders.

"I'll pay for a new mattress."

"No, thank you. I want to sleep on the mattress where my blood gushed out."

Ricky shook her head. Jeffrey was always independent, never taking a cent from her, valuing his independence to an unbelievable degree. He had even moved out of her home while he was still very sick, and needed more operations, insisting she not visit him in the hospital.

"You told me you liked working for the small police department in a town in Long Island. What happened to that job?"

Jeffrey poured himself another glass of Sunny D. "I told one officer the truth about my being shot. They fired me. It doesn't pay to tell the truth, does it?"

"The truth is that you should have kept that information to yourself; that's not lying, just looking out for your own good." Jeffrey's mother, feeling helpless, said goodbye to her son, leaving Jeffrey to his own devices and poor judgment.

The next time she paid Jeffrey a visit he seemed in better spirits. He showed her the police dog he adopted after the police department retired him. He ordered the dog to stand in the dirt yard tied to the pole. "He listens to everything I say," Jeffrey bragged. Now he was in control of a dog to order around, a miserable beast who obeyed his command for hours.

His mother felt heartbroken for the unfortunate dog, and for her son who didn't have compassion for an animal. She was relieved when Jeffrey said the dog bit through the rope and ran away. She hoped that somehow Jeffrey wouldn't get control over his children, but she kept this opinion to herself.

As Jeffrey hadn't seen his children since the shooting, he joined the organization Father's Rights for any help they could give him, especially emotional support. He learned from the organization that 'The Oprah Winfrey Show' was featuring a program "Fighting Back: Open Season on Husbands?" They couldn't get him on TV, but

Oprah would talk to him on the phone. He was satisfied with this and agreed.

When the program was televised, the attorney for Father's Rights said, " . . . if a woman can go out and buy a gun three days before she shoots her husband, she also had the option of moving out of the apartment or seeking some kind of help. You don't go buy a gun because somebody's hitting you. That's not an answer in today's world."

After a commercial break, Oprah said, "I think the point we're trying to make here, whether or not there's open season on husbands is, if you have the energy to plot to kill somebody, hire somebody to kill somebody, why can't you take that same energy to use to get yourself out of the house?"

Then it was Jeffrey's turn after Oprah said, "Caller, you're on the air."

"Well, my wife unfortunately decided—as you said, Oprah, no one should beat up on anyone else. And that's no spouse, male or female, should beat up on the other spouse or should hurt the other spouse. My wife took a .357 Magnum pistol in the middle of the night, woke me up, carefully aimed at the middle of my chest with that firearm and squeezed the trigger."

That's all that was said on the air, but Jeffrey found that some emotional pressure had been released and he looked for more opportunities to vent. But again anxiety overwhelmed him. Every time he fell asleep, Lena shot him. He realized that the PTSD was ruining his life.

A few weeks later Jeffrey asked his mother to accompany him to Queens Court. He'd try to get some of his possessions back from Lena and maybe he could recover some money that she illegally took from him.

Ricky sat in the wood-paneled courtroom a row in back of Lena and watched her murmur prayers from an open prayer book. She observed that she wore a black skirt and a long-sleeved sweater top with a metallic gold thread running through it. From her ear lobes large round black and gold earrings dangled and on her head she had a wig with long auburn hair held back with a red plastic band. Next to her was a yellow plastic shopping bag, no purse. When the clerk called her name she rose with her lawyer to go to the Judge's chambers. The noticeably obese woman with double chins carried a purple umbrella and had an arrogant haughty expression on her face.

Ricky's heart pounded. Her hands were clammy. She felt like doing "something" to her. Death would be too easy for her. Ricky prayed for justice.

At that point there was no justice, just a very disappointed, wounded young man. Jeffrey had gained nothing by going to court.

Chapter 28

THE ATTORNEY FOR FATHER'S Rights recommended a psychiatrist and Jeffrey followed his advice. Dr. McDonald's office on Park Avenue was in an elegant neighborhood in Manhattan. The stylish waiting room, in beige and browns, with Danish Modern furniture impressed Jeffrey. He gazed with interest at the oil paintings in primary colors done in dots, lines, and squiggles. Jeffrey felt lost in modern art, his taste leaning more to Rembrandts and Renoirs, but still and all he hoped this doctor could help him. Soft classical music played in the background.

A middle-aged receptionist with a curly head of hair greeted Jeffrey and told him he would have a wait of ten minutes until the doctor was free. It turned into a half-hour as Jeffrey turned the pages of the *Reader's Digest*.

Finally, the receptionist ushered Jeffrey into a large office with a pile of papers in front of the doctor, a man with wide shoulders who looked like he belonged on a football field.

Dr. McDonald asked him to tell him about himself and Jeffrey gave him a history of his life up to the time he was shot. He said that his stepfather physically and sexually abused him, knowing it wasn't true, but he was looking for sympathy. He hesitated before he told the psychiatrist about the PTSD. Dr. McDonald said it was only natural since Jeffrey's very life had been threatened. He prescribed Valium.

Jeffrey noticed Dr. McDonald taking notes on a lined piece of paper. He put down his pen when the receptionist interrupted saying there was a private call on a line in her office. When Dr. McDonald excused himself and left the room, Jeffrey took the opportunity to snatch the piece of paper and put it into his suit pocket. When the doctor returned he didn't seem to notice that the paper had disappeared.

Once at home, Jeffrey read the paper and found the diagnoses of his mental illness. The psychiatrist had written Anti-social personality disorder, Borderline personality disorder, and Pseudologia fantastica. He wrote that Pseudologia was first found in 1885, maybe 50 cases documented since then. In other words Jeffrey's diagnosis placed him in a small, elite group.

He raced to the library and looked up the definition.

The Dictionary of Psychology read, "Pseudologia fantastica, also mythomania, or pathological lying is one of several terms applied by psychiatrists to the behavior of habitual or compulsive lying. It was first described in the medical literature in 1891. One definition of pathological lying is the following: *"Pathological lying is falsification entirely disproportionate to any discernible end in view, may be extensive and very complicated, and may manifest over a period of years or even a lifetime."*

"The defining characteristics of Pseudologia fantastica are that, first; the stories are not entirely improbable and often have some element of truth. They aren't a manifestation of delusion or some wider form of psychosis: upon confrontation, the person can acknowledge them to be untrue, even if unwillingly. Second, the fabricative tendency is long lasting; it is not provoked by the immediate situation or social pressure as much as it originates with the person's innate urge to act in accordance. Third, a definitely internal, not an external, motive for the behavior can be clinically discerned. E.G. long lasting extortion or habitual spousal battery might cause a person to lie repeatedly, without the lying being a pathological symptom. Fourth, the stories told tend towards presenting the person in question in a good light. For example, the person might be presented as being fantastically brave, knowing or being related to many famous people.

"Pseudologia fantastica is not currently listed as a symptom in the Diagnostic and Statistical Manual of Mental Disorders (DSM), nor in The International Statistical Classification of Diseases and Related Health Problems."

Jeffrey leaned back in his library chair and took a huge breath. He always suspected that he was a unique person in the world. He lied because it made him feel good and, now that he knew there was a word for it, he took pride in it. He always wanted to boost his self-esteem or see himself as a hero or a victim. It wasn't in the DSM which meant he wasn't psychotic or even had any kind of mental disorder.

Then he turned to the definition of antisocial personality disorder which said, " . . . a pervasive pattern of disregard for and violation of the rights of others that begins in childhood or early adolescence and continues into adulthood."

That's a lot of crap. I always stood up for the rights of others. I'm not a sociopath or a psychopath. That psychiatrist needs a psychiatrist. How dare he label me as a person without remorse or empathy for others? Did he know I worked as a volunteer in a hospital? No one who doesn't have empathy would ever work in a hospital. I took a course in CPR and saved a man's life when he had a heart attack. I even visited him in the hospital. He died three days later through no fault of mine.

Jeffrey continued reading, checking out Borderline personality disorder or as they call it BPD which includes a switch between idealizing and demonizing others. Combining this with mood disturbances can undermine relationships with family, friends, and coworkers. *Nonsense, I always got along with my mother except when she didn't like my lying and told me so. There were months I refused to talk to her, but then I always started speaking. My friends never got hurt by me. It wasn't my fault if Sally's portfolio lost thousands of dollars and she turned on me. I was gracious to Lena who turned out to be a murderer. I don't have BPD.*

A day didn't pass that Ricky wasn't worried about her son. There were times in her life she laughed, but inevitably her thoughts turned to Jeffrey, a man who was on a rocky roller coaster in a downward spiral.

Chapter 29

THE FOLLOWING YEAR JEFFREY underwent thirty-four excruciating operations. He became so well acquainted with medical terminology and procedures that he could fool any doctor into thinking he was one of them. When he said he was a surgeon, they believed him. He was still addicted to Stadol, and could see no way out. The pain he suffered was horrific and the post-traumatic stress syndrome continued. What kept him going was the hope of seeing his children.

Being on Geraldo Rivera's show, Jeffrey considered was an accomplishment, but Rivera accused him of lying in front of millions of viewers. Jeffrey had sent in falsified tapes of Lena calling his insurance company to ask, if he was murdered, would she still collect the millions of dollars in his will. Jeffrey felt he wasn't really lying, just exaggerating. He was embarrassed when the truth emerged, but still felt justified. He wasn't sure if she shot him to collect the insurance, wasn't sure of her motivation.

Jeffrey lived like a victim of fate, until fate did catch up with him when he was brought before the United States District Court, Eastern District of New York. An investigation and analysis of the handwriting on the sign-in sheets uncovered the illegality of the exams Jeffrey took for men for the National Association of Securities Dealers. He was named first and then six more men were indicted.

He had no choice but to plead guilty, and was sentenced to jail. He feared for his life and figured the only way he could protect himself was to select the biggest, most fierce criminal, and make friends with him. He found a six-footer, muscular black man who was imprisoned for attempted murder. His name was Teddy Anderson, nickname Devil, and, when Jeffrey told him he was a lawyer, innocent of the charge against him, Devil also said he was innocent and befriended him. The other prisoners didn't dare to assault Jeffrey, and eventually came to him for legal advice, and he promised to help them.

After Jeffrey served his sentence, he was released and kept in touch with Devil and the other guys who needed his help.

Jeffrey was of the opinion that he would finally get custody of the children so he searched for an apartment with four bedrooms in walking distance of a Yeshiva where his children could get both an English and Jewish education. He found the perfect apartment on the second floor of a private home in the neighborhood of Bensonhurst, a mixed neighborhood of Italians and Jews, where shopping was close and stores were plentiful. The apartment had an alcove in the front of the house that Jeffrey turned into an office.

But not seeing his children made Jeffrey even more depressed, and he began to think that Lena might take them to Israel so he wrote to the United States Department of State to make them aware that he had custody and they should deny passports to the children. They agreed, and Jeffrey was relieved that at least he could locate them someplace in the United States.

Since Jeffrey didn't have the financial resources to hire an attorney, he represented himself *pro se*. By then he knew a great deal of law having studied it while in prison. He wrote out an Order To Show Cause citing himself as the Plaintiff and Lena as the Defendant. He wrote, "Notice: The purpose of this hearing is to punish you for contempt of court. Such punishment may consist of a fine or imprisonment or both as provided for under the New York State Family Court Act."

Lena hadn't shown up or paid alimony to Jeffrey or given him custody of the children. The judge ruled that the marriage between them was dissolved by reason of the cruel and inhuman treatment of the plaintiff by the defendant, and it was further adjudged that custody of the infant issue shall be with the plaintiff and the defendant shall pay child support to the plaintiff in the amount of $100 per week per child and maintenance of $50 per week to the plaintiff.

When Jeffrey appeared in court to have the order enforced, Lena never showed. The judge signed the order and nothing came of the useless piece of paper. Jeffrey thought he could use it for wallpaper in the bathroom. He considered Lena devious and evil, his sworn enemy.

Lena wrote an article in a woman's magazine about the abuse she had endured from her husband and how she had been driven to shoot him. They paid her $5,000 for the article and Jeffrey's shrunken stomach burned with anger.

Although Jeffrey should have been wary of women by now, he still hadn't learned his lesson and repeated the same mistake. He had met a caring nurse in the hospital and he invited Anita to his new apartment. He confided to her that he would set off fireworks on July 4th; of course it would be safe, but exciting. What did Anita do? She notified the police that Jeffrey had a bomb. The bomb squad was summoned and one of its members, in protective clothing, entered and searched through everything. They brought in a specially trained police dog who didn't find any bombs. Meanwhile they did find that Jeffrey was in possession of six sticks of dynamite, M-80's, a device that appeared to be a timer, a pellet gun, a derringer, and false identification. Jeffrey felt violated.

He was arrested and jailed on Rikers Island.

This time they put a doctor in his cell, an OB/GYN who was in jail for murder in the second degree.

The doctor was short, bald, and pale as cauliflower. He hung his head as he related to Jeffrey the sad story of how he had done an abortion and how unfortunately the patient had bled to death.

"It wasn't my fault," he cried. "I have a wife, who stands behind me, and three lovely children. I don't know what to do. I feel my lawyer isn't trying enough for me."

Jeffrey felt sorry for the poor fellow. "I'm also innocent. I've been trained in law; maybe I could be of help."

"That would be great. I'd appreciate it so much."

"Think nothing of it." Jeffrey sat down on the cot fastened to the wall. "What exactly do you want me to do?"

The doctor bit down on his lips. "Could you prepare an Affidavit in Support of Motion to Appeal for me?"

"Why not? I have nothing else to do. I'll prepare it and there's no charge."

They didn't keep Jeffrey in jail long, and as soon as he was home he kept his word and prepared the document for the doctor.

Unfortunately, it wasn't accepted and the doctor was transferred from Rikers Island to an upstate prison.

One morning after Jeffrey opened his mail, he found a membership card from the American Society of Notaries. He signed it with his distinguished flourishing signature and realized he had been a notary for thirteen years, a record to be proud of, having notarized many documents, all legal.

Jeffrey should have anticipated trouble from Lena, the murderer, and it came at him with a vengeance. She went back to court seeking custody and support for the children; the gall to say that they have always resided with their mother and that the respondent father has not been a part of their lives for the past 7½ years, as if he had deserted them. She was granted custody and support and Jeffrey vowed that he would never support them as long as they lived with their evil mother. He still had no idea where they were.

His emotions were so fragile that he kept clenching and unclenching his fists trying to settle himself down, drinking Sunny D by the gallon.

A few times, Jeffrey's friend, Stuart, came to the apartment to find him unconscious. Stuart dialed 911 and Jeffrey was taken to the hospital, a victim of diabetic shock.

When he was released in a weakened condition and told to avoid sweets, Jeffrey never listened. He kept himself busy with correspondence with the prisoners he knew from Rikers Island. He attempted to keep their spirits up and somehow that raised his spirits; otherwise, he felt he really would have lost his mind.

One day when the streets were packed with snow and ice, Jeffrey found two letters in his mailbox. He sat at his kitchen table with the big container of Sunny D in front of him and read the letters from Devil and Henry who were both still in Rikers.

Devil wrote *"What up, Jeffrey? By the time you recive this letter, I hope it fine you in the very best of health. Have you recive back the thing that I could not have? I think you for everything you doing for me here. Write me back soon. A man in need is a man indeed (smile). You is the best friend I have. Love, Devil"*

Jeffrey smiled when he read the letter from the big guy who had protected him when he was in jail. Once out, he began sending him presents to express appreciation, and Jeffrey guessed he was so deprived that he felt Jeffrey was his best friend. Then he turned to a long letter from Henry.

"In the Name of God, Most Gracious, Most Merciful—Hello Jeffrey, Shalom—First off let me say I appreciated the phone call to my wife yesterday immensely. I guess you can see the rock and hard place I'm between because although I love her very much I can't be honest and say I'm in love with her at this point in my life. I plan on proceeding with my divorce and I'm hoping I don't have to use 40 more days on another service affidavit. I say this because I really don't want to put this on a back burner and in your profession time is money, which is business, which I respect on all accounts.

Jeffrey took a gulp of Sunny D and kept reading.

"Now the paper I sent her was in the event she signed it, there would've been consent to divorce if not then within 20 days if there was no contest, I had 20 more days to wait to proceed by default with the receipt. Can you swing that for me, and if you want something, give me a minute to get it for you, and my word bonds me, I'll honor the debt. I already have a person whose willing to mail it certified

for a half pack of cigarettes. I've had hard times and in my past I weathered them tastefully. I'm better at giving help than asking for it from someone who'll need it a little more often than myself. That's why I asked you about my child's case and my wife's future. As for my cases I'll get it together on my own in due time once I get to the proper prison setting. There are very sharp minds in those libraries chiding time away. Like I said there are magazines that had a few resources for constructing a solid defense in a suit. Plus they have something called a Cut Board set up now to deal with the cutting in this jail. The Feds are in charge I heard, they don't have senseless razor fights in their prisons.

"I know you are busy and I'm cutting this short but I hope you don't forget these matters. I've learned a lot about life since I committed to God. There are brothers I won't deal with even when I was selling drugs in this facility before I became Muslim. Why? Because all they're about is self-indulgence and from Benny's own mouth, he's smoking reefer and that in his condition in an indication mindset, I call brain lock. I know you don't know a lot about drugs and the effect on persona, but from both ends of abuse I can give you the whole of them—pain, pleasure, success and losses. I know you're busy so I can't tie up the phone. I'll be writing more even though the dorm is noisy. Hopefully I'll be gone soon. Take care and Happy Chanukah. God bless you and your family. Henry"

Jeffrey finished reading both letters, sat back and gulped down the rest of the Sunny D. He planned on sending both guys cigarettes which in jail is used like money. His chest swelled with pride realizing that now he had real friends. They didn't know he wasn't a lawyer, but Jeffrey figured it didn't make any difference. He acted like their lawyer and didn't rip them off. His life would be satisfactory if only he had his children.

When the doorbell rang, Jeffrey peered out the window. The snow was falling like Niagara and, in the midst of heavy snowflakes, Sally stood dressed in her auxiliary police uniform. When Jeffrey buzzed to let her in, Sally shook the snow from her coat and removed it. She hadn't forgotten that Jeffrey was the cause of her losing thousands of dollars, but luckily for him she had forgiven him.

"How are you doing, Jeffrey?" Removing a stack of papers from the kitchen chair, Sally plopped down, her short legs dangling, not reaching the soiled linoleum.

Jeffrey threw the papers on the floor from the opposite kitchen chair and sat down. "I'm alive. How are you?"

"Great, except I feel like an icicle," Sally moaned. "My toes and fingers are numb. Crazy weather we're having. What's new with you?"

"To tell the truth, I'm absolutely livid as Lena applied for custody of the children and got it, and now I have to write to the court.

"But everything isn't dark as I just heard from my friends in jail, Devil and Henry. I need to send them some cigarettes. Half the guys in the pen have suffered more injustice than I'll ever know, still and all my life hasn't been a bed of roses. Listening to what happened to the other inmates wised me up to what a prize pain in the butt I was being."

Sally rubbed her fingers to warm them and frowned. "Don't compare your pain with the other inmates. You've suffered trauma more than anyone I know, and your enemy is still fighting you."

"She'll never stop as long as she's alive. I could have

her rubbed out, but I don't believe in murder. She'll get justice, but not from me." Jeffrey picked up a pencil and began doodling the picture of a gun.

"You have the right attitude." Sally pushed herself off the chair and strode toward the refrigerator that was covered completely with all kinds of magnet signs. The apartment was a shambles, messy, and dirty. It seemed every piece of mail that came into the place was either on the furniture or on the floor. Nevertheless, Sally was hungry and needed a nosh. "Do you have anything interesting to eat?"

"I'm loaded with junk food." Jeffrey went to the freezer that was packed with ice cream. "How about having some Rocky Road ice cream?"

"Thanks. I was freezing before, but I warmed up."

Jeffrey cleared the table, dished out two huge plates of ice cream, and he and Sally ate in companionable silence until Sally, too upset to hide her feelings, scolded Jeffrey. "Your pancreas has gone the way of silent movies, and you're taking a big chance by eating ice cream, drinks with sugar, candy, and God knows what else. Are you planning to go into diabetic shock?"

"I appreciate your concern but please don't worry about me. Now I don't want to hear another word about what I eat or drink. Understand?"

"Okay, I'm sorry. You're my friend and I'm concerned about your health. I was on my way home when I stopped off, and I better go now before the snow buries me alive," Sally said, looking unnervingly serious.

After Sally left, Jeffrey put the dishes and spoons in the dishwasher that was already full, added soap, and turned it on. Miserable and lonely, Jeffrey reread the letter from Henry. Then he tried to cheer himself up by thinking

Reva Spiro Luxenberg

about what happened in jail when elections were held for Inmate Grievance Representative. He had decided to become a candidate as he had always been interested in politics, knowing he could stand up for the inmates' rights for the three-month term. He smiled as his chest swelled remembering how he had won by a landslide with 102 votes, beating out the next two candidates who had 34 and 15, the men applauding vigorously, an exhilarating victory.

A week later Jeffrey opened what looked like the invitation he had been expecting. Arthur was getting married in February and he asked Jeffrey to be his best man. Arthur, at nineteen, seemed like a joyful puppy, and his fiancée, Ruth, seventeen, was a girl who was so lovely she could have been a model.

All the sugar he consumed made Jeffrey look like a puffed out pastry causing him to rent an extra-large size black tuxedo. Like a fat cat with fish in his dish, he looked forward to the wedding, but agreed with his mother that Arthur was too young to marry. His half-brother had completed a college course that prepared him to be an Emergency Medical Technician and Arthur had a job that provided him with the independence to live a married life. Jeffrey hadn't married until he was in his twenties, but a few years difference hadn't made him any smarter in choosing a mate, or even his mother who had married at the age of twenty-eight.

The weather was favorable for an afternoon wedding and the warmer weather allowed for picture-taking outside the synagogue. Inside in the lower level, the bride and groom looked like the Prince and Cinderella. The band played loud Jewish music, and the crowd was boisterous, as the young people danced in circles while Jeffrey watched from the sidelines, too weak to join in.

He enjoyed the food and for a few hours he tried to forget the shooting.

In March, on a day when the wind blew horrifically at thirty miles an hour, Jeffrey went to see his black friend in jail. Devil and he sat opposite each other as Jeffrey leaned forward and whispered, "What's up?"

"I'm goin' to trial for stabbing my baby's mother. I ain't got a chance to get off. I'm real scared that they'll put me away for twenty years."

Jeffrey couldn't let that happen to the friend who had saved his hide in jail. "You'll get off. I'll see to it."

"How?" Devil lowered his voice so much that Jeffrey had a hard time hearing him. "She got me real mad when she called me an animal. I did stab her and she's hurt real bad."

Jeffrey considered what he could do, took a deep breath, and bit down hard on his lips. "When you go to court, I'll appear as a defense witness. I'll say that I overheard a conversation on the phone between you and the plaintiff when she threatened to shoot you. You only stabbed her in self-defense." Jeffrey sat back smugly and smiled.

Devil's dark eyes opened wide. "You'd do this for me?"

"What are friends for? You'll be acquitted and we'll celebrate."

"I ain't never had a friend like you. I'll never forget you as long as I live."

When Jeffrey testified, he was accused of perjury, especially for saying he was a lawyer. Devil was sentenced to twenty years and Jeffrey was brought to trial for perjury.

Before the trial, he called his mother and, as his hand shook from the effects of the Stadol, he spoke in a pleading voice. "Please come to court as my witness. I can't stand going back to jail. They sent my friend who defended me upstate to prison, and the other guys in Rikers may attack me when he's not there. I can't trust those murders and thieves. All I did was say I was a lawyer, and I know enough law that I could be one. Please show up. Please."

Ricky dressed in a conservative navy suit, wore a plain beret, and sensible shoes and the day of Jeffrey's trial she came to court in a nervous state. The court officer made her sit in the corridor as she wasn't allowed to hear any testimony and could be present only when she herself testified. What could she say in her son's defense? He already implicated himself when he said he was a lawyer. She wiped the perspiration from her forehead and twisted the handkerchief into a ball.

When Ricky was called to testify, she tried her best. "My son has always lied. As a child I never knew when he was telling the truth. This is an emotional problem. He can't help himself. I ask for mercy from the court, Your Honor."

She returned to the corridor and waited a half-hour until Jeffrey came out smiling.

"Did they pardon you?" Ricky asked in a strained voice.

"The judge is reserving his decision. Come with me across the street. I have to meet some people."

Jeffrey rushed through security, his mother doing her best to follow his fast pace. In the hallway of the court building across the street, Jeffrey met with two well-dressed black women. When the meeting was over, Ricky asked him what was going on.

"I'm representing the younger woman in divorce proceedings," Jeffrey said as he grinned.

Ricky took a breath. Jeffrey was like a leopard that couldn't change his spots. He was soon sent back to Rikers.

Chapter 30

"I'M TAKING A SABBATICAL," Ricky said to her son on the phone.

"For how long and what kind of sabbatical?" Jeffrey asked.

"I'll be away for a year researching special education in Pennsylvania, Ohio, Florida, Louisiana, and Mississippi. I'll keep in touch."

Ricky travelled with a friend. She interviewed the chairperson in charge of special ed in various settings and assessed how different schools viewed the placement of handicapped students. One state included students who were high achievers under the umbrella of special ed. In her opinion, this removed the stigma that cast a dismal spell over some of the handicapped students who were labeled Emotionally Disturbed.

When Ricky lived in Biloxi, Mississippi she was enchanted with the colorful city and the courteous people she met. Southern hospitality lived up to its reputation. She and Jeffrey spoke often on the phone.

One day she said to Jeffrey, "I believe a change of environment might do you good. Fly here and I think the gloom you feel may lift."

"I don't go anyplace. I don't know if I should come to Mississippi," Jeffrey whined.

"It's very pretty here and it's much different from Brooklyn."

"I haven't got the energy to pick myself up, pack a suitcase, get a plane reservation and fly down South."

Ricky pondered about what she could tell her son to induce him to leave when he was so depressed. Suddenly an idea popped into her head.

"There's a gorgeous aquarium with a huge tank for a sea turtle that swims in a circle. I've never seen anything like it. You'd love it here. Also there are lectures about animals every Sunday by the expert, Jack Hanna, a respected TV personality."

"Really? A sea turtle?"

"Yes. You just have to see it as it stares at the people who stare back."

"Is the aquarium crowded?"

"Not at all. What do you say?"

"Okay, I'll come. I'll stay at Kessler Air Force Base in the Officer's quarters."

Somehow Jeffrey motivated himself to join his mother in Biloxi. He showed her around the base like he owned it. Every other day they went to the aquarium and Jeffrey managed to laugh and crack some jokes.

"Let's go gambling," Ricky suggested.

Jeffrey wasn't a gambler but he looked interested. "Where are the casinos?"

"Right now it's against the law to build casinos. There's a gambling boat that takes us ten miles out into international waters, and once we're there they turn on the slot machines and we play."

They didn't come back winners but gambling was a helpful distraction.

The next morning Ricky drove to Gulfport where she and Jeffrey visited art galleries. They looked at handsome old Audubon prints with pictures of birds.

Once again Jeffrey showed off his wide knowledge. "John J. Audubon was an ornithologist, a naturalist, and painter who died in 1851. These are rare prints and we should buy as many as we can."

They both bought many prints to the delight of the owner of the gallery.

A pier was close to where Ricky had an apartment in a fifteen-story house and in the afternoon they fished on the pier and looked at the shrimp boats that were docked.

"Boy, oh boy," Ricky exclaimed. "See that one. It belongs to me. The name painted on the side is Ricky's Treasure."

There were many activities and sights to see in Biloxi. They stood on the sidewalk and watched the Marti Gras parade pass by. Pretty girls on floats threw necklaces of cheap beads. Ricky was prepared with her umbrella, opened it, and held it like a bowl.

"That's a good idea," Jeffrey said. "You caught an umbrella full of necklaces. What are you going to do with them?"

"I don't know. But it feels good to get something for nothing. There's a lovely restaurant near the lighthouse. Are you hungry?"

Jeffrey cocked his head. "I could go for a bite."

"Let's walk to Magnolia Mall. The Fountain is one of the prettiest restaurants I have ever seen," Ricky said as they strolled through the streets of Biloxi.

Inside, Jeffrey admired the glass-enclosed dining

room and outdoor gazebo with a large tree that shaded the customers from the sun. The salads they devoured were unusual.

"I like this Southern hospitality and their exceptionally good food," Jeffrey said as he wiped his mouth with the cloth napkin.

When they left the restaurant, Jeffrey found a seagull that couldn't fly. "Let's call the park service."

"Okay," Ricky said.

They wrapped the seagull in the cloth napkin that Jeffrey had put in his pocket and took it back to Ricky's apartment. Jeffrey paced the floor while they waited for the ranger to pick up the sick bird.

The next day they called to learn the seagull had died. "I hope he's in bird heaven," Ricky said.

"It's a shame," Jeffrey said. "There's pollution in the Gulf and the bird must've been poisoned. Oil spills and debris are killing our planet."

Ricky stood at the window gazing at the slick oily water of the Gulf. "I hope not," she said with a sigh.

*　　*　　*

Grandma's 100th birthday took place in the Golden Lake Nursing Home in Staten Island on a mild October day when the leaves on the trees exploded with a pallet of russet, ocher, and gold.

Ricky lifted two shopping bags from the trunk of the car. One contained a birthday cake with pink icing and three large candles. The first candle was shaped like a one and the other two were zeros. She couldn't put a hundred candles on a cake since the flames could, God forbid, burn down the nursing home. The second shopping bag had birthday plates, napkins, paper hats, and a gift-wrapped present for her mother.

As Ricky strode to the entrance, she noticed one patient in a wheelchair was busy feeding a flock of pigeons. Two patients sat at a table watching the pigeons. Inside, a few patients were making their way with their walkers to the day room where the crafts session was about to begin.

Grandma's astonishingly withered face lit up when she saw her only child. Her wrinkled skin was covered with brownish blotches and there were stiff white hairs sprinkled on her chin. When she recognized Ricky, a glint became visible in her watery, glazed eyes. Unfortunately, the ophthalmologist had refused to do a cataract operation for such an elderly patient. There seemed to be a pleasantly soft aspect to Grandma's false-toothed smile. Sitting in the wheelchair she appeared as a gaunt figure wrapped like a cocoon in a thin cotton blanket, dressed in a sweater with felt slippers on her feet. Her silky white hair speckled with black was fixed in a bun, and her cheeks were painted with pink rouge.

Ricky said, "Happy birthday. How are you, Mama?"

"Zaier gut," she replied in a thin voice. She spoke little and had reverted to Yiddish, the first language she had learned speaking to her parents and grandmother. Although she was born in Bridgeport, Connecticut and spoke English well, her mind was playing tricks on her sending her back to a happier time.

"I'm glad you're well," Ricky said. "I have a present for you." Ricky tore the gift wrapping from a box and handed her mother a baby doll.

Her mother took the doll in her wrinkled spotted hands and cradled it to her flat chest. "A shainen dank."

Jeffrey marched in wearing his Army officer's

uniform decorated with additional shiny medals and highly polished jet black shoes. He had put on pounds from Sunny D and high calorie snacks and the uniform stretched tightly across his chest. His face was a mask but underneath Ricky knew there was a boiling cauldron, as he still wasn't able to see his children and there wasn't a moment he didn't yearn for them. Bending down stiffly, he kissed his grandmother on her leathery cheek.

Ten minutes later, Arthur showed up with his pretty young wife and chubby year-old son, Bernie.

Grandma's party took place in a private room. The old woman's memory was dwindling like sand through an hour glass. Although the baby was placed in her lap as she sat in the wheelchair, her daughter didn't know if she recognized that she was the great-grandmother of the pink-cheeked baby boy. She petted him and kissed his head, smiling all the time.

"Bobbeh," Arthur said. "This is my son."

"A good-looking baby," Grandma said in Yiddish.

Ricky placed a paper crown that read "Happy Birthday" on her mother's head.

Jeffrey had notified the Staten Island Advance of the centenarian's birth and a photographer from the newspaper took a picture of the four-generation family. It would remain a memento of a spectacular day in the long life of a woman who had lived through five wars starting with the Spanish American War.

Jeffrey's life was crumbling. He was arrested and served six months for perjury, coming out a broken man. He called his mother daily. It was costly, but by cheating the phone company he managed.

Chapter 31

Ricky retired and moved to New Castle, a small city in Pennsylvania where her friend lived. She liked the idea of living in harmony with 25,000 people. She no longer felt comfortable in the metropolis of New York City. When she was a child each neighborhood seemed like a small town, but the neighborhoods in New York had changed and she felt the need to live in a town where she would try to recuperate from the agony of having a son who was steeped in lies and deceit.

Many times Ricky drove back to see her mother in the nursing home in Staten Island. One day she observed how a male attendant was teasing her mother by taking away the doll she always had with her. Her mother was kept in a wheelchair even in the afternoon when she dozed, her head hanging down. This was a form of abuse. Ricky investigated a nursing home in Pennsylvania not far from her and it appealed to her.

She drove 425 miles, stopped off halfway, and stayed overnight in a motel. The next day she put her mother in the car and drove the 425 miles without stopping until she reached the nursing home. They welcomed her mother. Every day the attendant put her to bed for her afternoon nap. No one teased her. They treated her like she was made of gold and Ricky was happy she had transferred her. Ricky visited and ran the Bingo game bringing small inexpensive items for the patients who participated. By this time her mother's mind no longer was able to adapt to the game, but, when the patients were given musical instruments, her mother banged on a small drum.

The time came for her mother's 101st birthday. Ricky had bought an old Victorian house and made a birthday party for her mother who was brought by van to the home. A musician who played the violin was hired by Ricky. Her neighbors, Arthur, his wife and baby, and Jeffrey were invited. Arthur drove them in his car. As an Emergency Medical Technician, he was used to driving ambulances and had become adept at driving all kinds of vehicles.

When Jeffrey stepped through the front door wearing his Army officer's uniform, Ricky whistled. He had put on even more weight but the uniform still looked great on him.

"My son, you look terrific," Ricky said.

Jeffrey gave her a big smile. "You approve of my dress blues?"

"You bet. I like the gold buttons, the gold braid, the white shirt with the bow tie, and especially the medals. Very nice."

Jeffrey grinned. "It was General George Washington who prescribed blue dress coats. Dark blue is our national color."

"You always were smart," Ricky said.

Jeffrey beamed.

Arthur entered, accompanied by his pretty young wife and Bernie, an active toddler who ran around the living room.

They hugged and kissed Grandma who took Bernie's small hand and kissed it. They all applauded.

The birthday cake with 101 candles was on a plate on a carved antique oak sideboard. Ricky lit the cake and everyone sang 'Happy Birthday.' Quickly Arthur blew out the candles to prevent a blaze. The violinist played some lively tunes as the family, friends, and neighbors partook of the festive dishes followed by a slice of birthday cake. Ricky was pleasantly surprised when Mayor Johnson arrived and presented a congratulatory certificate to Grandma who gave him her toothless smile.

"Thank you, Mayor," Ricky said. "I can't imagine the Mayor of New York City coming to congratulate my mother. I appreciate your visit. It's a real honor."

Soon it was time for Grandma to go back to the nursing home for her nap.

"I wish I could keep Grandma here," Ricky said to her children.

"Can't you?" Arthur asked.

"No. She needs attention day and night and I don't have the money to pay for three aides. She seems to have adapted well where she is and I can go see her whenever I want."

"Let's go exploring," Jeffrey suggested.

"Good idea," Ricky said. "There's an old mill in town that's interesting."

Arthur drove them in his old car and they walked around the mill and took pictures.

Buggies came along the road and stopped at a parking lot down the block. Amish men and their wives stood around socializing. The men wore dark blue trousers and white shirts and the women wore white caps on their heads and long blue muslin dresses.

"Don't take pictures of them," Ricky warned. "It's against their religion to be photographed. They're nice people, very friendly and courteous. I needed a bathroom downstairs and an Amish man built it for me."

Arthur looked surprised. "You mean they built that tiny bathroom where I can hardly fit with my wide shoulders?"

"Yes," Ricky said. "It's big enough for me. I converted the dining room into a bedroom and needed a convenient bathroom. There was a small porch off the kitchen and I wondered if the Amish could build a bathroom on it. I heard they were excellent carpenters."

"How did you find an Amish man?" Jeffrey asked.

"I drove to one of their farms and inquired. It seems that Andy Byler wouldn't drive his buggy to my house, but he was amenable to be a passenger in my car, so I brought him to look at the porch. He agreed to build the bathroom and asked for the modest sum of $6.00 an hour and an extra dollar when he needed the help of his son."

"Boy, that's a bargain," Jeffrey said. "In Brooklyn that would have cost at least $10,000."

"This isn't Brooklyn," Ricky said with a smile. "I'll tell you something else that's amusing. I play golf on a course near the Bylers and every time I drive past their house I stop off and talk to Nancy, Andy's wife. Well, one day when I drove home from Brooklyn and was on the highway, my car had an altimeter problem so I stopped at a dealership, traded it in, and bought a new car. I always waited for Nancy to come out of the house so we could talk; well, the next time I waited, and waited until she finally came out."

"Why didn't you knock at her door?" Arthur asked.

"I didn't want to interrupt anything she was in the

midst of doing like quilting or cooking. Finally Nancy came out and said she didn't know it was me because I was in a red car, not the usual white one. I told her I needed to buy a new car because the old car was dangerous. She nodded and said that she had the same problem. I couldn't imagine what she was alluding to. She said she had the same difficulty with a horse who wouldn't stick to the road and she had to trade him in."

Ricky's sons laughed at her tale. It was a good time. But later Jeffrey revealed some bad news. He had played the market betting on options with his IRA that was worth $150,000. In three days he lost everything and couldn't get it back.

Her son's judgment was failing fast.

Chapter 32

WHEN GRANDMA WAS 103, her heart beat like a young woman's, but her bones were as fragile as egg shells. The femur cracked in her left leg when the attendant in the nursing home helped her into the wheelchair. She was hospitalized and, when they administered oxygen her mind cleared somewhat.

Her mother's eyes opened wide as Ricky stood by her side. A tall attendant came over to lift her more comfortably in the hospital bed. When he left, Ricky's mother said two words that indicated her mind was still functioning. She whispered, "Big. Black."

"Yes, Mama, he is a big, black man."

Those were the last words that Grandma uttered. Unbelievably she went into three comas and came out of them. It wasn't time for her to die.

Arthur came to Grandma's side. He draped his prayer shawl around his shoulders and said a prayer in Hebrew for her.

Grandma reached the advanced age of 104 and still her heart kept beating. Her broken leg couldn't be set because of the brittleness of her bones. She had lost a great deal of weight and now she was a mere fifty-five pounds, a thin layer of skin over brittle bones. Her hands were purple from the tubes that entered her body and she seemed to be in another world.

Ricky didn't know if her mother could hear her, but she leaned her face close to her and said, "Don't be afraid to die, Mama. You have more people on the other side than here. And don't worry about me. I'll be all right."

Jeffrey yearned for his beloved grandmother to keep living on and on. He couldn't face the reality of her coming death. Fancying himself as a lawyer, he wrote a legal document to the administration of the hospital trying to frighten them into keeping her alive. It was a complete lie written without his mother's knowledge, from his mother's viewpoint, and signed by him as a witness with his notary public's seal. In part it read:

"Please take notice that the above named individual is the sole child of the patient and she advises the hospital that the orders contained within this document to comply in toto with the following.

1. *Access to the chart concerning my mother must be available for inspection by myself personally on a regular basis or to my children via proxy from the initial date of admission to aforecited hospital for the purpose of understanding the medical condition of my 104-year-old mother, the needs that she has, and the diagnosis and prognosis according to the physician providing her medical care. In my absence I shall designate one of her grandchildren to act as my agent in fact and respectfully request that the hospital provide full and total disclosure of any and all medical concerns without reservation to my authorized agent."*

Ricky kept reading with grave concern. Jeffrey had taken on the job of keeping his Grandmother alive at all costs, even pretending that this was written by her. Her wishes, expressed to the doctor who had handed this paper over to her, were clear. *Keep my mother alive without extraordinary means. Don't let my son frighten you. I know you're doing the best you can.*

The second paragraph of the lying document consisted of medical advice given by Jeffrey with his limited medical knowledge. He was capable of sounding off, and Ricky told the doctor not to pay attention to anything her son had written.

2. *Of great concern is the site of the central I.V. line which is currently placed in the femoral area. The question of eventual infiltration or sepsis or putrefaction is addressed at this time. Instructions to the hospital are that, upon medical determination that the central line must be moved, permission is granted to move said line to an alternate site, but that said alternate site must not be subclavian as the possibility of pneumothorax is too great. The hospital or any of its agents should contact me via telephone prior to movement of the central line or via beeper, both of which numbers may be found in the front of the chart.*

The beeper was Jeffrey's.

Ricky had nightmares that night after the doctor had turned over the so-called legal document to her. She was haunted not by the eventual death of her mother who had no decent quality of life, but by the nerve of her lying son.

Ricky watched her mother take in huge gasps of air.

It was December 7th, the day of infamy, that her mother passed on to the next world. She died when her kidneys could no longer function. Ricky stood by her mother's side in the Intensive Care Unit and she recited prayers to help her on her way to Heaven. In death her mother's face was peaceful and Ricky noticed that her hair that one would expect to be white was sprinkled with black. Her mother had a long life, longer than most people.

Arrangements had to be made for her mother's transportation to her cemetery plot in Queens, New York. She had reserved a burial plot next to Ricky's grandmother. Her husband was buried close by.

At the funeral home, the director explained that a special coffin had to be put on the plane according to the law. Ricky paid for it and, when she notified Jeffrey that his grandmother had died, he questioned where his grandmother's body was now.

"She's in the morgue of the hospital."

"You can't leave her body alone," Jeffrey said.

"It's freezing where she is. I can't stay with her. She'll also be put in a special container on the plane and I can't accompany her."

"Yes, you can," Jeffrey insisted.

Ricky ignored what he said.

Arthur couldn't go to the funeral as he was in Denmark in a demonstration against terrorism, so Ricky wrote a eulogy for her mother as she sat on the plane. There was no family left to attend the funeral. All close relatives had died.

Ricky stood shivering beside the open grave. The gray sky was covered with black clouds and a winter storm seemed imminent. Jeffrey showed up late with a friend, a stout young man who wore a plaid winter coat with a muffler tied around his thick neck. Ricky didn't know him.

Jeffrey looked at her with rage in his eyes. Ricky paid him no attention. He was in one of his angry moods. She knew eventually he would talk to her. She read the eulogy in a strained voice, feeling relieved that her mother would no longer suffer in this world.

Chapter 33

THE WINTER IN PENNSYLVANIA had been tough for Ricky who had constant pain in her back from arthritis. Furthermore she had been snowbound for a week. Contemplating the beneficial effects of warm weather had turned her mind to relocating to a warm state like Florida or Arizona. Jeffrey and Arthur encouraged her to move on with her life. Retirement had its advantages.

She had kept in touch by mail with her first cousin, Monroe, who lived in Phoenix who was seventy-six years old and a cousin she had never met. Monroe, the middle son of her Uncle Morris, her mother's brother who had been a millionaire, had died when Ricky was an infant. infant. Her mother had separated herself from her sister-in-law with the excuse that seeing her might prevent her from marrying again. Sometimes her mother had some peculiar ideas.

Before Monroe passed away this would be an ideal time to finally meet him. She could spend the winter in an area that would be conducive to her health.

Ricky packed a suitcase and flew to Phoenix, the home of three hundred days of sunlight all year round, huge palm trees, and all species of cacti. She stayed in a hotel for a week in Scottsdale, found a furnished condo, and moved in for the winter.

She met Monroe who was tall, charming, and handsome. He embraced her and introduced his present wife who, when she got a chance, berated her husband unceasingly. Ricky disliked her from the outset. Monroe told her a different version from her mother's about the way her uncle had died.

"My father had lost his money when the depression hit in '29. He then began to sell insurance and called at a store in Manhattan. Next door they were operating a still making whiskey during Prohibition and it blew up. The men in the store ran to the front and saved their lives, but my father ran to the back door and he was buried under debris for three days until they dug out his body."

When Monroe paused, Ricky said, "I'm sorry about your father. My mother always told me the explosion was from a chemical experiment. Now I know the whole truth."

Ricky's thoughts dwelled on Jeffrey who was still obsessed with the unsuccessful plan to gain custody of his children.

After the first winter in Scottsdale, and now that her mother had died, Ricky felt she could buy a condo and remain in the comfortable climate of the Southwest. She purchased a condo with two bedrooms and two bathrooms and invited Jeffrey to stay with her.

It took a lot of persuasion to change Jeffrey's mind to fly to Arizona. She told him about the sunny climate, and about meeting her cousin Monroe, and she offered to finance the whole trip if he would come for two weeks. Reluctantly he agreed.

When he showed up, he was impressed with the

climate, the beauty of Scottsdale with its palm trees, and the upscale shops in the indoor mall. Ricky made him comfortable in her second bedroom adjacent to its own bathroom.

Monroe showed up with his critical wife. Jeffrey with interest cocked his head when Monroe spoke about his father and told them that he had married the daughter of the man who reintroduced Hebrew as a language in Palestine. Monroe suffered from the lack of conveniences and, when his wife wouldn't move to the United States, he divorced her. He had married a second time, lived in South Carolina, and had entered the antiques business. When his wife died, he married his present wife.

Jeffrey said Monroe impressed him with his debonair ways. He told his mother he was glad he had come to Arizona to meet him. In fact he liked Arizona so much, he was contemplating relocating. Ricky hoped he would move near her as she took it to mean he was getting on with his life, not dwelling on the fate of his children.

Ricky drove Jeffrey to the Phoenix Zoo and watched as his spirit soared. One of his many interests had always been the love of animals. He snapped pictures of the Galapagos Tortoises as they munched on a large green salad, their jaws clicking noisily when they bit down, some of them hundreds of years old.

The Asian elephants, the largest land mammals, captivated both Jeffrey and his mother. After strolling past more exhibits, Jeffrey pointed to the bighorn sheep that stood rigidly on the peak of a mountain. It seemed to Ricky that Jeffrey was more at peace in the zoo than he had been for many years.

He reclined on the grass next to the lake tossing crumbs to the ducks. His face was tranquil and his dark eyes were lit with a calmness that Ricky hadn't seen since he married the woman who had shot him. Most of their conversations still revolved around his deep longings to see his children.

Another year passed, and when Ricky opened her mail she found a Rosh Hashanah card from Jeffrey. It read,

"Dear Mother, My sincerest wishes for the very best in this coming New Year. May God inscribe you in the book of health, wealth, happiness, and may all of us merit pleasure from Grace, Dan, and Bernard . . . the next generation. I do try to be a dutiful son, but sometimes that does not come across that way. I ask you for your forgiveness for any errors I made toward you, either accidentally or deliberately. Love, Jeffrey."

Ricky wiped the tears from her eyes with her hand, and determined that she would try her best to get Jeffrey to come again to stay with her. When in January he sent her a photo of his car buried under many feet of snow, she begged him to return to Arizona where one needed sunglasses for protection. This time Jeffrey readily acceded to her wishes and, when he was comfortably settled in once again in her condo, she drove him to Rawhide, a popular tourist attraction.

Jeffrey snapped a picture of his mother on a colorful stagecoach and she took one of him on the same stagecoach. They strolled through Rawhide that featured an 1880's western town. Jeffrey played skeeball in an arcade, picked up a shotgun in another, hit the bull's-eye, and won a prize of a big box of hard candies. A cowboy with bow legs stopped them and spoke to them for a few minutes. He told them he originally came from Maine but settled in Arizona and worked for Rawhide doing odd jobs including being a gunfighter and rodeo rider. He guided them to a theater where a gunfight would take place in fifteen minutes.

Seated on a wooden bench under a bright sunny sky, mother and son watched when a group of belligerent locals challenged a gunfighter in front of a building with a sign that read Saloon/Hotel. More gunfighters showed up and began shooting and climbing buildings until they dropped out of sight. Punches were exchanged. Explosions ripped the air. Heart-pounding shootings took place. Cowboys engaged in daring falls from buildings. When it was over, an appreciative audience applauded loudly. Joy ran in Ricky's heart and curved her lips. Her son seemed happy, even if it was for just a few hours.

But on the way home Jeffrey confided that, ever since he had been shot, he had nightmares of being shot over and over.

"In the beginning it wasn't so bad, and I thought it would go away, but it keeps getting worse. I see her pointing the gun at me, pulling the trigger, and I see my blood spurting out. The excruciating pain is overpowering. I stay up as late as I can to avoid sleep at any cost. Arthur is working nights as an EMT and he and I talk for a long time in the middle of the night. Eventually sleep overcomes me and then I wake up after a couple of hours, my heart pounding, breathing rapidly, nauseous, covered in sweat. I'm not interested in my hobbies, stamp and coin collecting. I'm emotionally numb. I'll never be able to work again. I can hardly concentrate. If there's a noise in my apartment, I get startled and feel jumpy. I'm always afraid she'll come back and finish me off. I'm angry at everybody, including you, even though I know you wish me well. I wish that somehow I can be cured of this post-traumatic stress disorder. The PTSD is making me a nervous wreck."

Ricky paused for a moment as she digested the

horror of Jeffrey's plight. His feeling of depression and hopelessness was overwhelming. She breathed heavily.

"Jeffrey, maybe there's an answer. I've been going to a chiropractor for my aching back. A month ago he began to share his office with a homeopathic doctor. Maybe that doctor has a way to help you."

"I don't think there's anything that will help. I've been taking tranquilizers and the condition still persists."

"It's been ten years now that you have endured this pain. I don't know if this doctor has anything to relieve your suffering but I believe you should try."

"I don't agree, but all right, you can make an appointment for me."

Dr. Hoffman was able to see Jeffrey in a couple of days. Ricky and Jeffrey sat on wooden chairs in front of Dr. Hoffman's desk. He was a man in his thirties, with an engaging smile and a soft manner. Jeffrey went into detail about why the PTSD had occurred. The doctor listened attentively.

"I believe I have something that will completely relieve your condition." Dr. Hoffman stood, walked over to a cabinet, and drew out a bottle of pills. "Take one every night before you go to sleep."

"What is it?" Ricky asked.

"It's the treated venom of a snake," the doctor answered calmly. "It sounds dangerous but it's not. It's worked for other patients and I think it will work for you. After you go home and run out of the pills, call me, and I'll send you more."

"I don't think it will work," Jeffrey said on the drive home.

"You never know until you try," his mother said.

Chapter 34

THE SNAKE VENOM WORKED. Jeffrey flew home and the PTSD was gone, never to return, no more nightmares of being shot. Ricky was relieved, but when Jeffrey called her, his depression seemed to increase. He called daily always dwelling on his unfulfilled desire to see his children. There were no words that Ricky uttered that could comfort him.

The following year, when Jeffrey came to stay ten days with his mother, she decided to take him to a place he had never been, Las Vegas. When the plane landed in McCarran International Airport after a deep descent, Ricky was sick with motion sickness. Her ears were clogged and she looked like a ghost.

"Let me rest for a half-hour and then I'll be better," Ricky said in a weak voice. "Meanwhile you can play the slots in the airport."

"I'll sit with you," Jeffrey said. "I don't like to gamble. The last time I gambled I lost $150,000."

"I remember."

"It's really the fault of my broker. I had a three-day, non-prudent trading binge. It is surely the obligation of the broker to protect accounts from such downside risk."

Ricky didn't know if she should believe Jeffrey who was adept at lying. She remained silent, hoping that she made a good decision to bring her son, who wasn't a gambler, to Sin City, the city made for gamblers. Jeffrey remained next to her looking like he was brooding.

When Ricky felt better, they took a taxi to the hotel New York-New York. In the taxi, Jeffrey whispered that he had stopped using Stadol. She would believe him if she didn't see him inject himself every four hours. She could hardly believe that he had stopped on his own. If it was true, then he did something amazing. That drug was ten times stronger than heroin.

When the taxi stopped at the hotel, Jeffrey said, "Look, Mom, across the street at the MGM Grand they have a huge figure of a lion out front. I like the buildings and bridge here. It's a replica of Manhattan."

The rooms in the suite were comfortable, and Jeffrey was intrigued when he peered out the window at the roller coaster. "It simulates a jet fighter's barrel roll," he said with the assurance of King Solomon. "Did you know that Las Vegas was founded in 1905 when Grandma was 15, and they brought in legalized gambling in 1931?"

"No, I didn't know that." *Thank God, his mind is still functioning.*

Jeffrey stood at the window in his room watching the careening roller coaster, people screaming with excitement and fright. He remembered the time he was healthy and thrilled to the roller coaster ride he had taken with Ann. After all the surgeries, he could no longer board a roller coaster with half a stomach. His life had changed forever.

It was Thanksgiving when Ricky decided to persuade Jeffrey to come back to Arizona for a change, hoping she could somehow lift his spirits. He took the next plane out, rented a Lincoln, and drove to her complex.

"I made turkey, sweet potatoes with pineapple and

marshmallows, and cranberry jelly," Ricky said after she greeted her son.

"Thanks, Mom, but I'm not hungry. I need a nap and later I'll eat."

"Suit yourself, Jeffrey. Is there anything on your mind?"

"My abdomen is all scarred. It's embarrassing. When I go to a pool I have to wear a T-shirt to cover up. I'd like to find a plastic surgeon to correct it."

"Okay. We'll look for a plastic surgeon. But are you sure you want to suffer the pain after having forty-two operations?"

"I'll live with the pain. It goes away and I'll feel better when I look better."

The next morning Jeffrey said he wanted to skip the plastic surgeon. He woke up feeling nauseated and weak and he wished to go to a general practitioner. Ricky belonged to a group for seniors, a group for which Jeffrey was ineligible. She reached for her reading glasses on the kitchen table, searched in the phone book, and located a doctor close by.

The ordinary-looking waiting room had a dozen chairs, ten of which were occupied. One old woman kept coughing like the braying of a donkey. A teenager sat with a bandaged head, and a mother held a crying toddler on her lap.

Jeffrey strode to the harried receptionist who sat with a phone to her ear behind a marred wooden desk.

"I need to see the Dr. Parton right now."

The receptionist ignored Jeffrey as she kept listening to someone on the phone. When she hung up after three minutes, she said, "Sorry, sir, you'll have to wait your turn. There are ten people ahead of you. Just write your name on this list, fill out this form, and I'll make a copy of your insurance card."

Jeffrey handed her his insurance card and took the form. "I need a pen."

With an annoyed expression the receptionist pointed to a vase filled with artificial flowers.

Jeffrey lifted a red flower from the vase and found the stem was a pen. He worked fast and brought the form back to the receptionist. "I have to see the doctor immediately."

"You'll have to wait."

Jeffrey's face reddened. "Don't you triage your patients?"

"No, sir, this isn't an emergency room."

Jeffrey's voice became loud and strident. "I'm very sick and I demand to see Dr. Parton."

The doctor, a man with broad shoulders and an angry look, left his examining room and strode over to Jeffrey. "Young man you are disturbing my patients. I refuse to examine you. Leave my office at once before I call the police to remove you."

Jeffrey face reddened. He took the form, tore it to shreds, and grabbed his insurance card that lay on the receptionist's desk.

"I'll drive you to the emergency room at the hospital," Ricky said as they entered the car.

Chapter 35

"I DON'T NEED TO go to a hospital," Jeffrey said quietly. "I feel better already, but I want to go to the police station."

"Why?"

"Don't worry. I won't report that ass of a doctor. I want to get a badge that says Scottsdale P.D." Jeffrey removed a badge that read Detective, Police Department, N.Y.C. and flashed it in front of his mother.

Ricky capitulated to her sick son's whim. She was used to his lying, but his explosive behavior and volatile temper frightened her. At the police station Jeffrey marched in like he owned The Bank of America. Ricky stood outside hoping that he wouldn't be arrested for impersonating a New York City police detective.

Five minutes later Jeffrey emerged, a big smile on his face, and a badge from the Scottsdale Police Department. Ricky's blood pressure went up and down like the mercury in a thermometer.

She drove Jeffrey back to her condo without uttering a sound, trying to compose herself. Her son seemed calm now but she didn't know when the volcano would blow. At home Ricky went into the kitchen to prepare tuna fish sandwiches for lunch. Her hand shook so much she cut her finger with the knife as she was mincing the celery to mix with the tuna. She moved to the bathroom for a Band-Aid and stood in astonishment at the sight she saw.

Jeffrey was standing staring down at her pet box turtle, Murray, swimming in the bathtub that Jeffrey had filled with water. The agitated turtle was obviously trying to escape, moving its legs faster and faster, trying not to drown.

Ricky grabbed Murray and brought it back to its aquarium. "This is a land turtle I picked up in Kentucky ten years ago. It's afraid of water. Why did you do this?"

"It looked like it needed to swim," Jeffrey said as he released the water in the tub.

Ricky's knees went weak. *Jeffrey's mind is severely affected. My poor son, I better watch what he does. Please help him, God. He's very sick.*

Overnight the rain came down in torrents. The condo was on the ground floor. Outside the living room there was a patch of ground the size of two cars. Ricky sometimes let her turtle walk around the patio but today the rain was so heavy that water seeped under the glass sliding door and formed a pool on the tile in the living room. Ricky mopped it up. It didn't happen often and she was used to the inconvenience.

Jeffrey took it to heart. Unknown to Ricky, he drew up a legal document of complaint, signed his mother's name, and dropped it off in the condo office. That afternoon the head of the condo board rang her bell.

Mr. Borden was a popular person who always stood up for owner's rights. He wore navy pants, a crisp white shirt, and a crimson tie and it was rumored he had his four-room condo furnished like a millionaire. Frowning, he handed Ricky the document.

"Why did you turn this into the office?" Mr. Borden

said. "When there is a problem, everyone knows to come to me first."

Ricky read the words on the paper all in legalese. Her name was signed at the end of the document and notarized by Jeffrey.

"I'm sorry. Please disregard this paper. I never wrote it. I didn't sign it. I never brought it to the office." Ricky tore the paper in half.

"Who wrote it, if not you?"

"My son is the author. It is true there's a problem of water seeping into my living room after a heavy rain. I'd like something to be done, but believe me, I never threatened the condo with legal action."

That night Ricky didn't get a moment of sleep. Jeffrey seemed to be getting worse. He would wind up in prison again, in a mental hospital, or God forbid, dead.

The next day the torrential rain continued and Ricky put towels next to the glass sliding door to absorb whatever water seeped in.

Jeffrey watched her with interest but stood by silently. After a few minutes Jeffrey suggested they play chess.

"I know I taught you when you were a child," Ricky said, "but now you're so good that I wouldn't be a challenge."

"I don't care. I just want to play. I'm not interested in watching the news or soap operas, or stupid game shows. How about it?"

"All right, but on one condition."

"Which is?"

"I'll play one game of chess if we alternate it with a game of Scrabble."

"That's unfair, Mom. You know I can't spell. You'll win all the time."

Ricky grinned. "So what? You'll win every chess game."

They sat at the glass dining room table with the wooden chess board Ricky had gotten in Israel. She took out the pieces and Jeffrey lined them up. He selected black giving her the advantage. Ricky's forehead creased as she concentrated moving each piece slowly. Meanwhile Jeffrey looked at the aquarium on the stand next to the table. Murray sat quietly on top of the rock facing away from Jeffrey. In five moves Jeffrey called, "Mate," and the game was over.

The next game they played was Scrabble and Ricky won it hands down. No contest.

Jeffrey conceded. Something was on his mind. "My father told me that you tried to kill me when I was a baby."

Ricky had heard this before, but this time she didn't deny it as she had done in the past when Jeffrey had raised the issue. "Did you father tell you how I tried to kill you?"

"Sure. He said that when I was an infant you walked to Old Country Road and pushed my carriage into traffic. He rescued me."

Ricky smiled and nodded. "How can that be? You were eight days old when I was put in a hospital. I never wheeled you in your carriage until you were fourteen months old and I was granted custody."

"Who should I believe? Who is telling the truth, you, or my father?"

"When you die, you'll learn the truth. Is there anything else on your mind?"

"Yes," Jeffrey said as he picked up the rook and turned it over in his hand. "I don't know how long I'll live. Nobody knows that. But I think I'll die before you. In that case I want you to hire a lawyer and prosecute Lena for murder. Will you do that?"

"If that's what you want, Jeffrey. But would you like lunch now?

"Good idea. I'd like an egg salad sandwich on rye and a glass of Sunny D."

Jeffrey always liked the way Ricky prepared the egg, chopping it and adding sweet relish and mayonnaise. She wished he wouldn't keep downing that sugary drink. He didn't take his diabetic condition seriously and it could come back and haunt him. Ricky remembered her cousin, Buddy, who died from diabetes when he was twenty-one.

Chapter 36

JEFFREY REMAINED WITH RICKY another two days.

One night when the moon shone like it was lit up with a search light, he announced, "I'm going for a drive."

"Okay, when will you be back?"

"Soon."

After an hour when Jeffrey rang the doorbell and Ricky opened the door, her son looked like he had been caught in a fiery furnace. His face was crimson and his eyes were wide with fright.

"I'm leaving right now," he said with a wavering tone.

"What's wrong?"

"I went to the drug store with a phony prescription for a woman I know who is on tranquilizers. They had me wait a long time. I got scared and left. I think they called the police."

Jeffrey packed quickly and for the first time in his life he asked Ricky for one hundred dollars. Ricky drove to the bank, pressed her code on the ATM, and took out three hundred.

Ricky handed Jeffrey the money. He didn't thank her but put it quickly into his pants pocket. He didn't say goodbye, just opened the door of the rented Lincoln and without another word left.

Ricky trembled. Her heart raced. She sat on the sofa, her head cradled in her hands. Jeffrey had never been this far from reality. He had caused her problems, but not as severe as the ones he caused himself.

For the next two days she didn't have the strength to talk to him. She just let the phone ring.

When she finally answered the shrill ring of the phone, Jeffrey told her he was sick. He had caught a germ on the plane and was sneezing and coughing.

He called his mother daily for a week, but then the calls stopped and Ricky sensed something was terribly wrong. She knew Jeffrey was low, despondent, and weak. He didn't have his children. He didn't have his health. He didn't have money. The only consolation he had was Milky Ways and Sunny D. He didn't care about his diabetes. He didn't care about his life.

Ricky kept calling but couldn't get through as there were too many messages. She called Arthur but couldn't reach him for a couple of days. When she finally made contact with Arthur, he told her he had been in the hospital with an abscess. It was nighttime in Brooklyn, but Ricky insisted that Arthur go to Jeffrey's apartment.

Is my boy sick or dead? Ricky sent a message to God to help her son.

Chapter 37

THE SHEETS ON JEFFREY'S bed were filthy. He was too weak to wash them. He grew weaker. Dizziness overtook him. Fear became his companion.

Jeffrey grabbed the phone and held on tightly. Desperately he tried to dial 911, but couldn't. He closed his eyes, said *Shema Israel,* and he never opened his eyes again.

He became a lost soul.

* * *

Arthur called his friend Manny and woke him up. It was 3 a.m.

"I'm sorry to bother you, but my mother thinks there's something very wrong with Jeffrey as we both can't reach him."

"I'll get dressed and come over ASAP," Manny said.

Twenty minutes later Arthur drove his car while Manny sat in the passenger's seat. Both were silent. Arthur bit down on his lips hoping that Jeffrey was just sick and not dead. For the last few years the brothers had become close, talking every night, Jeffrey unburdening himself and Arthur encouraging him to try to enjoy life.

As soon as Arthur reached the staircase he smelled death. It was a familiar odor as he had come across it many times in his work as an Emergency Medical Technician.

Manny and Arthur covered their noses. Jeffrey had given Arthur a key to his apartment. They entered the foyer, raced to the bedroom, and found Jeffrey on the floor, his hand clutching the phone in desperation. They covered him with a sheet and carried him down the stairs. Arthur's eyes were wet with tears.

He called his mother, but she had gone to bed and unplugged the phone.

Early the following morning Arthur made the most difficult call of his life.

He didn't have to say a word when his mother asked in a weak voice, "Is Jeffrey dead?"

"Yes. Manny and I found him on the floor next to his bed, his hand tight around the phone. You'll have to come to New York for the funeral."

"Where is he now?"

"In the morgue."

Ricky groaned, "He asked that he have an autopsy so Lena could be prosecuted."

"An autopsy is against Jewish law."

Ricky placed her hand on her chest where she felt a rock. She gasped, "But that was his last wish. I want him to have an autopsy. I promised him. I can't go back on my word."

Chapter 38

Rᴉᴄᴋʏ ᴀᴛᴛᴇᴍᴘᴛᴇᴅ ᴛᴏ ᴘᴀᴄᴋ a suitcase but she was adrift like a sinking boat. She packed some stockings but couldn't focus. The same thing happened with her clothes. She couldn't decide what to take and kept going back and forth into her closet. Her mind was numb with overwhelming grief.

The phone rang.

"Hello." Ricky clutched a tissue.

"Hello, this is Dr. Walters in the morgue in the hospital. I understand you want me to autopsy your son. Is that right?"

"Yes."

When Ricky hung up the phone it rang again. She answered teary and weak.

"This is the Rabbi from the New York City Fire Department. Your son, Arthur, told me you have given permission for the doctor to do an autopsy."

"Yes. I just got off the phone with him."

"This is against Jewish law."

"I know but I promised my son I'd do it. It's the only way that his wife can be brought to trial."

"But even then it wouldn't guarantee she'd be convicted. It's eleven years since she shot your son."

"But I promised him."

"If you promised your son you would eat non-kosher, would you still keep your promise?"

Ricky was silent. She really didn't want Jeffrey's body to be violated. "All right, I agree. I'll call the doctor back."

When Dr. Walters answered the phone, in another minute he would have started the autopsy.

"I changed my mind," Ricky said. "Please cancel the autopsy."

JetBlue had a late afternoon flight. Ricky climbed the staircase to Alice's condo. Her finger shook as she rang the bell. Alice's waterbed had caused a flood in Ricky's kitchen and ever since that time they had become friendly. When Alice's husband left her, she decided she didn't want a waterbed. The handyman had advised her to empty the water from the bed in the kitchen sink and as a result it had caused a mess in Ricky's kitchen. It took an hour for Alice to mop up the water and, as she did so, she kept apologizing. Afterward they became close and Ricky had introduced Jeffrey to her. Ricky liked Alice, a woman who had compassion and a loving nature.

When Alice opened the door, she was shocked to see Ricky looking like a drowning dog with bloodshot eyes.

"Honey, what's wrong? You look like Hell."

"Jeffrey died," Ricky gasped. "I'm going to New York this afternoon."

Alice put her arms around Ricky who was bent over, clutching a wet tissue. She drew her in, indicating a chair in the dining room. Ricky plopped down and put her head in her hands.

"I'm so sorry," Alice said. "How do you feel?"

"Like I was run over by a truck."

"Have you eaten anything today?"

"I can't eat."

"You have to try. I'll make you some toast and tea."

Ricky nibbled on a corner of the toast and slowly drank the tea after it cooled.

"Will you please take my mailbox key and get my mail. I don't know how long I'll be gone."

"Of course, and I'll go get Murray and take good care of your turtle. Is there anything else I can do?"

"No. I can't think of anything. I can't think about anything but that my son is dead. I'm walking around in a fog."

Alice's expression was sad. "I'll drive you to the airport."

"A parent shouldn't have to bury a child," Ricky said.

Alice nodded. "You're right. It's horrible."

Ricky sat in the window seat in the plane. She bit down on her lips trying not to cry. She wanted no attention, no sympathy. She looked out the window where clouds were gathered like soap bubbles but she didn't see them. Her mind drifted to the first time she met Lena. There was something about her she didn't like. She shouldn't have told Jeffrey to call her. He wouldn't be dead if she had told Lena a lie like he was engaged or he was married. Lena had pressed her for information about Jeffrey, and that pressure had made her uncomfortable especially when Lena insisted she had to meet him, but then Ricky considered that Jeffrey was an adult and could make up his own mind.

She was one hundred percent wrong.

Now she felt deep guilt. It was her fault for not recognizing how dangerous Lena was. Perhaps it was better that Jeffrey had died. He could have landed back in jail or gotten hooked again on Stadol. He had been so depressed. He had been living a life of desperation. He wanted his children, was obsessed with seeing them. Maybe it was time for her to die, too. She never considered suicide but maybe God would take her, then she'd be reunited with her son and her parents.

Chapter 39

AT THE AIRPORT, ARTHUR met his mother at the luggage carousel. They embraced and held each other for minutes while their eyes filled with tears. Jeffrey was gone and both of them would miss his daily calls even when he had been kvetching about not seeing his children. He was the most unusual person both of them had ever come across. He was very good and very bad, and you never knew when he'd change. He was like a mirror with two sides. He epitomized the saying, "When he was good he was very, very good, but when he was bad he was horrid."

Arthur lifted his mother's suitcase and carried it out to his car. He had moved to a two-bedroom apartment, and when Ricky entered she stood at the threshold and cried, "Why are you living like this?"

"I can't afford to pay a higher rent."

"But the linoleum in the kitchen is old and torn and there is a hole a foot deep next to the sink."

"I know. The landlady won't fix it. Just watch your step. I'll bring your suitcase to the second bedroom. I made all the arrangements for Jeffrey's funeral. It'll be tomorrow."

That night Ricky sat in front of the computer and with a broken heart wrote the eulogy that Arthur would deliver at Jeffrey's funeral. She included all the good things that Jeffrey had done in his life and omitted the bad.

The next day should have been overcast and teeming with rain, Ricky thought, but instead the sun shone when Arthur drove Ricky to the funeral home. The room was packed with people and there was an overflow into the street. Jeffrey's coffin was at the front of the room. The Rabbi spoke but Ricky didn't hear a word he said.

When Arthur stood up to give the eulogy, he broke down a few times, his eyes overflowing with hot tears, but he persisted and then the service was over.

Ricky approached the white pine coffin, placed her hand on it, and whispered, "You're going upstairs. Don't make a fuss. Don't change the rules. Don't start any committees. Behave yourself."

As the funeral procession moved along on the FDR drive on the way to the Beth David cemetery in Elmont, Queens, Arthur pointed to a plane that flew overhead. "Look, it's Air Force One. Jeffrey would like that," he said weakly.

The service at the cemetery became a haze in Ricky's mind. She knew that Jeffrey had been buried not far from his father's grave and that was all right with her.

Next would be the shiva, the mourning period of seven days. Ricky sat on a box in the living room. She wore a black hat and a plain green dress. She had no makeup on, and she held a tissue in her hand to wipe the tears that kept flowing.

Twice a day Arthur's friends came to the apartment and said Yiskor, the memorial prayer for the dead, the prayer that glorifies the Lord. The next morning Ricky got up at 5 a.m. and collapsed in the foyer. She was too weak to yell for help and lay there until Arthur's son found her an hour later.

"Don't worry," she said. "I didn't have a heart attack. Just call Daddy and he'll pick me up."

Arthur and his friend helped Ricky up and put her to bed. They sent for a doctor who pronounced the condition a virus and ordered fluids and bed rest.

Five days later when Ricky was feeling better but still sitting shiva on the box in the living room, the bell rang. When Arthur opened the door he was handed an eviction notice which he examined with an angry look. "I didn't pay the rent this month because I was in the hospital and then in mourning for my brother's death. And this is the result?" he whined.

"What will you do?" Ricky asked with sympathy in her voice.

"I'll move out," Arthur said as he paced the room, "of this overrun miserable wretched apartment."

"When shiva is over, I'll help you look for another apartment."

"No!"

"What do you mean by 'No'?"

"I mean that I'll never be under the thumb of a landlord again. I want to buy a co-op."

At the end of the seven days of mourning Arthur bought The Jewish Press and his mother found a listing of a co-op in a luxury building in Brooklyn in a nice neighborhood that was selling for $55,000.

They drove there and parked in front of the building that stood fourteen stories, next to a cemetery, on the wide thoroughfare of Ocean Parkway. A doorman asked for their destination and opened the front door. He guided them to the superintendent's apartment.

"We called," Arthur said, "and would like to look at the apartment for sale."

The superintendent, a tall muscular man with a small mustache, grabbed the key from a board and led them to the elevator. They emerged at the eleventh floor and entered an apartment with two moderate-sized rooms and a kitchen large enough for just one person to fit comfortably.

Arthur moved to the window and looked down. "Mom, come here."

Ricky stepped alongside him and gazed at a pool below. The only other pool, in an apartment house she had seen, was in Sally's house.

"The pool is open in the summer for the residents and we have 24-hour doormen. This is a safe house to live in," the super said.

"I like it," Arthur said quietly to his mother.

Ricky agreed. "We'll return after my son applies for a mortgage."

The mortgage company was in mid-Manhattan. Parking was impossible so Ricky and Arthur took the subway.

They sat at the desk of a young attractive woman dressed in a gray business suit who listened politely as Arthur explained that he had found the ideal co-op for himself and just needed a mortgage.

The woman nodded. "Okay. How much can you put down?"

"Well," Arthur said seriously. "I'm getting paid tonight so I'll be able to pay $100."

The woman looked at Ricky and both of them smiled simultaneously with the bond of sympathy and understanding.

Ricky said, "I'll buy the co-op. I'll give you a check for one thousand dollars now and send you the rest when I go back home to Arizona."

And so the co-op was bought in Ricky's name with her money. They shopped for furniture with Ricky's credit card. Arthur wanted the condo to be strictly modern and Ricky agreed.

I'm no more the mother of children and what I've saved I want Arthur to have. This is my time to be generous. I have one child left and he deserves to live in a decent place with decent furniture.

After six weeks of living with Arthur in Brooklyn, Ricky returned to Arizona, but her heart would never be the same. It was scarred when Jeffrey died. If Lena hadn't shot him, he'd still be alive, healthy and active. She should've divorced him, not picked up a .357 Magnum and shot him in the chest. She murdered him even if the death certificate reads Cause of Death, Undetermined.

Alice told Ricky about the organization Parents of Murdered Children. The meetings were sad especially when the other parents related how their child had been murdered. At one meeting the President announced that they were offering a memorial to each child by way of erecting a stepping stone on the grounds of the State Capitol in Wesley Bolin Plaza in Phoenix. She could buy one and have Jeffrey's name engraved on it. Good idea, Ricky thought.

On the day the memorial service took place, Ricky peered at the stepping stone with Jeffrey's name, and dates of birth and death, and her eyes filled with burning tears. Overcome with such grief that she couldn't bear to hear the speeches, she raced to her car and left.

At home Ricky sat at her desk, opened a ring box, and

lifted a bullet Jeffrey had given to her to demonstrate how his insides had been penetrated. Ricky took out a ruler from her desk drawer and measured the one-and-a-half inch bullet. The tip was black, the adjacent color, bronze, and the rest was an antique gold. She held the flat end up and saw that it was inscribed R.P. 357 magnum. Ricky put the bullet down and cradled her head in her hands staying that way for fifteen minutes while a ton of hot tears dripped from her eyes.

Two months passed before Ricky had a dream that woke her, shivering and perturbed, with the memory of her son telling her he wanted a tombstone taller than his father's in the cemetery. It would be expensive but Ricky understood she had to do it. Jeffrey had broken the clutch of Heaven to bring her a message.

The mortgage went through without a hitch, and once again Ricky flew back to Brooklyn to help Arthur decorate his new co-op. After a few days, she returned to Scottsdale and joined a grief group. The other members had lost their mates. She was the only one whose child had died and they couldn't begin to understand the grief of losing a child. The social worker offered individual counseling and Ricky took advantage of the once-a-week counseling. What saved her sanity was going out for lunch after the meetings with the women. One night they even went to see a play. When the audience laughed at the dialogue, Ricky couldn't even smile. She clung to life as there was no choice. Nothing she could do would ever bring Jeffrey back.

Her mind was often filled with the tragic story of Job in the Bible. He started out as a rich man, the owner of thousands of animals, the father of three daughters and seven sons. His faith was tested when he lost his wealth and his ten children. As a result he cried, "Man that is born of a woman is of few days, and full of trouble." He complained and kvetched to his three friends who criticized him. Job longed to return to the previous time. "Oh, that I were as in months past, as in the days when God preserved me," he moaned. But Job never sinned by charging God with wrongdoing. And then the Lord spoke to Job telling him of all His mighty powers. Job asked for repentance, and the Lord blessed him with even more wealth that he had before and especially with three gorgeous daughters and seven sons.

Ricky remembered the time when her grandchildren, seven and five years, respectively, were hidden away. Somehow she learned where they were. She yearned to just see them, not even to acknowledge who she was. At a wig store Ricky bought a wig of white hair, put Murray the box turtle in its travel cage, and drove to the religious colony where Lena hid out in New York State.

Her heart beat rapidly as she found the address. She was fearful of Lena who she knew hated her guts. Once a person shoots a gun with the intention of killing a person she very likely could do it again. Luckily she observed a "For Sale" sign on the lawn in front of the large frame house. Children were playing in the yard, but by their light coloring Ricky surmised these weren't her grandchildren. They crowded around her, surveying the turtle in the cage. She took Murray out and let them have a closer look.

A short elderly man with a salt and pepper beard emerged from the house.

"Can I help you?" he asked with a Jewish accent.

"Yes. My married son is in the market for a house in this vicinity. He asked for my help as he's very busy working." Ricky hated to lie. She used to say that lying is a sin and it's easier to tell the truth, especially when you had the burden of remembering your lie.

"I'll be happy to show you the house," he said as he led the way to the front door. "It has ten rooms, three bathrooms, central air-conditioning, two freezers, two refrigerators, and a new kitchen."

Inside, the house had worn furniture and was clean. One room had a wall filled with Hebrew books. Ricky kept snapping pictures of the rooms indicating she was impressed with the house.

The elderly man nodded. "There is a small house in the back of this one. It has four rooms, two bedrooms. It can bring in rent to help with the mortgage. Right now it's rented to a widow with two children and she's paying $8200 a year. She's quiet and pays the rent on time. She left fifteen minutes ago."

"I'd appreciate if you could show me the house." Ricky's knees almost buckled. She had a near miss meeting up with the dangerous Lena.

"I don't think she'd mind if I let you in. The price for both houses is $325,000."

Ricky took photos of the small house, looking for pictures of her grandchildren but no pictures were displayed. She started to feel her heart beat faster and faster. She was afraid that Lena would return any minute, pull a .357 magnum from a drawer and shoot her.

"Thank you for showing me your home," Ricky said. "I'll tell my son and he'll get back to you."

On the way home Ricky's breathing was shallow. She thanked God for sparing her life and keeping her away from Lena. At that time Jeffrey was too ill to look for his children although he knew exactly where they were.

*   *   *

A difficult two years passed for Ricky after Jeffrey's death—mourning was hard work. She and Sally spoke often on the phone. Ricky convinced Sally it was time for her to retire.

"What will I do with myself?" Sally asked.

"You'll buy a computer and get on line," Ricky said.

And that's what Sally did. Twice she stayed for ten days with Ricky in Scottsdale. The friends spoke about Jeffrey's tragic life and his death. They had a lot in common, and felt close to each other. They went shopping in the upscale Scottsdale mall, and sightseeing to Sedona, a city surrounded by red-rock vistas sporting the most spectacular scenery in the world.

There came a time when Sally told Ricky she had learned how to use her computer, and had gone on the Jewish Chat site. She had been corresponding with Joe, who seemed like a nice man who had lost his wife fourteen years ago. She wanted to come to Arizona and stay with Ricky so she could meet Joe, who lived in his own home in Phoenix. Ricky agreed.

But it wasn't to be. Sally had driven her car up the Catskill Mountains and the car had rolled over a mountain and she had a badly broken ankle that didn't heal for a year.

"You go meet, Joe," Sally said.

And that's how Ricky met the man she dated for two years. They were married by the Lubavitcher Rabbi in Phoenix in a wedding that they both enjoyed. Ricky wore a white lace dress with a veil, and Joe was decked out in a tuxedo. Fifty people were present for the ceremony and the catered meal. Unfortunately, Arthur couldn't come as he had contracted a virus. Ricky had friends at the wedding but no family, but now she had a devoted, decent, honest husband. They went on many cruises to Mexico, Alaska, Hawaii, and Brazil, and twice took trips on a riverboat in Europe, visiting Hungary, Romania, Holland, and Belgium.

This was the happy marriage that Ricky had always yearned for. Joe had a good sense of humor, was generous, and optimistic but twenty years had passed without Ricky seeing her grandchildren. Every year on their birthdays she signed a birthday card and bought a gift for each that she hoped one day she'd be able to give them. Her heart was heavy until she learned that her grandson was attending a Yeshiva in Connecticut. Maybe he would talk to her, and maybe not. She couldn't bring herself to call, but made an appointment to meet with the same Rabbi from the Lubavitch synagogue in Phoenix who had officiated at her wedding.

Ricky sat on a hard chair in his office and softly told the story of her son being shot by his wife and dying eleven years later. The Rabbi listened in silence with a poker face, his long beard hanging down over the collar of his white shirt under a black suit, a black yarmulke on his head.

"I came to ask a favor of you, Rabbi," Ricky said in a hoarse whisper. "My grandson is in a Yeshiva and I was told by a third party that he's doing very well. He's as brilliant as his father. Will you please call and ask if he'll talk to me?"

"Why don't you call him yourself? He'll probably be interested in talking to you, and, if not, what do you have to lose."

At home Joe encouraged Ricky to call Dan. Her hand shook as she pressed the button and dialed the number.

When a student answered, she asked to speak to Dan, telling him that his grandmother wanted to talk to him.

At first, when Ricky said that she was his grandmother, Dan was confused. He thought he was talking to Lena's mother and then, when he learned it was his father's mother, he was overwhelmed. He asked many questions and the conversation went on for an hour even though he said he was due back in class, but he couldn't stop asking questions. Ricky, with shallow breath, held the mobile phone in her hand and paced the living room of her home. She described where she lived in a ranch house that overlooked a golf course and a lake and told him she was happily married. He wanted to know if his father had been observant and she told him that he had eaten kosher and kept the Sabbath.

A few months later Dan arranged to meet his grandmother and her husband in a Rabbi's home in Monsey, New York. Arthur and his friend drove them to their destination. His friend spoke about the possibility of Lena's being there and how she could shoot them. Ricky didn't accept that possibility but her heart beat fast as she climbed the steps of the Rabbi's brick home.

His wife welcomed them and brought in refreshments, but Ricky's stomach had tightened and she couldn't eat or drink.

The bell rang.

The Rabbi opened the door and Dan stepped in. Ricky and Dan stared at each other without saying a word. Ricky's eyes widened as Dan stood at the door in a black suit, a dark beard, and his father's eyes and expression. It was like looking at her son again and she was astounded.

The Rabbi motioned them to the dining room table and he and his wife exited to give them privacy. Ricky had agreed not to talk negatively about his mother and she kept her word. A few minutes later the door opened and Grace crossed the threshold holding the leash of a large grayish-white dog. Grace wore a sweatshirt and offered a slight smile. She joined them at the table.

They knew that their mother had shot their father. They didn't know what caused it. No one knew what happened in that bedroom because there weren't any witnesses. Ricky agreed. They wanted confirmation that their father was a liar, and Ricky said he was since the time he was a child. They asked many questions about their father and Ricky provided the answers.

After talking a while, Dan said he wanted to tell Grandma about the condition of his mother. Grace objected but Dan proceeded to relate that his mother is convinced that Jeffrey is alive. She believes his reported death is a plot to cover the fact that every day he comes to kill her or harass her. She doesn't have a moment of peace. She hears noises in the house and believes he's torturing her.

No retribution had to occur for Lena to be punished. God took care of her in His own way, Ricky thought.

When they said goodbye, Ricky embraced and kissed her grandchildren. It was a highlight of her life.

But after seven happy married years with Joe, he died and Ricky lived alone once more.

Epilogue

AFTER THAT FIRST MEETING, Ricky and her grandchildren kept in touch by phone and e-mail. Dan married but couldn't invite Ricky to the wedding as he had invited his mother. He lived in Jerusalem and continued with his Jewish studies until he became a respected Rabbi. Dan married a sweet woman who was from a large family in Switzerland, and was willing to live in Jerusalem.

Arthur married a respectable woman, and had two stepchildren and two more biological children. He became a computer doctor and a Top-rated e-Bay seller. All his children attended Yeshivas.

Arthur's son, Jonah, always wanted to go to the Wailing Wall to celebrate his bar-mitzvah, and Ricky decided to go, too. Arthur, his wife, and younger daughter, Rachel, also came along. Ricky was surprised that Nat, her divorced husband, was willing to travel eleven hours for the trip and spend the large sum that it cost. Nat had never remarried and lived in a small co-op in Brooklyn, and spent many weekends with Arthur and his family. Ricky and Nat stayed in the same hotel and got along peacefully. Ricky was overjoyed once again to meet with Dan, his wife, and see her three great-granddaughters for the first time.

Grace, a beautiful young woman, had been studying in North Dakota, taking classes to become a geological engineer. She fell in love with a modern orthodox Jewish man with a beard, and told her grandmother she was sorry she couldn't invite her to the wedding in Atlanta, as her mother was coming. Still and all, she wanted Ricky to come to the religious celebration and dinner, the Sheva Brochas, the night after the wedding. Ricky was delighted, and rejoiced with the newlyweds. Again, happily she met Dan, his wife, and her great-granddaughters.

Jeffrey did change some of the rules in Heaven. He organized committees of angels and kept track of their duties. He ran elections and helped with disagreements. Sometimes he annoyed the angels, but he made Heaven a better place by being there. And he did learn the truth. His mother had never tried to kill him.